PRAISE FOR PAT WHITE AND
GOT A HOLD ON YOU!

"Wrestling romantic? Absolutely! *Got a Hold on You* made this skeptic a believer. . . . White's single-title debut delivers a potent punch of humor and romance."
—*Romantic Times* (Top Pick)

"I laughed and smiled all the way through Ms. White's . . . debut. Her sexy, fast-paced read is a delight. . . . You've got to read this one—it's a hoot."
—*Old Book Barn Gazette*

"This wrestling romance takes off faster than a flying dropkick."
—Harriet Klausner

"What a blast! *Got a Hold on You* is a wonderful book. This is a hilarious romp and highly recommended."
—*Scribes World*

"This book rocks! Charming, fresh, funny—I couldn't put it down."
—Suzanne Brockmann,
New York Times bestselling author

"White mixes today's wrestling world with 1980s wrestling nostalgia; adds warm smiles, quirky characters, and a sympathetic couple and cooks up a perfect diverting read."
—*Booklist*

ABLAZE

"I'm Loverboy Luke, the baddest, sexiest, pro wrestler of them all. I can set a woman on fire with a touch of my finger."

Didn't she know it. Alexandra had a hard time breathing against the desire building in her chest. She wanted to pull her hand away, but couldn't move.

I'm Loverboy Luke, the baddest, sexiest pro wrestler of them all.

Something unsettling rang in his words. She shouldn't care, but couldn't ignore the unusual tint of his blue-green eyes.

"I don't believe you," she blurted out.

"You don't think I'm the best in the ring? Or you don't think I can light a woman on fire?" The huskiness of his voice sent shivers across her back.

Get up! Run for your life!

"Because my stats prove the first," he said. "And I can easily prove the second." He leaned even closer and her breath caught in her chest. He was about to kiss her . . . or worse.

"I need . . ." she said.

"What, honey? What do you need?"

Other *Love Spell* books by Pat White:

GOT A HOLD ON YOU

RING AROUND MY HEART

Pat White

LOVE SPELL NEW YORK CITY

*This book is dedicated to
the "high flyers" of professional wrestling,
whose talent keeps us on the edge of our seats,
and often ends their careers before their time.*

LOVE SPELL®

September 2004

Published by

Dorchester Publishing Co., Inc.
200 Madison Avenue
New York, NY 10016

ISBN 0-505-52609-3

The name "Love Spell" and its logo are trademarks of Dorchester Publishing Co., Inc.

Printed in the United States of America.

Visit us on the web at www.dorchesterpub.com.

ACKNOWLEDGMENTS

I'd like to thank my writing buddies for not calling me crazy for writing pro-wrestling romances, at least not to my face. Thanks to Suzanne Brockmann and Laurie Brown for helping me "pin" Loverboy Luke. Thanks to Wendy Blythe Gifford for your advice and friendship, and Crystal Bright-Hollomon for the laughs.

Thanks to my brother, Bob Sherman, for knowing almost everything about every match since the first Wrestlemania. Who needs the Internet when I've got you?

Thanks to Steve Hooper at Stampede Wrestling in Calgary for answering my questions about the business, and for the tour of CPR—Larry's favorite part of the trip!

Finally, thanks to Patt and Jeff for always making me proud, and thanks to Larry for his incredible wisdom, and for being my real life hero.

RING AROUND MY HEART

Chapter One

Good God in heaven. What had she gotten herself into?

Alexandra Hayes stared in disbelief at the man in the wrestling ring below. He sparkled like a mirror ball in full spin at a Saturday night discotheque.

"That man needs help," she muttered from the sky-box overlooking a nearly full Centurion Stadium in St. Louis.

"I hear you're just the woman for the job," said Cosmo Perini, owner of pro wrestling promotion company Brawlers and Maulers, better known as BAM.

"I'm a public-relations expert, not a shrink."

Cosmo laughed, an explosive sound that shook the glass. "Oh, there's nothing wrong with Loverboy. Nothing that a handful of women and a bottle of scotch wouldn't cure."

"Since Whitford and Hayes Inc., provides neither of those services, I'm wondering why I'm here." She squared off at him. She was taking a chance, but she had to act the part of tough-talking businesswoman.

1

The gorilla-sized man glanced at the floor. "I've offended you. I'm sorry. I have this way of moving my mouth without letting my thoughts go through my brain first. Let me try again."

She nodded for him to continue. Truth be told, she'd done everything in her power short of breaking the law to secure this client. She wondered if impersonating a seasoned PR woman carried prison time.

"Pete and me love this business," he started. "We've been wrestling since we were two and our papa threw us down on the cement floor in our basement and told us to go at it. Pete almost went to the Olympics, but he got bit by the neighbor's dog, Pickles, and—sorry, I'm rambling again."

The crowd cheered and she glanced at the ring. Loverboy Luke Silver jumped up and down and thrust his fists into the air as if leading an aerobics class. With wiggling hips and a sultry smile, he shed his garish costume to the beat of rock music. He tossed his shimmering vest over the top rope and reached for his belt buckle, his hips jerking right, then left, then right again.

When Alexandra was spending six years earning her bachelor's while waitressing at Dixie's and raising little Riley solo, she never pictured herself ending up here, consulting for this questionable form of entertainment. Then again she was nearly broke, and going to the ex for money was out of the question.

"I'll do anything to save this company," Cosmo continued. "I know just how to do it and that's where you come in." He pulled two beers from the minibar and offered her one.

"No, thanks." She needed to keep her wits about her.

He motioned for her to sit in a gray-cushioned stadium seat.

"We need to get the kids back," he started. "Like in the eighties: larger-than-life heroes and ruthless villains. We need to get back to the basics. Good, clean violence."

She blinked. Had she heard him right?

"And some real wrestling," he added.

She glanced at the ring. "As opposed to a striptease?"

Loverboy had shed everything but a pair of skin-tight, silver shorts with a pink heart plastered across his firm buns. He interlaced his hands behind his head and rotated his hips counterclockwise. A tall, twenty-ish woman with big, yellow hair tumbled over the barricade in an attempt to reach the superstar.

"Loverboy gets carried away sometimes," Cosmo said. "But he's a good kid. One of our best high-flying wrestlers. What we need from you—" he paused and fingered the lip of his beer can—"we need you to fix him."

She glanced at the thirty-something wrestler who pranced from one corner of the ring to the other, flinging his long blond hair and grabbing himself in places that would land eight-year-old Riley in his room without dinner.

"And which part of him is broken, exactly?" she said.

"You've got a helluva sense of humor for a suit," he chuckled. "What I mean is, his character needs to be tamed. You know, civilized. I've got my eye on two other guys I want to make heroes, Oscar the Louse and Flamboyant Floyd, but Loverboy's my Number One guy. I'm hiring you to make him a superstar. Teach him how to talk to the press, behave at charity functions. Smooth him out around the edges. We need to bring wrestling back into the mainstream, make it okay for families again."

She glanced ringside. Two women scaled the three-foot metal guardrails, sprinted into the ring and tackled Loverboy to the mat.

"The fans seem to be having fun," Alexandra said. "Besides, you've got a nearly full house here."

"I gave half these seats away. Parents are sick of what wrestling's become. I suppose I can't blame 'em. It used to be wholesome, family entertainment."

"Right," she said as one of Loverboy's assailants ripped open her blouse, exposing a black lace bra. Four security guards pulled the women from the ring. Loverboy jumped to his feet and mooned them for good measure. Miss Black Lace fainted dead away.

It would be a scorching day in Alaska before she'd bring Riley to a spectacle like this.

"You sure you're committed to making the change?" she said.

"Yes, ma'am."

"And Loverboy down there?"

"He'll do what he's told. He's a loyal employee and a good man, even though he lives for the spotlight."

Wonderful.

"This scheme will either be our greatest success or the end of wrestling, at least for the Perini brothers." Cosmo's eyes dimmed as he picked a thread from his brown suit.

Pro wrestling was obviously the promoter's life and he was trusting his future to her, Alexandra Hayes, a woman who'd earned her degree two years ago at age twenty-nine and worked only briefly at a mediocre PR firm before going out on her own.

But she'd chased this dream because she had good instincts, knew how to say things and when to say them. Too bad those instincts were nonexistent in the male

4

department, and too bad for Cosmo that her biggest client to date had been a start-up company that specialized in outerwear for Chihuahuas.

Cosmo was a big boy. He'd reviewed her resume and still asked her to come to St. Louis for this meeting. Alexandra had heard through the grapevine he'd interviewed some of the big guns as well.

Why had he picked her? Cosmo was either a poor businessman or very trusting . . . or very desperate.

She knew the feeling.

"I can't help wondering why you chose my firm, Mr. Perini."

Here it comes. Aunt Lulu always said Alexandra's petite features and round eyes telegraphed "pushover." Cosmo probably thought he could bargain her monthly retainer down to a buck fifty.

"Truth is, I need to keep this hush-hush." He took a generous swig of beer. "No one can know we're in trouble or what we plan to do about it. The other wrestling promoters would swoop down on us like crows on road kill. If I hire a big PR firm they'd brag about taking on a wrestling organization to boost their own client base. I need someone discreet, unknown."

Unknown. Yep, that about described her.

"About my retainer—"

"I have to watch my budget. I can only offer six thousand a month plus expenses."

She nearly fell off her chair. A roar from the crowd drew Cosmo's attention, thank God.

Six thousand, six thousand. Figures rattled off in her brain. Riley's math tutor, braces, a new car. God, what she wouldn't give to trade in her '87 Chevy Caprice station wagon.

Hallelujah! Why look a gift horse in the mouth? If the man was willing to pay a hefty retainer, who cared about his motives?

"Would I be able to use you as a reference once the job is complete?" she asked.

He nodded. "You civilize Loverboy Luke, teach him how to be a gentleman and I'll personally take out a billboard on Interstate 80 saying you're the best PR gal north of the equator."

"Thanks, I think."

"When can you start?" he asked.

"I—"

"Tonight, after the show? At least come backstage so I can introduce you around."

"I'll need to draw up a contract."

"A formality. I'll check Loverboy's schedule. He's on the road three weeks out of the month. You might have to tag along."

She'd known there had to be a catch.

"I can travel one, maybe two days per week," she said. "I do have other clients." *Not to mention an eight-year-old boy who needed his mom.*

"Seven thousand a month."

"No, it's not the money, Mr. Perini."

"Call me Cosmo."

"Really, I have previous commitments and—"

"Eight."

"Mr. Perini—"

He stuck up his finger.

"Cosmo," she repeated. "It's not the money."

"Ten."

"Please, stop. Six thousand is fine." What was she saying?

"Twelve. Fifteen. Name your price." He stood and

6

extended his hand. "I'll be back in a few minutes. You think about it. I have someone waiting." Cosmo smiled and lumbered out of the skybox, leaving Alexandra in more than a bit of shock.

They say miracles happen every day. Maybe this was God's way of making up for the past six years of hell. She glanced at the wrestling ring. A giant black man whacked Loverboy in the chest with a steel ladder. She would never understand this, the abuse, the violence, the disrespect for one's own body. A chill danced across her shoulders.

"Your job is to make them look good, not judge them," she muttered, repeating Professor Englestein's lesson aloud.

The crowd cheered as Loverboy did a double back flip and kicked the giant's chest, then did a hip wiggle, thrust, grab.

This man looked beyond help.

Cosmo raced to his office as fast as his sixty-seven-year-old legs would carry him. Everything was on the line, and until Pete got out of jail, Cosmo was on his own.

He pushed open the door to his office.

"Well?" a deep voice said from the corner. Shadows hid the man's face, as usual.

"She had a problem with the travel," Cosmo said.

"How big of a problem?"

"We'll work it out. Maybe I can reduce his schedule."

"Well done, Mr. Perini." He tossed a thick envelope onto Cosmo's desk.

"I hope you're right. She seems awfully . . . green."

"She's the one," said the man Cosmo had privately named Mr. X.

A cheer drew the man's attention to the arena. Who

was he, anyway? A millionaire wrestling fanatic? Someone who owed Pete a favor? A spy from a competing wrestling group? Cosmo squinted to make out the guy's face. No luck. Well, even if he worked for WHAK or OW, Cosmo would come out on top. He'd take the guy's money and prove to Pete he could run a promotion as well as the next guy.

"The new angle with Loverboy is a good investment, isn't it?"

"Yes, sir. That kid's the best thing we've got."

Cosmo had found Timothy Lucas Silverspoon in Goober's Gym twelve years ago and thanked Lady Luck ever since. The kid's charisma and wild antics had saved BAM from bankruptcy more than once. Loverboy was loyal to BAM and Cosmo knew he had a good heart. Sure, the kid acted arrogant for the crowd, but he always helped the boys with new moves so they wouldn't get too banged up.

"Whatever the Hayes woman wants, I'll make sure she gets it," Mr. X. said.

"I'm still not sure we should go with her, being so inexperienced and all."

"I'll check in next week."

Cosmo heard the dismissal and took his cue. He snatched the envelope from the desk and left the office, shutting the door behind him. He knew the drill. Meet, get orders, leave, and allow his new, silent partner privacy and the ability to disappear without anyone catching sight of his face.

Ambling down the hall, he considered Mr. X's decision to hire the girl from Sycamore, Illinois, to groom their new breed of heroes. How the hell was that slip of a girl going to deal with Loverboy, a self-confident ladies' man? Hell, he'd have her under the sheets before she could say press release. And make him into a gentleman? Cosmo chuckled aloud at that one. For all his good qualities, Loverboy Luke could be a stubborn, arrogant son-of-a-gun.

But stranger things had happened, like fans embracing heels and turning on heroes. Sometimes you just didn't know what to expect.

"Come up here and say that!" Loverboy Luke called from the ropes to the front row of fans.

"Riptide Ralph's going to kick your ass!" a skinny teenage boy shouted back.

"Yeah? Not if he's unconscious!"

Luke sprang over the top rope and drop kicked Ralphy in the gut. The beefy wrestler stumbled back-first to the mat. Luke took a bow. The crowd went nuts, tossing peanuts, cheese-laden nachos, and half-consumed plastic cups of beer. Good thing they didn't sell it in bottles.

He dropped to his knees and applied a sleeper hold to Ralph's neck.

"Easy," Ralph mumbled.

"You can do this, Ralphy," he said between gritted teeth. "Nice and easy."

"You're nuts."

"Just like we practiced."

The ref got in Luke's face. "No choking. One!" He thrust his forefinger into the air in warning. "Two, three—"

Luke ceremoniously released the hold and strutted to the corner of the ring. He grabbed his mirror from the mat and admired his reflection. He ignored the bloodshot eyes, pale skin and scarring above his left eye. The fans couldn't see those things anyway. All they saw was an obnoxious, cocky, son-of-a-bitch. The kind of guy they loved to hate.

He puckered his lips and laid a big wet one on the mirror. Jeers bounced off the ceiling, rattled the rafters and pierced his eardrums.

Jeers that energized him. Protected him. And kept anyone from seeing what he really was.

Heart racing, he tossed the mirror to Nedra the Nymph. He spun around and watched Riptide Ralph fumble his way to the corner. With any luck Ralphy Boy would get it right this time.

Nedra handed Loverboy the microphone. "What's the matter, you pigheaded donkey?" Luke taunted. "You tired? You too old for this? Or has the burned-out, ex-football player run out of guts?"

Ralphy flexed his pecs three times and motioned for Luke. "Come on, you pretty boy, good-for-nothin' piece of soap scum."

Soap scum? Whatever.

Luke dropped the mike and took off, sprinting the twelve feet to his opponent. Just before contact, he sprang and Ralphy pushed, sending Luke flying over the ropes as planned. Only Ralphy's heart wasn't into this move. Instead of landing in the first row of planted spectators, Luke fell short and hit the guardrail—back first.

"Shit!" he muttered under his breath, flopping to the floor. Back surgery was one thing he didn't need right now. He knew how long it took guys to recover, if they ever did. Panic burned his gut.

"Get up, you worthless piece of trash!" a fan screamed.

"You're not so hot now, are you, Loverboy?" another shouted.

Luke played possum, wondering when the wrestlers were going to listen to him and trust his instincts. A guy could get hurt like this.

With a fistful of Luke's hair, Ralphy jerked his head back. Luke pushed himself to his knees and felt a definite crack across his lower back. Great.

"We're not done yet, Loverpunk," Ralphy shouted, tossing him under the bottom rope into the ring. He rolled to center ring, sprawled on his stomach.

The crowd was hot, all right. They were more than ready for the Riptide Rush. Luke could roll onto his back and let Ralphy nail him in the gut when he came down, but what he had planned would be more dramatic. Watching Riptide, their hero, shatter Loverboy's spine would be sweet justice for Luke's devilish antics. The way they figured it, he deserved to be punished.

Didn't he know it.

Through half-closed eyes he spied Ralphy working up the crowd with his patented chest-pounding, feet-stomping howl. Sounded like a lovesick hyena.

Luke braced himself. Breathe. Focus. Shut out the pain.

Ralphy balanced on the turnbuckle, stretched his arms and jumped. Luke sucked in his breath just as Ralphy's bony knee hit his lower back. He bit down, hard, and tasted blood.

Couldn't this monster-sized rookie get anything right? Flat to flat. Belly to back. Where the hell was his head?

Ralphy turned him over and casually pinned him with a lateral press. If the storyline didn't require

11

Loverboy to lose this one, he'd be sorely tempted to pound the lights out of Idiot Riptide.

"One! Two! Three!" the ref shouted, slapping the mat.

Ralphy jumped to his feet and thrust his fists into the air. The crowd cheered his victory.

Luke rolled under the bottom rope and limped up the ramp. Nedra came up beside him.

"You okay?" she asked, batting her red false eyelashes and handing him the microphone.

He wished she'd stop worrying about him. He didn't deserve her compassion.

"I'm fine," he said, forcing a smile to make her feel better.

He spun around and pointed at his opponent. "This isn't over, Rip-tush!"

The crowd booed, shouted obscenities, and threw coins.

"Next week, at Fall Maul you're mine, got it?" Luke said. "For the title this time. I let you win tonight, you giant squid. I wanted to check out your moves. I know what you got now, you brainless kumquat. You'll be wishing you'd picked croquet instead of wrestling for your second career!"

He tossed the mike to the floor and stormed up the ramp, Nedra by his side.

"I'm worried about you," she said.

"I'm fine, baby. Just fine." He smiled at the crowd and a little boy caught his eye. The kid couldn't have been more than six. While all the adults around him were booing, hissing and shoving their thumbs down, this little guy cheered and waved.

And something broke inside.

He ripped his gaze from the audience, stuck his nose

in the air and sauntered out like he was king and they were mere peasants.

Pushing through the black curtain, he pulled away from Nedra.

"Later," he said.

"You sure you don't need to see a trainer about your back?"

"You worry too much," he said with a peck to her cheek.

"We're all going to O'Shea's Pub after the show." She looked hopeful.

"Maybe I'll see you there."

She smiled and her brown eyes lit up. *Aw, honey, don't get your hopes up. You wouldn't want me if you knew who I really was.*

A man who hurts those who get too close. A man who let his best friend die.

He ambled toward the locker room and only when he was alone in a dressing alcove did his knees buckle. He gave in to the pain then, shut his eyes and balled his hands into fists. Kneeling on the cold, cement floor, he gritted his teeth and pressed his forehead against his closed fists.

With all his lecturing and rehearsals, this was what he tried to spare the rookies: the paralyzing pain. He couldn't bring back Bubba, but maybe he could help save a few of the boys from unnecessary pain.

And maybe even death.

Yet some of the boys didn't take the work as seriously as Luke. They figured if they could deliver a swift kick to the chest, they were in; they would take their place center stage and bask in the attention and glory.

There was a lot more to pro wrestling than that.

13

To Luke it was about going to the edge and back again, stirring up the crowd and being the best "bad" there was. That would keep him in the number one spot—where he needed to be in order to take care of Bubba's family.

"Let it go," he said, dragging his body into the shower. The pressure of hot water soothed his muscles and eased the tension in his neck, his back. Nothing would work for bone. Nothing that Luke would consider.

Wrapping a white towel around his waist, he stepped into the locker room toward his gear. He unzipped his duffel bag and something flew at his face.

"Jesus!" he cried, jumping back and almost losing his balance thanks to the jolt of pain up his spine. Two dozen multi-colored condom packages littered the floor, the bench and his duffel bag.

Merlin and Mook snickered from the corner of the room.

"Funny, very funny. Did Oscar put you up to this?" Luke said.

"Who?" Merlin said. Mook shrugged.

"Tell that old married bastard that if he wants to get some piece of ass, he should stick with me. I do the easy ones, the hard ones and every one in-between. Hell, there aren't enough rubbers here to last me a week," he said in keeping with his image. Even the boys didn't know the real Luke Silver. He liked it that way.

Mook cleared his throat. "Um, behind you."

He turned to find Cosmo standing in the doorway with a short brunette.

Luke blinked twice. And blinked again.

Cosmo put his hand on her shoulder. "Loverboy, I'd like you to meet—"

"Lexy? Lexy Whitford?"

14

Chapter Two

Lexy? No one had called her Lexy since the third grade. She studied the nearly naked beast, a handful of multi-colored condoms clenched between his fingers. His long hair fell in tangled waves down his shoulders; light brown hair dusted across his chest and down his stomach to disappear below the skimpy white towel.

"Sorry, I thought you were someone else," he said, turning his back to her.

Lexy. Lexy. She racked her brain. Who used to call her that?

"Loverboy, this is our new PR gal," Cosmo said. "She's coming on board to redefine things a little. Teach you how to behave in public."

"Jesus, Cosmo, I'm a grown man. I know how to behave," he said, snatching a T-shirt from his duffel bag.

She took a few steps toward him, wanting to see his face again. She had the absolute *worst* memory when it came to faces and names. Although selective memory came in handy when she wanted to forget nights of forced passion with the ex.

"Alexandra Hayes." She stuck out her hand.

He looked at it, then narrowed his eyes.

"And you know who I am." Arrogance dripped from his voice.

"Loverboy Luke Silver," she said, the name sounding all wrong. She withdrew her hand and gazed into his striking blue-green eyes. Her stomach did a double back flip. One too many cups of coffee, no doubt.

Loverboy glanced away and rifled through his bag.

"Have we met before?" she asked.

He turned to her, a slight curve to his mouth. "Lady, that is the sorriest excuse for a pick-up line I've ever heard. Even *I* gave that one up years ago."

"I'm serious."

"So am I, sweet cheeks." He winked, grabbed his bag and headed for the dressing alcove. She followed him.

"You called me Lexy," she said.

"Got you mixed up with someone else."

He started into the alcove and she touched his shoulder. Glancing down at her hand, a wry smile played across his lips.

"Sorry, babe, there's only room for one."

"But—"

He ripped the curtain closed. Drat. She didn't know which she hated more—not knowing who this man was, or having to deal with his cocky attitude. She'd had enough of cocky.

This was business, and in order to do her job she needed to know everything about Mr. Loverboy. She had to focus on his strengths and mask his weaknesses, know him inside and out, anticipate his response to things and teach him new, appropriate responses.

"I wasn't done talking to you," she called through the curtain.

Nothing.

"Mr. Loverboy?"

He was purposely ignoring her. An all-too-familiar feeling. She ripped open the curtain.

"Hey!" he protested.

He'd slipped on a navy T-shirt but still wore the terry towel around his waist. "She's the one who needs a lesson in manners, Cosmo."

"How do I know you?" she asked.

"Obviously not well enough." He smiled, then snapped the towel from his waist.

Any other woman would probably swoon at the sight of him, semi-hard and, she suspected, larger than most. Unfortunately Alexandra's libido was almost non-existent—yet another reason David went wandering. His ego couldn't take his wife being lukewarm about something as sizzling as sex. Oh well, there were worse things than being frigid.

Like being unemployed and childless, if she failed to earn a decent living.

She wavered at the thought.

"She's goin' down!" One of the wrestlers called.

"I'm fine," she said, staring into Loverboy's eyes, her fingers gripping the curtain for support. She wouldn't let him think his hard body had any effect on her. "Must be low blood sugar," she said.

"I've got some candy, if you're interested."

The twinkle in Loverboy's eyes made her want to slap him upside the head. "Oh, you do, do you?"

Cosmo cupped her elbow and snapped the curtain

shut. "My fault, my fault. They need their downtime after a match. Let's wait outside. He'll be easier to talk to when he's not crowded."

Cosmo led her to the door.

"Have Oscar clean up this mess of condoms," Loverboy ordered the other wrestlers.

Alexandra heard the metal rings of the dressing curtain scrape open. She glanced over her shoulder at Loverboy.

"I've got my own supply." He looked her straight in the eye and shot her a half smile, a wolf's smile. "Now if I could only find someone to help me break them in."

She shook her head and wondered how on earth she was going to work with this man. Cosmo led her into the hallway.

"Sorry about that," he said. "See, that's what I mean. The boy needs a lesson in how to deal with people." Cosmo shoved his hands into his blazer pockets.

"No need to apologize. He doesn't scare me." She waved him off and leaned against the cement wall.

"You sure? You looked a little pale in there."

She stood straight. "Mr. Perini, don't think a little sexual intimidation has any effect on me. I'm immune."

"Excuse me?"

"Never mind. Let's focus on business. I'd like to see your story lines for the next three months and your promotional schedule for Mr. Loverboy." She paced a few steps and back again. Think, plan, execute. Keep your mind trained on the objective. Shoo away the nagging thoughts brought on by the utterance of a childhood nickname.

Lexy. The name evoked memories of Checkers, her cock-a-poo, the tire swing out back in the old house, and her little brother, Christian, hooking himself to the

18

suspended dog run cable and sailing into the neighbor's rose bushes.

Lexy. Who had called her that?

"I'll get you the story lines ASAP," Cosmo said. "The promotional schedule is nil at present. Once he turns from heel to hero and the fans take to him, we'll set up a tour." She remembered the blonde bimbos falling over themselves to get to the wrestler. Obviously the reason for the case of condoms.

"Now, explain this to me again," she said, pulling a small notebook from her briefcase. "He seems awfully popular as he is."

"Popular as a heel. We want him to get over with the fans as a hero."

"Get over what?"

"That means, get popular with the fans."

"But he's popular now, isn't he?"

"We need a hero, a good guy who can draw the same kind of loyalty. Wrestling hasn't had a baby face like that since the Hulkster back in the Eighties. Only a handful of guys have that kind of charisma, and Loverboy Luke is one of them. I'm telling you, if we don't do something radical, we're going to lose all our fans to Steel's Outrageous Wrestling. I can't stand the thought. That's not wrestling, it's porn."

The door to the locker room swung open and Loverboy sauntered out, buttoning the cuff of his denim shirt.

He glanced at Lexy. "You still here? Let me guess, you want a one-on-one with yours truly."

She stood tall, but still barely came up to the breast pocket of his shirt.

"Sorry to disappoint you, Mr. Loverboy, but this is strictly business."

"I'm sorry to hear that." With that mischievous smile, his eyes roamed the contours of her body.

She fought back the anger-induced adrenaline rush and narrowed her eyes in warning.

"I'm hiring her to straighten you out," Cosmo said. "You're going to be seeing a lot of each other."

"I know what I need right now, Cosmo, and it isn't lessons on how to talk, walk, or handle the media. Now, if she was offering something else . . ."

Her heart pounded with irritation. He was too close. The man didn't know the meaning of personal space.

"But then I have a feeling she's the one needing lessons in that department. Isn't that right, babe?"

She gritted her teeth. For the first time in months she felt that familiar burn bubbling in her stomach, and once again the words caught in her throat.

"I'm outta here," he said.

Loverboy walked away, awfully fast, in her opinion. Why did she get the feeling he wanted to escape her presence more than he wanted a hot and willing woman?

She shoved the notebook into her purse. He probably couldn't stand the thought of being around a cold, asexual creature. He had to sense her lack of desire. "Disturbing." That was the word David had used. Disturbing and devastating to his ego. If men valued anything, it was their egos.

"Loverboy, hang on." Cosmo chased after him, his loafers scuffing across the cement floor. "I want you to go with this one, kid. It's important."

"It's a waste of time."

"I don't think so." Cosmo hesitated. "You want to keep wrestling, don't ya?"

"You threatening me, Cosmo? Is that what you're do-ing?" He dropped his duffel bag to the floor and backed Cosmo against the wall. Alexandra automatically took a step back, and she was a good fifteen feet away.

Scary when provoked. She made a mental note of that.

Cosmo's eyes widened and he swallowed hard. "It's not a threat, it's a reality check. We need to carve out a new piece of the market. If you want to keep fighting, we need to make changes."

"What kind of changes?"

"New characters, new heroes," Cosmo said.

"I could never do that."

"You've got to try."

"Bullshit. I'll quit first."

Alexandra stared at him in disbelief. The man was morally opposed to becoming a good guy?

"Think real hard about this, kid," Cosmo said.

Loverboy clenched his jaw, then marched towards Alexandra. There was no way she was going to back down. She'd backed down way too many times in her life. This was business and represented a big job, big money and a way to protect her son.

He closed in and her legs started to move of their own volition—backward. She held firm, planted her hands on her hips and cocked her chin up a notch.

He towered over her, the scent of his musk after-shave tickling her nose. If he got any closer, he'd be in-side her.

"Go back to wherever you came from, little girl. I'm not working with you now, tomorrow or ever. Got it?" he said, his turquoise eyes ablaze.

She held firm, but didn't speak. No sense provoking

him further. He marched away, damp hair trailing down his back.

The man was madder than a penned bobcat and probably just as dangerous—to the wrong person.

But for all his grunting and physical intimidation, she sensed he wouldn't hurt her physically. Something told her he was a gentle man, though he'd never admit it.

Where did that come from? What the heck did she know about men anyway? Especially this one?

Loverboy stormed past the waiting press and adoring fans who'd been lucky enough to snag backstage passes. The steel door slammed behind him.

She looked at Cosmo.

"He'll come around," he assured her, leading the way toward the exit, where a cab was waiting.

"You still interested?" He chewed nervously at his lower lip.

Cosmo reminded her a little of Dad: well-meaning, but not completely together.

She smiled. "Don't worry, Cosmo. I can handle him. By the end of our three-month contract you'll know you've made the right decision."

Now, if she could only convince herself of that.

Luke directed the limo driver to pull into the alley behind O'Shea's Pub. He checked his watch. Eleven fifteen.

"Give me twenty minutes," he said to the driver. The man nodded.

Slipping on his silver silk jacket, he made for the back entrance. He had to find Sam. The bouncer was always good at picking just the right girl.

He took a deep breath, still messed up about tonight's

turn of events. Make him into a hero? Were they nuts? His heel persona was what made him a success with fans. They recognized true bad when they saw it.

Besides, he couldn't risk people liking him and wanting to get close. God, if anyone knew how bad he really was . . .

Don't go there.

He climbed the back stairs and knocked twice. Sam, the bouncer, swung the door wide. "Heard Riptide did a number on you."

"He's a slow learner."

"Yeah, tell me something I don't know. Sucked as a defensive lineman, sucks as a pro wrestler."

Luke chuckled. They'd all thought bringing in a "real" athlete would add class to pro wrestling. Sometimes it worked, but not in Ralph's case.

"What have you got for me?" he said, following Sam through the back hallway toward the bar.

"A blonde, cute, with a smart mouth, or a brunette. She came with a pack but she'd dump them for a night with you. Both have been drinking since nine."

Luke pulled a fifty from his wallet and slid it into Sam's palm. "Which one would you pick?"

"Brunette. Easy on the eyes, easy on the ears. The blonde's got this voice that cuts right through you."

"Talking isn't a priority," he said to keep up the pretense.

Luke cracked open the door and studied the women. The brunette was cute, with an oval-shaped face, warm smile and—

Another smile drifted across his thoughts. Sparkling amber eyes and a turned-up little nose.

Lexy. She didn't even remember him.

"I'll take them both," he said. "Where are the cameras?"

"Everywhere." Sam pointed to a couple of tabloid photographers.

"Thanks." He pushed through the door into a crowd of screaming fans. Making his way toward the bar, he ignored the knot in his chest. There was a time when he'd lived for the adulation. He was Loverboy Luke Silver, the best pro wrestler in BAM, the most outrageous athlete to step into the squared circle. Then Bubba died and now Luke lived to make up where he'd failed so miserably.

Flash bulbs popped, blinding him, irritating the shit out of him. The bartender handed him a Chivas on the rocks and Luke raised his glass to the fans.

They cheered, shoved pictures and Sharpie pens at him and showered him with praise. This was real. He was a superstar. Even the Colonel couldn't deny that.

Why the hell was he thinking about the old man?

He navigated through the swarm of fans and made his way toward the sweet-looking brunette. As he extended his hand to introduce himself, the blonde shimmied up beside him.

"Hey, there, handsome," the blonde said.

He eyed the blonde, then the brunette. "You're both so cute, I can't decide who to take home tonight." The snapping of more flashbulbs blinded him.

Out of the corner of his eye, he caught sight of Nedra's sad eyes and half frown. He smiled, trying to ease her pain. She grabbed Curtis the Crippler and kissed him.

Everyone had his own way of dealing with the pain.

"So, which one of you is going to get a private lesson with Loverboy Luke?" he asked.

"I've got some interesting holds I'd like to try on you," the blonde boasted.

Too pushy. He didn't need pushy. He needed nice and . . . submissive.

"Sissy! What the hell do you think you're doing?" A tall, lumberjack-type guy appeared, grabbing the blonde's arm.

"Getting some real male attention," she said.

The guy glared at Luke as if he were the Antichrist.

Great. His body ached in more places than he dared admit. A fight was something he didn't need right now.

"Hang on, big guy," Luke said, trying to avoid a confrontation. "I've got my girl for the night." He pulled Miss Brunette toward him. She tumbled off her stool into his arms.

"What, my Sissy ain't good enough for you?"

What the hell? He couldn't win.

"Didn't say that, man." He put up his hand in a defensive gesture.

"Good, cuz Sissy's the best woman here. She's cute and funny. Except for that mouth of hers, she's just about as perfect as any girl can get."

He took a step closer and Luke readied himself for battle. Every muscle in his body was tensed; that salty taste filled his mouth.

"Cal?" The blonde placed her hand on her boyfriend's chest. "Did you say, perfect?"

Lumberjack hissed through his teeth.

Luke held his position.

"Cal? I'm perfect?"

Lumberjack looked down at her. "Sissy, you are the most frustrating woman I know. But yeah, you're pretty perfect."

She jumped into his arms and kissed him on the mouth, the cheek, the forehead. Relief spread across Luke's shoulders, then pain settled in his chest. Must have cracked a rib on the way over the ropes tonight.

"Well, kid, looks like it's you and me." With an arm around the quiet brunette's shoulder, Luke led his catch of the night toward the front door. He waved at the fans, smiled and winked for the cameras. Wouldn't they love the pictures they got tonight? Loverboy living up to his reputation of rake and scoundrel, sweeping a lucky female off her feet for a night of unrelenting sex.

He nodded at Sam on his way out and led her to the limo.

"What's your name?" he asked.

"Hmmm?" She glanced into his eyes with a mix of admiration and inebriation.

"Your name?"

"Does it matter?"

It should, it really should. What was the matter with everyone?

They climbed into the limo and she nuzzled against his shoulder. Maybe he'd go through with it for a change. He had the sudden urge to screw someone hard and all night long. But not this little thing. He should have taken Nedra home. She would have jumped his bones till sunrise. Then maybe he could put the luminescent color of amber out of his mind and wash all images of a chestnut-haired beauty from his heart.

No. He wouldn't let ghosts of the past eat away at him. He'd come too far and fought too hard to get here. He was Loverboy Luke Silver, the toughest bastard in pro wrestling. There was no room in his life for sentiment or compassion or . . . love.

He reached for the minibar. "Want something?" he asked his "date."

"No, thanks." She shot him an unfocused smile. She'd be out before they reached the bed.

The limo pulled around the corner to the Hilton, where a line of fans waited outside.

"You want to go around back, sir?" the driver asked.

"No." He glanced at the nameless brunette. "Bring us up front." Appearance was everything.

Taking a deep breath, he grasped the brunette's hand and opened the door.

Hotel security struggled to keep the fans from swarming Loverboy and his female. Fans shoved programs, eight-by-ten glossies, even bras in his face. "Sorry, don't have much use for one of those," he joked.

"Sign it! Sign it!" a well-endowed woman pleaded.

"No time for autographs, sorry," he said, working his way through the crowd.

The brunette stumbled and he cupped her elbow. "You okay?"

"Sure." She gazed at him with empty eyes.

"Come on." He scooped her into his arms and posed for the cameras. The flashes popped like a strobe light. He smiled, then escaped into the lobby, where he carried his prize to the elevator.

He punched the concierge floor button, still cradling the woman in his arms. She felt like a sack of cement. Like all of them. Lifeless, dead weight. He couldn't remember the last time a woman warmed him to the inside of his bones. He'd turned that off years ago.

If you don't feel, you won't hurt. He'd learned early on that although his persona attracted women, they never really wanted to know what lay beneath. They wanted to screw Loverboy Luke, but didn't care about the real Timothy Lucas Silverspoon.

Who the hell was *that*, anyway? Luke closed his eyes. Whoever he was, he'd died seventeen years ago when he walked out the front door of the Colonel's five-bedroom home.

The elevator doors opened and he made his way to Room 1412. With careful balance and quick fingers, he unlocked the door and carried the girl to the bed.

"Where are we going?" she mumbled.

"Shh. Just relax." He gently laid her atop the pale print comforter and took a step back.

"No, come here." She beckoned with her hands.

She grabbed hold of his shirt and jerked him forward. Quite a grip for a drunken little thing. She pulled his lips to hers, the kiss tasting of rum and desperation. His own desperation spiraled through his chest like a roller coaster out of control.

He broke the kiss. "Hang on. I'll make us a drink."

"Okay." She smiled, her eyelids closing, opening, then closing again.

He ambled to the minibar and poured two miniatures of whiskey into a plastic cup. "Whiskey okay?"

He glanced over his shoulder. She was out cold.

Standing, he gritted his teeth against the back pain and went to the girl, pulling the comforter across her body. She had a nice enough figure. Any other man would jump at the chance to nail this beauty. But not Luke.

He took a step back and shoved his hands into his pockets, fingering his bronzed eagle's feather key chain. Touching the cool metal usually calmed him, brought him back from the vortex of anger threatening to eat him alive.

He made for the balcony, grabbing his drink on the

way. Drinking wasn't like him either, but tonight he needed something extra to quiet the storm.

The crisp, fall air slapped his cheeks as he stepped outside. St. Louis was a pleasant enough city, not overwhelming like New York or Los Angeles. Just right. It kind of reminded him of . . . home.

He took a quick swallow of booze, cursing the walk down memory lane. How did he get here again?

Lexy.

What trick was God playing on him, reminding him of the past? Of hiding in tree houses and chasing after a runaway mutt. Of sailing paper airplanes into her second-story bedroom window, and walking to school far enough behind her so she wouldn't see him. Of taking the blame when the Anderson twins had set her up for putting gum in Miss Connor's brush. He'd protected Lexy and had earned her gratitude, even though he knew she didn't particularly like the geek from next door.

After the gum-in-the-brush incident she'd let him walk beside her to school. She didn't complain about his gifts of wax lips or Smarties. She'd accepted him, as much as she could, anyway.

Then Kevin died. Luke's fault. He should have done something, should have stopped him—

"Shit." He pounded a closed fist on the metal balcony.

Forget the past, make the future. The words he'd lived by since he'd gone out on his own. But the past was back, haunting him with the memory of Lexy . . . handing him her bandanna to dry his tears, touching his hand, crying alongside him at the loss of his brother.

"Enough," he said, wanting the torture to end, but knowing it never would.

He glanced through the sliding doors at a sleeping Miss Brunette. She'd dream up plenty of stories to tell her friends about her fabulous night with Loverboy Luke.

Loverboy Luke—a ladies' man, a selfish bastard. The persona that kept anyone from getting too close and seeing what a true bastard he was.

Glancing out over the city, his eyes watered from the biting wind. He was exactly where he wanted to be—successful, famous, and autonomous. He didn't need anyone.

He placed his half-empty cup on the ledge and studied the woman on his bed. How many faceless, nameless women had he hoped would drive away the pain and give him completeness? No one could. Now it was all a game, going through the motions, acting out a role.

Except Loverboy Luke was more than just a role. It was his life, his soul. Without it, he was nothing.

Chapter Three

It bothered her all the way home. Alexandra couldn't shake the feeling that Loverboy's true identity was extremely important. The cab turned the corner of Newberry Court, her quiet suburban Chicago street lined with duplexes and single-family homes. She dug into her purse for her wallet.

Lexy. She hated the name. It reminded her of a toy poodle with a diamond-studded collar and manicured nails.

How could Loverboy know the dreaded nickname? She'd never met him before today. Had she? He certainly wasn't forthcoming with his true identity. Had they been childhood sweethearts?

No, one thing she did remember was her list of disasters. There'd been Petey Carson in the fifth grade and the kiss by the railroad tracks. Tasted like licorice.

She'd gone steady with tennis star Hank Sikes in middle school. Gave herself a mild concussion trying to impress him with her patented forehand. She couldn't look him in the eye after that, not that she could look anyone in the eye thanks to the swelling. And that was before high school.

Forget high school. None of those boys called her Lexy, nor were they worth remembering. She closed her eyes and focused on Loverboy's voice, unusually low and gravelly, so unlike that of a child's.

Lexy? Lexy Whitford?

The rich rumble rolled around in her brain, teased her memory, and irritated her senses.

Nothing. Nada. No dice.

"Oh, forget it," she muttered under her breath.

The cabby pulled into her driveway. "Twenty-five dollars," he said.

Gritting her teeth, she handed him thirty. It was getting expensive to leave your house these days. Cripes, it was expensive to live. She visualized the stack of bills waiting on her kitchen counter and wondered if Cosmo would consider sending her an advance on her services.

She slammed the white cab door shut and slung the briefcase over her shoulder. Aunt Lulu's side of the duplex was dark. A soft, purplish glow emanated through Alexandra's living room sheers. Lulu must have fallen asleep in front of the TV again after tucking Riley in bed. Yet it was only 8 P.M.

She trudged up the drive and realized how lucky she was to have Lulu around, no matter how eccentric her aunt was. Alexandra had been devastated when her mom and dad moved to Florida, but she hadn't let on. She'd smiled her brightest smile and told them how great it would be for her mom's health.

Alexandra was strong, but there were days she'd worried about parenting Riley on her own. Then in walked Aunt Lulu, crystal ball in one hand and ice skates in the other. Alexandra had resisted at first. She had her hands full with Riley, and felt like she couldn't take on the added responsibility of watching over her aunt.

Two years later, Alexandra found herself depending on the seventy-year-old woman for more than a neighborly cup of sugar. She filled in for Alexandra when work and college had sapped all her energy. More importantly, the woman loved Riley with all her heart.

Lulu never had her own children. Her first love was her career as an exotic ice skater for The Palms Resort in the Caribbean.

Sticking her key in the front door, Alexandra thanked God for her good-hearted aunt. She pushed open the door and shrieked at the sight that greeted her.

"Lulu!" She dropped her briefcase to the carpet and stared in disbelief at her aunt, dressed in a pink leotard, poodle skirt, and high heels. The costume was topped with a purple wig and shiny gold earrings.

"Hey Mom!" Riley jumped out of the kitchen, wearing a navy suit, chewing on an unlit cigar and waving a toy gun.

"What are you doing?" Oh God, he should be doing homework or watching Nickelodeon, not playing cops and hookers with his aunt.

"We're play acting," Lulu said, putting an arm around Riley and grabbing the cigar. "I'm Patsy Poodles and the boy is Phil Marlow. You just walked in on the interrogation."

Riley waved his gun in the air. "Yeah, I'm the big dick."

"Riley!" Alexandra said.

"Oh, relax," Lulu said. "He means he's the lead detective. We got work to do, don't we, Riley?"

He studied the floor and bit his lower lip.

"Oh, don't worry about Mama," Lulu said. "She just had a rough business trip, didn't ya, Ally-ooops?" She pulled off the lampshade and tossed it to the floor, then handed Riley the lamp. "Go for it."

Riley glanced at Alexandra and she couldn't help smiling. Those big green eyes always did that to her.

He redirected his attention to his aunt. "Time to talk, Poodles."

"You got nothing on me," Lulu said, sitting on the sofa and crossing one leg over the other.

"You were seen at the docks. You tossed Clyde into the swamp and made off with the shipment of paper umbrellas."

Lulu squared off at Riley. "I got no use for paper umbrellas, Marlow. You'll just have to find yourself another stool pigeon."

The exchange continued for a few minutes and Alexandra relaxed. Her son had come a long way since the divorce, loss of his grandparents, and subsequent emotional withdrawal. She couldn't help thinking her aunt had something to do with that.

Okay, so maybe she'd overreacted. A little fantasy play wasn't such a bad thing, was it?

The microwave beeped. "Popcorn!" Riley cried, racing into the kitchen.

She narrowed her eyes at Lulu.

"Don't go giving me that look. The boy was having a meltdown about missing his mama. I had to do something to distract him."

Panic fluttered in her belly. If Riley melted down when she'd been gone twenty-four hours, how could she travel two or three days at a time working for Cosmo?

"How'd the business trip go?" Lulu said.

"Good. Bad. I don't know."

"Well, was it good or bad?"

"Good. He's throwing money at me."

"So what's the problem?" Lulu said.

"There's travel involved."

"No sweat, as long as it isn't on the weekends. I got the lead in *Annie Get Your Gun* on ice. Rehearsals start next week."

"All the more reason why I can't take this job. You said Riley had a meltdown. I can't travel."

"He'll be fine. What kind of money are we talkin'?"

"Lots."

"Make it work. You've been waiting for a chance like this. Don't let it pass."

"But—"

Lulu stuck out her index finger to silence Alexandra. "Ally-ooops, you gotta learn to let go, let nature work its way with the boy. He isn't going to become a man if he's always clinging to your skirt."

"He's only eight!"

"I had a paying job when I was eight."

"That's against the law and you know it."

"Collected skate guards the rich kids left on the railing at the Wintergarden. Sold 'em for five cents a pair. By the time I was ten, I had enough money to buy a used pair of skates."

"This is about Riley. I can't leave him for two or three days at a time."

Riley poked his head through the kitchen door. "Parmesan?"

"Sure," Alexandra said.

"Chocolate syrup for me," Lulu said.

35

"Chocolate syrup on popcorn?"

Lulu jutted out her chin. "Could be worse things."

"Like dressing up as a hooker."

"I beg your pardon, missy. Patsy Poodles did not sleep with anyone she wasn't married to. Although I think she was married about twelve times, or was it thirteen?" Her brows curved in concentration.

Riley trotted up to Lulu, handed her a bowl of popcorn and a can of Hershey's, then sat on Alexandra's lap. "I like parmesan too, Mom."

She smiled. A natural, immediate response whenever he got close. The boy had a round-cheeked grin that lit up his face and a sweet way about him that lit her insides. He was the brightest spot in her life. Without him, she'd be lost.

"Riley, honey, can you go change for bed?" Alexandra said.

His lips curled into a frown.

"No, you're not going to sleep, but I want you to get ready. I think you and your aunt are done with the investigation."

He glanced at Lulu.

"Go on. We'll finish tomorrow." She looked at Alexandra and muttered, "Or maybe not."

He jumped off Alexandra's lap. "I'll put you away, Poodles!" he cried and raced to his bedroom.

"Getting back to our conversation . . ." Alexandra said.

Lulu ignored her and squirted syrup on her popcorn. The woman's eyes lit up and her tongue danced across her lower lip.

"Lulu!"

"What?" She jerked and dripped syrup on her tutu.

36

"Nuts." She dabbed at it with her finger, then stuck it in her mouth.

"What if David had shown up tonight?" Alexandra said.

"He didn't."

Alexandra kicked off her pumps and paced across the short-pile living room carpet to the bay window. "He would have freaked out if he'd seen Riley like that." She turned to Lulu. "He already thinks Riley should spend more time with him to strengthen his personality."

Lulu snorted.

"David is looking for reasons to take Riley away from me," Alexandra said.

"You're paranoid. That man wants to play daddy about as much as he wants a double root canal."

"Not if the new wife pressures him. She wants kids. Playing mommy to Riley would convince David what a great mother she'd be."

"And I'm the queen of Egypt."

Alexandra straightened a stack of Riley's school papers sitting on the walnut desk. "I can't take the job."

"Hogwash. You need the money and the career boost."

Alexandra ambled back to her favorite swivel rocker. How cruel to see the light at the end of the tunnel, the opportunity of a lifetime and have to let it go.

Lulu got up and shoved the can of Hershey's at her. "Get a grip."

She looked into her aunt's eyes, appreciating the woman's attempt to help. "Thanks." She took the can and fingered the syrup as it oozed down the side.

"You're going to take this job because it's time good things happened for you and the kid. We're going to

37

work it out, the three of us. The show will work rehearsals around my schedule. If they balk, I'll step down and let my stunt double take the lead."

"That's not fair to you."

"There will be other shows. This is just one of many for a talented star like me." She sidled back to the sofa and dug her manicured fingers into the popcorn.

"I honestly don't know what I'd do without you some days," Alexandra said.

"And others you'd like to send me packing, I know, I know." She waved her off. "Now, give. What's the deal with this new client?"

"They're based out of St. Louis, an established business trying to change the perception of their product." Did she dare say more? Admit it was sweaty men beating each other to a pulp for entertainment?

"What kind of product?" Lulu said.

"Um . . . well . . . it's kind of radical."

Lulu leaned forward, the metal bowl of chocolate-covered popcorn cradled in her hands. "Kinky sexual devices?"

"Aunt Lulu!" Her cheeks flushed.

"What?" She sat straight. "You said radical."

"It's a sport, not a sexual device."

"Let me guess, let me guess." She tapped her forefinger to her chin. Her eyes lit with excitement. "Bikini square dancing!"

"No."

"Surfer kick boxing?"

She shook her head.

"Badminton on ice?" she asked, hopeful.

"Nope."

"Well, come on. I'm dyin' here."

Alexandra sighed, placed the can of Hershey's on the end table and clasped her hands together in her lap.

"Alley-ooops? It can't be that bad. Spill it."

"Professional wrestling," she blurted out.

Her aunt froze, dangling a piece of chocolate-covered popcorn between her fingers. The woman was completely speechless.

"The money's great," Alexandra said defensively.

Lulu slid the popcorn bowl to the table, her mouth still partially open in shock.

"He kept upping the ante when I sounded unsure. Seven thousand, ten thousand a month. Heck, I could probably talk him into twenty if I really tried."

Lulu blinked.

"I know, I know. Pro wrestling. It wouldn't be my first choice. I'm a complete klutz at sports. Not that you'd call pro wrestling a sport. My first order of business is to fix this egocentric jerk, Loverboy Luke. Can you imagine me trying to refine a testosterone-charged ladies' man?"

"I gotta go." Lulu jumped to her feet and raced out the door to her side of the duplex.

Great. If Aunt Lulu had this kind of reaction, Alexandra could only imagine what David would think.

David. Another good reason to decline working for Cosmo. Too bad. She wanted to find out who Loverboy really was and why the tone of his voice had such a strange effect on her body. Goose bumps crawled across her shoulders when he'd spoken her name, his tone resonating with such tenderness.

Tenderness. One more thing she hadn't experienced in a while.

"Mommy!" Riley ran into the living room and leapt into her lap. "Where's Lulu?"

"Aunt Lulu," she corrected.

"Where'd she go?"

"She got scared."

"Why, is it gonna thunder?" His eyes grew round.

"No, she ran off when I told her who offered me a job."

"Who, Mama?"

Just as she was about to tell him and ostracize herself from her entire family, Lulu burst through the door cradling a cardboard box.

"Whatcha got, Lulu?" Riley said.

"Aunt Lulu," Alexandra corrected again.

She dropped the box on the coffee table, pulled out a videotape and handed it to Riley.

"Set it up, kiddo."

"Movie night?"

"Better. Did your mama tell you who she's going to be working for?"

He shook his head.

She handed him the tape and he read the label. A full grin spread from ear to ear. "No kidding? Does that mean . . ." He looked at Lulu, expectantly.

"It's time. You're old enough, boy, especially if your mama's going to be working for them."

"All right! I'm old enough! I'm old enough!" He jumped up and down and Lulu jumped with him. The popcorn bowl danced from one end of the coffee table to the other.

"Lulu, what's going on?"

"Set it up while I explain a few things to your mom," Lulu directed Riley.

The older woman plucked a tape from the box and handed it to Alexandra. "You need to know about wrestling? I've got it all right here." She dug through the box. "All the rage when I was growing up. Favorites were Verne Gagne and Killer Kowalski."

"He ripped off some guy's ear," Riley said, hitting the power button on the TV.

"You let him watch wrestling?" Alexandra said, horrified.

"No, just told him bedtime stories."

"Killer Kowalski ripped off Yukon Eric's ear while trying to stomp him in the throat."

"Riley!"

Lulu dumped the box of tapes in Alexandra's lap. "If it's got a red 'C,' it's a compilation. The orange tapes are from the Seventies; blue ones are the Eighties, The Hulk and Andre. The purple is the Nineties, although there's not much worth taping the last few years, if you ask me. Too much sex and foul language, and not enough wrestling."

She studied another tape. "I've been a fan since I was nineteen and Sammy Cooch took me on our first date to see Verne Gagne square off against the Nature Boy Buddy Rogers. I've been hooked ever since."

"You never told me." Alexandra pulled out a tape marked *For the Love of Shooters*. "Sounds like a Western."

"Shush. Just sit back and learn. You'll know all you need to by Monday morning."

"This is gonna be great!" Riley clapped.

"Maybe Riley shouldn't be watching this. If it's anything like what I saw this afternoon—"

"This is real pro wrestling, not the nonsense you see in the ring today. It's like comic book heroes come to life."

Alexandra glanced at her son, sitting on the edge of the coffee table, rubbing his hands together. He was becoming a man and this was the first of many rites of passage.

"Riley, if it's inappropriate, I'll have to turn it off," she warned.

"Okay, Mama. Can I sit with you?"

"Sure, baby. Come here."

He curled up in her lap and stuck his hand in the popcorn bowl. No matter how grown up he wanted to be, he was still her little boy.

Lulu hit the "play" button.

"I'll share my popcorn," Riley said, tipping his head back to look into her eyes.

"You're a sweetie pie."

He smiled and his left cheek dimpled.

For once in her life, things had fallen into place. She had a great client on the line that her son was excited about as well. She was so used to struggling for everything she got that when things came easily she didn't know what to do.

But she was ready this time. Monday she'd meet with Cosmo at his Milwaukee office and they'd map out PR objectives. There was too much on the line to pass this up and it was all coming together so nicely. Why couldn't she just embrace it?

It was perfect.

He packed the loose-leaf tobacco into the bowl of his pipe and smiled.

He'd set things up nicely, if he did say so himself. He paced to the multipaned window of his living room, looking out across the street. A few kids raced by on their ten-speeds. He blinked and turned away.

It was the right thing to do. Loverboy had to be stopped.

Ambling to his favorite leather chair beside the fireplace, he struck a match and lit the fine, imported to-bacco. The woman would be Loverboy's Achilles heel, a constant reminder of who he really was, and what he'd become. And the woman? She'd pull herself out of financial trouble and comfortably support that son of hers.

He leaned back and took a long drag of tobacco. It couldn't be more perfect. In the end, everyone would get what they deserved.

Chapter Four

"That stunt you pulled off the top of the ladder last night was lunacy," said Johnny Walker, the BAM trainer.

Luke shrugged, trying not to wince at Walker's manipulation of his knee. "Would have been fine if Moth Man stayed where I told him."

Walker bent Luke's knee, slowly, assessing the damage. "Keep icing it. Rest it. Go for pictures if the swelling doesn't go down by tomorrow morning."

"I'm on the card tonight against Wolfman."

"I'll tell Cosmo you're out."

"It'll be fine." He sat up and Walker helped him to his feet. Luke hobbled toward his gear.

"Don't be stupid. You're killing yourself," Walker said.

"I'm fine." He sat on the bench and reached into his duffel bag, wincing as pain speared across his shoulder.

"The shoulder's bothering you, too?"

"Slept funny last night."

"You're coming apart at the seams, kid. Let someone fill in for you tonight."

"Nope."

"You're a pigheaded ass, you know that?"

"Yep."

The trainer ambled to the door and hesitated. "At least let me send Sandy down."

"Okay."

Walker closed the door and Luke leaned against the hard cement wall. Damn, he was only thirty-one and his body was letting him down. Then again, if he'd been a little easier on it up to now, things might be different. But taking the risks made Loverboy Luke what he was today. Going over the edge and making the fans jump out of their seats, night after grueling night, in one town after another. Towns that seemed to blend together. Where was he last night again?

Focus, dammit. He pulled a hand-held electronic game from his bag. A few minutes as a fighter pilot always helped calm him down.

Sandy, the masseuse, walked in with her tie-dyed backpack. "Johnny said you could use a quickie."

He placed the game on the bench and smiled at the unintentional come-on. Sandy was all business. Hell, half the guys had tried to nail her in the four months she'd been with BAM. She'd have none of it. There were rumors she was gay, probably started by bruised egos. All Luke cared about was that her fingers worked magic on his muscles.

"You've got a lot of toxins built up back here." She pressed her thumbs into the muscle above his shoulder blades. "You stressed about something?"

Other than the daily fear of losing it all because of the limitations of his body?

"No more than usual," he said.

"This isn't good." She got in front of him and raised herself up on the bench. He found himself staring at the crotch of her jeans. Her methods might be unusual, but they worked like no pain medication could.

"How's that feel?" she said through gritted teeth as she squeezed, then released, then squeezed again.

"Better. Don't stop," he moaned. And it was. The muscles started to uncoil, his mind drifted. He closed his eyes. Maybe he'd make it through the match, after all. His neck, his shoulders felt almost pain-free. His knee on the other hand . . .

"I don't suppose you could work your way down to my other injury."

"I don't do bones."

"I think it's a muscle problem."

"One muscle at a time, Loverboy."

Something crashed outside the door and he opened his eyes.

"What the hell was that?" He got to his feet to investigate.

"We're not done here," Sandy called after him.

He limped into the hallway and found Lexy realigning a row of folding chairs that had slipped to the floor. His heart rate jumped into triple time.

"What the hell are you doing here?" he said.

"I was looking for Cosmo." She shoved a chair in place, then stood straight. The chair slid to the floor and hit the cement with a crash. Her shoulders jerked.

Curse her for looking more beautiful than she had last Friday. Her short, chestnut hair danced away from her face, a beautiful face with high cheekbones and full lips. He balled his hand into a fist, cursing his body's natural reaction to her. He felt excited and not just sexually.

47

"Cosmo's not here," he said, reigning in his panic.

"Loverboy, get back in here." Sandy came out of the locker room, rubbing her oil-slicked hands together.

Lexy's eyes widened in horror. Good. Let her think she'd interrupted something sexual. An image of Lexy's hands on him, rubbing his tension away, made him grit his teeth even harder.

Digging his fingers into his palms, he vowed that would never happen. He'd never let her touch him. He valued his way of life too much.

"Sandy, this is our new PR gal, Alexandra . . . what was the last name again?"

"Hayes," she said, with a lift of her chin.

Not Whitford, her maiden name. Another reminder to stay away. She was married.

"Nice to meet you." Sandy nodded. "Come on, Loverboy, I've got to do Ralph after I do you."

"Wait a minute," Lexy said. "I need to go over a few things."

"That's what they all say," he chuckled.

"I'm first," Sandy said, grabbing his arm. "We'll be done in ten, fifteen minutes, tops."

Sandy pulled him back into the room.

"She's good at what she does." He grinned as Sandy shut the door in Lexy's face.

"Now, sit down so I can finish," Sandy ordered.

"Whatever you say, boss."

She repositioned herself and he closed his eyes. That scene should keep Lexy a safe distance away. He didn't know much about her as an adult but had to assume she didn't like womanizers. Most females didn't, unless they wanted a piece of Loverboy Luke to take home and show their friends. Sometimes he obliged, gave them one of his fingerless gloves, or a hand mirror. Once he let a twenty-ish blonde cut a few strands of hair to take home as a keepsake. She'd claimed it was for her nephew. Yeah, right.

"Relax," Sandy ordered, probably feeling the tension in his shoulders from the brief encounter with Lexy.

She could ruin everything, weakening his armor and exposing his shame. No, the past had no power over him. He'd even distanced himself from his family.

Then he thought of Sheila. The Colonel had cut her out of the family when she became pregnant. Bastard. But Luke stepped in, supported her and baby Katie. And now she had a family of her own, complete with new husband and second child.

He warmed at the memory of Katie as a newborn, all wrinkled and sweet-smelling. He wished he could have spent more time with her, watched her grow from a baby to a young girl. But he needed to stay on the road, work as many matches as he could to support his sister and niece.

Then the Colonel extended the olive branch, bringing Sheila back into the family. His sister was right to snatch it up, even if that meant Luke would fade from her life. He didn't want to threaten the rekindled relationship between father and daughter.

That wasn't the whole truth. Part of his detachment was born of pure survival. Feeling Katie's chubby arms around his neck had warmed something inside his soul. Something never to be warmed by a child of his own.

The price of stardom.

"Un-hunch your shoulders," Sandy ordered.

She grunted as she pressed and released, working the knots out of his shoulders.

If only she could ease the knot in his chest. A lead weight, more like it. Hell, it wasn't there before Lexy showed up.

"You almost done?" he said.

"Yeah." She pressed and poked some more. "Do you enjoy pain?"

"Nobody enjoys pain."

"I used to believe that. Then I met guys like you." She gave him a gentle tap on the shoulder. "You're done."

Wiping her hands on a towel she said, "I just don't get it. You go out there knowing you're going to aggravate the knee, the back and the shoulder. Nothing stops you, not the pain, orders from Cosmo, not even your own good judgment."

"Never had much of that."

"No kidding." She shoved supplies into her backpack. "It's your ego, isn't it? Being the star, having all those women throw themselves at your feet?"

He shrugged. If only it were that simple. Luke stood, working out the knee.

"Just for the record, thanks for working with Zero," Sandy said. "He'll live a lot longer thanks to your tips on ladder matches."

"Sure." Too little, too late, in Luke's mind.

She opened the door. "He's all yours," she said to Lexy, who waited outside. "I can't do any more for him."

Lexy didn't answer. She just stood there, gawking.

"In or out?" he snapped.

She stepped inside and shut the door. Silence hung between them. He rotated his shoulders, stretched out the knee, all the while feeling her disapproving gaze burn his skin. She obviously thought he'd just slaked his physical need on Sandy, then got up and gone about the business of preparing for a match. Let her think what she liked, as long as those thoughts kept her away from him.

"My son has *Master Game*," she said, eyeing the hand-held game on the bench.

Luke shoved it into his bag.

"We need to talk," she said.

He stretched his arm over his head to ease the shoulder into submission. Lexy didn't speak. She just stood there, waiting. For what?

"If you've got something to say, say it," he said. "Just keep in mind that I'm not interested in what you're selling. I'm a heel and have always been a heel and don't plan to change anytime soon."

"Cosmo said—"

"Screw Cosmo."

Her fingers tightened around the strap of her black leather briefcase.

Drive her away before she causes the kind of pain that will make your shoulder feel like a mild headache.

Intimidation. Seemed to work when he'd disrobed in front of her. She'd physically wavered at the sight of him. She was always too sweet for her own good. Then again, that was what made him love her.

No, the yearning of a kid wasn't real love. It was a crush, idealism at its worst, and he was anything but a naïve schoolboy.

He closed in on her, his bare chest dwarfing her small frame. He'd drive her away with the seasoned arrogance of Loverboy Luke. His trusty shield of armor.

"Maybe we *can* work together," he said.

"Really?" She took a step back and he pursued her.

"Sure." He gently took her hand and brought it to his lips. Damn if she didn't taste better than he'd imagined, like sweet honeysuckle.

"See, I like my job just the way it is," he whispered.

51

"Rather than us fighting over it, let's make a deal. You tell Cosmo I'm a hopeless case and I'll do something for you."

"I'll bet." Her tone dripped with sarcasm.

"Come on, baby. It would be a life-altering experience." He brushed her hair away from her face and feathered a kiss on her cheek. Absorbed in her scent, he lost himself for a minute, letting his lips linger. He thought he heard her moan.

"Um, no thank you," she politely said, then stepped away.

He realized the moan must have come from him. He ambled back to the bench, hoping the heat from the kiss hadn't lit his cheeks bright red.

"Mr. Loverboy, changing your persona is very important to BAM."

"So is my career." He sat on the bench and taped his knee for support.

"This will help your career. You'll be a hero, loved by everyone. Cosmo's got it all figured out."

"Forget it. I've seen too many guys turn, only to lose their heat. Fans don't like it. They like knowing the players. Why do you think KIK went tubes last year? Fans got confused, couldn't keep track of what the hell was going on. I've been a heel for fifteen years. I'm not changing now."

"You like being a bad guy?" Shock filled her voice.

"It's what I'm good at."

She crossed her arms over her chest, a chest concealed beneath a conservative gray suit and starched cotton shirt with a pressed collar. He guessed she had quite a figure under all those clothes.

"Cosmo could take legal action if you don't follow through," she said.

"Bullshit." He could barely hold onto his temper. Bubba's family needed his financial support. Luke couldn't lose money to legal fees.

"He'll sue for breach of contract."

Jumping to his feet, he ignored the crunching pain in his knee and cornered Ms. Alexandra Hayes against the cement wall. "He's going to what?"

"I'm just relaying the message." She readjusted her briefcase on her shoulder and cocked her chin up a notch.

"I think you're enjoying this, backing me into a corner." Panic squeezed his gut. Without BAM he was nothing. Worse, he couldn't help pay his penance and earn back some shred of self-respect.

You don't have the character to do anything worthwhile. The words echoed in his brain. Once, twice. The Colonel's words.

"Get out of here," he said through clenched teeth.

"We're not done."

"You don't give up, do you?" He took a step back and ran his hand through his hair.

He couldn't stand to be near her; he desperately wanted to kiss her.

He was losing his mind.

"You've got me over a barrel and you're loving it," he said. "I know your kind: cold, heartless, an ice queen."

She paled, then cleared her throat. "My job is to make a civilized hero out of this . . ." She waved her hand in his direction, "this arrogant child who still plays with video games. Let's be clear, Mr. Loverboy, I don't get paid to make you happy. I get paid to—"

Her ringing cell phone interrupted the lecture. Just as well. The fire in her amber eyes and the flush of her cheeks stirred something wicked inside his chest. In another minute he *would* be kissing her.

"Hello? Yes? I'll have to call you back. I'm in a business meeting. . . . What about him? . . . I can't talk about this right now . . ."

She shuffled to the corner of the dressing room and whispered into the phone. Whoever it was didn't take "no" for an answer. Luke wondered who had this kind of power over her and how he could get some. To drive her away.

He sat down and put on his skin-tight pants. He had no business getting into the ring tonight, but that had never stopped him before. The special bonus schedule Cosmo had put into Luke's contract only motivated him to wrestle more. For every match he fought over the standard 250 a year, Luke got an extra three grand. All Luke cared about was Bubba's family. He had let the guy die, the least he could do was support his family.

Which he wouldn't be able to do if they trashed his career. What the hell was Cosmo thinking with Luke's heel-turned-hero angle? He'd seen what had happened to Nasty Nick and the Barroom Boys when they turned. Six months later Nick and his boys were scrounging to get on a card in Beavertown, Pennsylvania.

He shuddered at the thought. Without wrestling his life was worth shit. He had nothing else. It wasn't like he'd had time to go to school or learn a trade, what with his grueling tour schedule.

He wouldn't run from his responsibilities. He had a family to take care of. Bubba's family.

Lexy snapped her cell phone shut and planted her hands on her hips.

"The old ball and chain?" Luke said.

"The ex-ball and chain, not that it's any of your business."

The ex? Hell. Her marriage had been one more reason to keep his distance.

She nibbled her thumbnail for a minute, her gaze roaming his body. Heat pooled in his gut. Pretty pathetic that a simple look could evoke this kind of visceral response.

"I need to find Cosmo," she said.

"You do that. Just make sure you tell him there's no way I'm turning baby face, got it?"

She didn't answer, her expression troubled.

"Did you hear me?" he said.

"Sure, right. I'll tell him."

She ambled toward the door and he wondered what had happened to her fighting spirit, her determination to civilize him and turn him into something he wasn't.

Defeat. He read it in her eyes. He suddenly wanted to reach out and wipe away the agony coloring her cheeks.

Knock it off.

He taped his wrist instead. Once, twice, six times to make sure it would give him the support he needed. When he finished, he glanced up. Lexy hesitated at the door, watching him.

"What?" he said.

"Do I really seem like an ice queen? No, don't answer that. I can't believe I just said that. Totally unprofessional," she mumbled, rushing out the door.

"Damn!" He tossed his boots across the room. He'd hurt her, bad, and didn't even know it. Of course not. He hurt people as easily as he breathed.

Someone knocked on the door. In three strides he gripped the handle, hoping it was Lexy, hoping for a chance to apologize.

He whipped it open and his heart sank at the sight of

55

Nedra, dressed in a low cut, skin-tight jump suit. "They need you in Hall B."

"I'll be there in a minute."

She nodded and walked away. One more person he'd hurt without even trying.

He grabbed his gloves, mirror and sunglasses from the bench. Anger and frustration simmered white-hot in his chest. He knew what he was and had accepted his destiny.

Then Lexy waltzed back into his life.

"Forget it," he muttered, heading down the hall toward his next opponent. Tonight was one night he really needed to beat on someone. Maybe then he'd release some of the hopelessness and rage eating him up inside. Maybe then he'd find some sort of peace.

"This is Luke's last match as a heel," Mr. X ordered Cosmo over the telephone.

"But I think—"

"I'm paying the bills. You'll listen to me."

"Now wait a minute, this is my promotion," Cosmo protested.

"We agreed that I'd call the shots where Loverboy is concerned."

These wrestling promoters didn't care about the talent, not really. But he sensed Cosmo had developed a soft spot for Luke.

If the promoter wanted to keep BAM afloat, he'd have to follow orders and give up control of Loverboy Luke. Yeah, like anyone had control over that kid.

"What's the angle?" Cosmo said.

"We end his heel career tonight and let the woman finish the job of turning him into a hero. I'll keep the money flowing until Pete gets back."

"Loverboy Luke won't just lay down because I say so."

"Leave that to me. Wolfman and I have an agreement."

"Wolfman is unpredictable and Loverboy's still on the mend, for Christ's sake."

"This conversation is over." He hung up and reached for his pipe. Wolfman had better not be unpredictable tonight. Everything depended on his sticking to the plan.

It was unfortunate he had to go to these lengths, but Loverboy was an obstinate, bull-headed ass.

There was no other way.

"Wrestling fans, say good-bye to Loverboy Luke: the heel, the womanizer and heartless bad boy," he whispered.

Chapter Five

Alexandra was sick of being bullied. First there was Loverboy's intimidation number in the locker room, then her ex's lecture via the cell phone.

Pacing Cosmo's temporary office in a skybox at Cincinnati's United Stadium, she cursed the bank's incompetence. Why would they contact David, of all people, about her delinquent loan payment? Heck, it wasn't delinquent. Their computers burped, showed her account past due, and now she was up against a wall.

David had scolded her like a father shaming his daughter for stealing M&M's from the corner drug store. Then, surprisingly, he'd offered to up his financial support.

His flaky wife must want to practice her nurturing skills again. After all, in David's book, increased support meant increased quality time with his son.

What a joke. His idea of quality time was dragging Riley to work with him on a Saturday morning and sitting him in a conference room with a stack of videos and a mug full of change for the vending machines.

Quality time. Right.

She sifted through the papers Cosmo had left for her to review. Working for BAM was more important than ever now. Her first paycheck would pay off some bills and allow her to sock money away for a rainy day. She was readying herself for a monsoon.

Other than the bank's mistake and David's subtle extortion, she had things under control. Except for one obstinate, impossible man named Loverboy.

She read over the story line designed to transform him into a refined, classy hero. She needed a miracle.

Kissing a woman's hand and smelling her hair without her permission was definitely not classy. Nor was getting a quickie from a hippie fan in the locker room.

"Disgusting," she muttered. She scanned the folder of press clippings and spotted last weekend's entertainment section of the *St. Louis Dispatch*. In Neanderthal style, Loverboy held a woman in his arms, a cocky grin lighting his face. His companion looked uncomfortable at best. Honestly, he didn't even know how to hold a woman properly. Definitely not classy.

Not that she knew classy from first-hand experience. On the outside David was all pressed-suit, good-manners classy, but beneath the surface he was a lying, cheating SOB who wanted to take her son and make him into his own image.

"Over my dead body," she muttered, grabbing a legal pad and mapping out her plan.

First, she'd teach Loverboy the meaning of personal space, how to walk properly and smile without it seeming like the come-on of the century. A shiver went down her spine at the memory of Loverboy, all testosterone-charged and ready for a fight. Yet she hadn't been scared. Something else had tickled her belly, something unusually hot and titillating.

"Oh brother." Of all the men to light her fire, it had to be a beefy wrestler with nothing to offer but his own stupidity.

What else would explain his choice of careers, one which called for abusing his body to the point of destruction? She shivered at the thought. Health was one of the most precious gifts of all. She remembered how Mom had struggled for months to regain the ability to speak clearly after her stroke. She'd had no choice about her disability.

Yet Loverboy welcomed the abuse that had to be eating away at his body, if not destroying it. Just last month a thirty-five-year-old wrestler had died of a heart attack.

She shook her head. Thirty-five-year-old men just didn't die of heart attacks.

It did no good to try to make sense of this crazy business. She needed to do her job and earn her retainer. Cosmo figured it would take three to six months to refine Loverboy, plenty of time for Alexandra to build a nest egg and maybe even line up her next big client.

Cosmo poked his head into the room. "You staying for the show?"

"Yes, sir. I thought I'd take another crack at Mr. Loverboy."

"Gave you a hard time, did he?" He hooked his thumbs onto his snakeskin belt and ambled toward her.

"He's a bit more of a challenge than I'd expected." And more of a jerk.

"Stubborn. Damn fool." He shook his head and studied the floor. Regret creased his brow.

"Mr. Perini? Are you okay?"

"Sure, fine. Listen, uh, you don't need to stay tonight. I'm sure you could catch a late flight back to Chicago."

He handed her an envelope and she peeked inside. Her first month's retainer! She suppressed a cheer.

"I'd better get down to the ring," he said. "The show starts in ten minutes."

"I'll stay for the show." She didn't feel right taking his money and running off. "I'll give Loverboy another shot."

"I've got a feeling he won't be in a talking mood after tonight's match."

"Why's that?"

"Just a feeling." He cleared his throat. "Well, the show starts in fifteen. Luke's on the card early tonight. Gotta get the fans worked up."

She shoved her legal pad into her briefcase. "I'll come down with you."

"I wouldn't want to keep you from your important planning."

"Monitoring the product is important. It will help with my strategy." Standing, she straightened her linen blazer and slung her briefcase over her shoulder. She started toward the door but Cosmo blocked her path.

"You should stay here. I'll have them bring you a drink."

"I'm not thirsty."

"Food then. Fried chicken, hot dogs, nachos and cheese"—he paused and smiled—"with extra jalapenos."

"I'm fine, really."

"We've got some bloody matches planned tonight." His eyes narrowed in warning.

Heck, she'd cleaned up plenty of blood when Riley

cut open his forehead last spring after his bike collided with Mrs. Slaw's prized Muskie mailbox.

"I'll be fine. Thank you for your concern."

"Luke's irritable tonight, more than usual," he said. "It's best if he doesn't see you."

"Well, he'd better get used to seeing me if we're going to work together."

"Yes, but not tonight. Not when he's wrestling."

"There will be other matches and I'll be at them."

"Other matches . . . yes, well, that's true, but . . ."

"But?"

"Okay, fine. I saw him in the locker room and he said . . ." He cleared his throat and ran his hand across his balding scalp. "You can't keep making passes at the man if you want him to respect you."

"Making what?"

"He told me you made the moves on him in the locker room. He had half a mind to oblige but was trying to get ready. Concentration is everything to these guys."

"As is storytelling." Her cheeks flushed with anger.

"He doesn't want you near the ring. Says it will ruin his concentration."

"Mr. Perini, did you or did you not just hand me a check for my first month's retainer?"

"Well, yes, but—"

"I'm here to learn about the business, to help you remold a character so you can boost your reputation and increase sales. You're paying me well and I won't let you down. I certainly won't let an arrogant beast of a man stop us from our goal." She motioned with her hand. "Shall we?"

"Oh, okay, sure." Cosmo opened the door and she strode past.

Not bad, she thought. She'd even convinced herself that the sexy grappler wouldn't call the shots. Wow, she was learning already. A week ago she thought a grappler was a rubber device used to open the top of a stubborn peanut butter jar.

Holding her head high, she marched down the hall into the elevator. Of all the nerve. Loverboy actually told Cosmo *she'd* made a pass at *him*? Egocentric, clueless moron.

Maybe he wasn't so clueless. Did he sense her unwelcome attraction to him? Well, any woman would naturally be drawn to such a muscular, charismatic creature. He exuded sex simply by breathing.

She'd thought herself immune to such things until she'd found herself wanting to reach out and run her hand down Loverboy's lightly haired chest. She couldn't help wondering if his professionally trained pecs were hard and firm to the touch, his skin soft, warm and . . . she closed her eyes. A sudden heat wave filled the cramped elevator as they descended to the ground floor.

"You sure you want to do this?" Cosmo asked.

She snapped to attention. "This is what you're paying me to do, Mr. Perini."

The elevator doors opened and they stepped out.

"I've got some people to see, but there's a reserved section up front," Cosmo said. "Show the usher your badge and he'll escort you."

"Thank you." She headed toward section 101 through the mob of fans. Dressed in her tailored suit, she stuck out like a nun in a strip club.

Men, women and children filled the lobby, sporting their favorite superstar's picture across their chests. She noticed a few T-shirts with Loverboy's obnoxious face emblazoned across the front. You'd never catch *her* wearing one of those.

"Ticket please?" the usher said.

She showed him the badge with the logo of a red-faced man baring his teeth and smoke streaming from his ears.

"Your seat is up front, sectioned off with red tape." He pointed.

Ambling down the steps, she ignored the curious stares. Most of the women accompanied their significant others or came in groups so they could thoroughly enjoy ogling the six-pack tummies and bulging biceps on display in the ring.

Then again, maybe the fans thought she was part of the show. One of Lulu's tapes featured a female manager named Sharon Shark who dressed in a three-piece suit and smoked a cigar, while her wrestler piroutted into the ring wearing a black tutu and tiara.

The things people did for money.

She found her seat in the front row next to a young couple with two kids. Her thoughts drifted to Riley. She wouldn't bring him to a show until BAM made it safe for families. It felt good to be a part of that process.

The lights dimmed, the crowd cheered and the children sitting next to her slapped their hands to their ears. She had half a mind to join them.

"Hello, Cincinnati!" the announcer boomed. "Are you ready for an exciting time?"

The crowd roared.

"On the card tonight we have some of the best and baddest superstars ever to step into the squared circle."

She glanced around the stadium. It was about two-thirds full. Not bad for a house show on a weeknight.

She wondered why BAM was so determined to change its direction. Dad always said if it ain't broke, don't fix it.

"Starting us off is the outrageous ladies' man, Loverboy Luke Silver."

Cheers and boos competed with the sultry sound of his jazz-rock music. Everyone stood and she joined the crowd. But she wouldn't clap for the jerk.

Loverboy pranced up the aisle, shunning the fans as he studied his reflection in his hand mirror. He rounded the corner, spotted her and froze.

Uh-oh.

She sat down and crossed one leg over the other. Cosmo said she was the last person Luke wanted to see tonight. Maybe this wasn't a good idea.

Women screamed and stuck out their chests to get his attention. Loverboy ignored them. His gaze was set on Alexandra. What would he do? Pull her into the ring and humiliate her?

Or would he kiss her?

Suddenly she wanted to jump from her seat and sprint up the aisle to the lobby. She'd be safe there. She surely didn't feel safe right now, with his eyes scanning her body, taking in every curve she'd worked so hard to conceal.

Casually brushing a speck of lint from her navy skirt, she acted as if every nerve ending in her body didn't tingle with anticipation at what might happen next. Or what she wanted to happen.

No, she couldn't allow herself to be drawn to him. She'd used bad judgment with David. But Loverboy . . . she'd known from the start the man was an arrogant womanizer.

"Loverboy, the ring's up here," the announcer said.

She glanced up. Loverboy towered over her, but his face didn't burn red hot with anger. On the contrary, he wore that "I-want-to-lick-you-till-you-scream" smile that made her nipples harden.

She narrowed her eyes. "What?"

In a ceremonious gesture, he untied the satin ribbon binding his long, ash-blond hair, pressed it to his lips and closed his eyes. The crowd roared. Her heart pounded. What was he doing to her?

When he opened his blue-green eyes she noticed the mischievous twinkle. She should have taken Cosmo's advice and hopped the next flight home.

He leaned over the metal guardrail and gently clasped her wrist between his fingers. So gentle. How could that be? The man was a rude, crude, sonofagun.

"For luck," he said, placing the ribbon in her palm. "I'll come for it later." He winked.

Lust dissolved into anger and she found herself wanting to slap him across his stubbled face. She hated the effect he had on her.

"Don't count on it." She shoved the ribbon in her suit pocket and crossed her arms over her chest.

His smile faded and she shifted uncomfortably in her seat. Why? She'd done nothing wrong. She wasn't here as Loverboy's personal cheerleader.

He ran the back of his fingers across her cheek and she automatically held her breath. She hadn't thought him capable of such tenderness. She couldn't move.

Luke swallowed hard. What had started as a challenge was spiraling way out of control. What the hell was he doing touching her like this? Asking for trouble, that's what.

He spun around and climbed the metal steps. He'd

been caught off guard, didn't expect to see her seated front and center, not after their confrontation in the locker room. He thought he'd scared her, that she'd flag the first cab she spotted and get the hell out of Cincinnati.

But that Whitford determination still pumped through her veins. She was determined, all right. She'd managed to keep her distance from him plenty of times growing up. Was that what this was about? Luke getting back at her for shunning him?

No, his objective in touching her was to ruffle her controlled, professional feathers. He had to do something to let her know who would always be in charge of their relationship.

Relationship? More like train wreck.

He strutted to center ring, swung his hips right, then left, his hands clasped behind his head. A group of female fans in the front row shrieked and tried to climb the guardrail, but security held them back. He wrapped his arms around the top rope and stretched, bouncing twice as he waited for his opponent.

Wolfman's music blared across the stadium. The fans roared on cue. Luke still didn't understand why he'd been pitted against another heel. Who would the fans cheer?

The crowd grew wild, ready for a good match. Luke hoped his injuries didn't give him too much trouble, not that it mattered. He'd wrestled before in worse shape.

Besides, they'd agreed in a strategy meeting that even though Wolfman made his name as a shooter with a reputation for playing dirty, tonight would be a "clean" fight. Neither wrestler would walk out in worse shape than when he stepped into the ring, which was a good thing considering the hairy beast had about one hundred pounds on Luke.

Wolfman stomped up the aisle, growling and baring his teeth. One little boy held up a Wolfman sign and the wrestler grabbed it and ripped it in half with his teeth. Looked like the fans would be cheering for Loverboy tonight. That was a first.

He waited for Wolfman to get close to the ring before he made his move, an idiotic one, maybe, but the fans expected nothing less.

Wolfman must have witnessed the scene with Lexy on the closed circuit TV because he hesitated in front of her, then turned to Luke. The roadie handed him a microphone.

"If I win, she goes home with me," Wolfman said.

Lexy's eyes grew round and Luke bit back smile. This was going to be fun. She didn't know Luke was scripted to win. Or would it offend her more to go home with him?

He grabbed the mirror and admired his reflection as if he couldn't be bothered with the challenge and didn't care about protecting Lexy's virtue.

"Did you hear me, punk?" Wolfman said.

Luke breathed onto the mirror, then swiped it with the heel of his fingerless glove.

"I'm taking your woman when I win," the beast shouted.

The collective roar from the crowd pounded Luke's eardrums. Out of the corner of his eye, he spied Wolfman get into position, moving away from Lexy and standing dead center in the empty aisle.

Deep breath. Swipe the forehead. Brush back the hair. Hand the mirror to Nedra. Stretch the neck. One more deep breath.

Clenching his teeth, Luke charged to the other end of the ring and flew through the top and middle ropes at

Wolfman. The burly wrestler caught him and they both went down as planned. He delivered six rapid-fire punches to the side of Wolfman's face. The beast countered by sending Luke flying into the guardrail.

They made it into the ring and for the next ten minutes exchanged holds and punches. It was a damn fine match.

Loverboy flattened Wolfman with a clothesline. The beast sat up and Luke applied a chin lock, waiting for the ref to crouch down so Luke could pass him the next set of moves.

The ref's attention was on Lexy. Her eyes glared and she clenched her jaw. Hell, he didn't care if she approved of him or not. *Sure, keep telling yourself that, buddy.*

But why did the ref consult her at this critical point in the match?

"Drop kick, leg drop, flip off the turnbuckle," Luke said between clenched teeth to the ref, who then passed the moves to Wolfman.

Wolfman grabbed for the ropes and the ref ordered Loverboy to break the hold. He did, and marched to the corner of the ring. The fans cheered as Nedra handed him the mirror. He'd make sure the fans' adulation was short-lived.

As he batted his eyelashes and puckered his lips, the ring suddenly bounced with the weight of his opponent on the attack. Luke spun around and kicked Wolfman in the chest, sending him over the top rope onto the floor. Hell, Luke didn't want to fight outside the ring. Why didn't the jerk just go down as planned?

Luke climbed the ropes and raised his arms to build up heat. A siren of cries filled the arena.

Luke dove at his opponent, but Wolfman didn't stay in position. Instead of Luke landing on his beefy opponent to cushion the fall, Luke landed on concrete.

Air rushed from his lungs and pain speared his knee. What the hell? Did Wolfman miss the signal?

Flattened like a pancake, he struggled to suck air into his lungs. His knee throbbed and his shoulder ached. Good thing he didn't brace his fall with his hands or he would have at least one broken wrist. Breathe, dammit.

Wolfman grabbed him from behind and flung him against the metal guardrail as if he fully intended to break every bone in Luke's body.

Maybe Wolfman had changed his mind and wanted to win this match. Maybe he wanted to try out new shooter moves and hadn't bothered to tell anyone.

Draped over the metal guardrail, Luke caught his breath and readied himself for Wolfman's next move. He should just stay down, submit and get it over with. He sure as hell would save his body some hard time with the chiropractor.

Picking him up like a rag doll, Wolfman stormed back to the ring, at least that's where Luke thought they were going. Instead, the beast dropped him back first onto another set of guardrails. Luke slid to the floor, stomach first, figuring the ref would count him out.

But not soon enough.

Wolfman shoved his boot into Luke's ribs, rolling him over. He did his patented laugh-bark at the crowd, looked at Lexy and nodded.

Luke's gut knotted. It couldn't be. She couldn't be behind this.

Reality slapped him like a virgin who'd been groped for the first time. She and Cosmo wanted Luke to turn.

What better way than to keep him out of the action for a while until they molded him into a perfect hero? Cosmo was determined to change Luke's character, no matter what the cost. And he'd hired the perfect woman for the job.

Lexy.

He closed his eyes. Sweet, sensitive Lexy. Hell, that girl didn't exist anymore. Then again, neither did Timothy Lucas Silverspoon.

Wolfman peeled Luke off the floor and shoved him chest first into the guardrail. Damn, how did this get away from him? He opened his eyes long enough to catch Lexy's smirk.

"How could you?" he said.

She paled and he knew he was right. She was his enemy, willing to do anything to meet her job objective and turn Loverboy Luke into some kind of loser, milquetoast hero. His high-paying career would crash and burn and he'd be forced to work local promotions in No Town, USA. Worse, he'd have no way to support Bubba's wife and kids.

Rage boiled up in his chest. They wouldn't strip him of his last chance to regain some shred of integrity.

Luke rolled under the ring, pulled out a few tools and tossed them at Wolfman. He stumbled back, giving Luke time to get the advantage. He applied a sleeper hold.

Like a beast fighting for his last breath, Wolfman cried out, then stumbled, ramming Luke's back into the metal ring post. Pain exploded in his chest and he let go, crumpling to the floor on his hands and knees. Wolfman collapsed against the ring apron and Luke knew this was his last chance.

Pumped with rage, Luke took three steps and drop kicked Wolfman in the side of the head. They both went down. Luke crawled to his opponent, draped his arm loosely across his chest and waited for the ref. The jerk took his time getting down from the ring. Once he did, he counted once, twice and hesitated. The crowd went ballistic.

Luke glared. "Do it or you're a dead man."

The ref slapped the floor for the three count and the place exploded. The ref tried to raise Luke's arm in victory, but Luke ripped it away. He didn't want the bastard touching him. He was in on this, on what could have ended Luke's career. Hell, it wouldn't have been the first time Wolfman did a number on one of the boys that turned out to be his last match.

But Wolfman wasn't in this by himself.

Luke got to his feet and wavered. He was hurt, bad. Hell, he could barely walk.

He ground his teeth and flexed his biceps in celebration. The fans roared. He couldn't remember the last time he'd won a match. Of course not, he was the master jobber, the guy who took the falls to make others look good.

The fans cheered, waved BAM signs, threw popcorn and jalapeno peppers. They were all on their feet except for the brunette in the front row who shot him a look of disapproval.

Pain setting his teeth on edge, he marched over to Lexy. "Let's go."

She crossed her arms over her chest.

He leaned across the rail. Damn her for smelling like fresh cut roses, crisp and sweet. "Over my shoulder works for me."

For a second he thought she'd refuse. Then she must have thought better of it, not wanting to be humiliated. Good thing she didn't know he lacked the strength to make good on his threat.

A security guard escorted her through the rail opening and she marched up the ramp. The crowd screamed out of control, but he could barely hear them, his rage blocking out all sound, all thought. What did she think she was doing? She wasn't a part of this violent, tragic world. She was in way over her head.

She strode confidently ahead of him and the second they pushed through the curtain, he stepped in front of her and backed her against the cement wall.

"What the hell was that?" he said.

"What?"

"You know what I'm talking about."

"Loverboy!" Cosmo cried running up to him. "Hells bells, I haven't seen a good old-fashioned shooter match in years. That was one of your best, kid."

"And it could have been my last." He didn't take his eyes off Lexy.

"Now, calm down, kid."

"Stay out of it, Cosmo."

Luke stared down Lexy. "You set me up."

"What are you talking about?"

"No more lies."

"You're worked up, kid," Cosmo said.

"You're damn right I'm worked up. Were you part of this, Cosmo?"

"Part of what?" He cleared his throat and hooked his thumbs onto his belt.

Luke turned his attention back to Lexy. "I could have been permanently injured out there."

74

"And this surprises you?" she said, with a raised eyebrow.

He wanted to wipe that smug look right off her face. Not with a clothesline or a body slam, or any other submission hold. He wanted to wipe that look off her face with a kiss.

For the love of God, man, get a hold of yourself.

"If I weren't a gentleman—"

"You've got to be kidding."

"Enough." Cosmo grabbed Luke's arm and yanked him away from her. Strange, the promoter had never chanced touching him before.

"It's perfect," Cosmo said. "The fans are starting to take to you. It fits right in with our plans."

"Not my plans."

"Well change them. Because this is the last time I'm saying it: Either turn or clear out."

"Fine." He limped toward the locker room.

He must have scrambled his brains out there. He couldn't just up and leave BAM. Sure, he had some money saved, but not enough to live on after a year's time. Besides, who would hire him, knowing he refused to play out a new angle?

And what the hell would he do if he didn't wrestle? He didn't have a college degree; he wasn't a master at anything. This insane career left little time for personal development. Not that he had much left to develop. His body degenerating, his mind sometimes a blur thanks to one too many knocks, Luke's future wasn't all that bright.

BAM was all he had and, up to this point, all he'd ever needed. Damn Lexy for threatening his future.

He flung open the locker room door and a few of the

guys cleared out. They knew he'd been set up and anticipated the aftermath.

As he ripped off his gloves, he realized just how deep he was in. Without wrestling he was nothing, a failure. He was Timothy Lucas Silverspoon. The son his father wished had died instead of Kevin. Dammit, if he'd only stopped Kevin from getting in that car.

The door squeaked open.

"Get the hell out." He turned and found Lexy standing in the doorway. "What do you want?"

Fear colored her eyes. He'd put that there.

His chest ached. "What?" he said, wanting her gone for too many reasons.

She closed the door and pressed her back against it. "I need your help."

Chapter Six

"You're kidding, right? You set me up in the ring and now you want my help?" he said.

"Set you up?"

"Don't act innocent. Go on, get out of here."

"I can't. I need to talk to you."

"We've tried that before. We're not good at it."

"Please." She took a deep breath and folded her hands in front of her. She looked twelve again, naive and trusting. He knew better.

"What do you want from me?" he said.

"I really need this job."

Pressing his thumb into the heel of his palm, he stared her down. He couldn't afford to care. Not about Lexy or her problems, or anything but his own survival. His own survival and the well-being of a fatherless family.

"What you need is not my problem," he said.

Pain sparked in her eyes, then determination. He wanted to look away, but couldn't.

The door burst open, shoving Lexy forward a few steps. Wolfman bounded inside the locker room. "What the hell was that? You nearly killed me!" he yelled at Luke.

Great. Luke had nothing left. His body was bruised, broken and ached like hell, and this sadistic lunatic was accusing him of being too rough.

"I thought that's what you wanted," Luke said, calmly, figuring out his next move. Everyone knew about Wolfman's explosive temper.

"I wanted to win that match," Wolfman roared.

Lexy took a step toward Luke, then another. Smart girl.

"Your winning wasn't in the script," he said. "Take it up with Cosmo."

"Cosmo is an idiot."

"Tell me about it." Maybe if he befriended Wolfman, he would be able to walk out of here in one piece.

"I write my own scripts!" Wolfman howled.

"Good for you. They're probably better than Cosmo's."

"Damn straight." He seemed to relax a little.

Luke didn't. Lexy edged behind him, using him as a human shield.

"It was a good match," Wolfman said.

"A great match," Luke agreed.

"I shoulda' won."

Luke didn't argue. He fiddled with the tape on his left wrist.

"I shoulda' won and walked out with that girl over there." He eyed Lexy, practically drooling.

Luke stood a little taller and planted his hands on his hips. Old habits die hard.

She huddled behind him for protection and her fingers touched his back. Warmth crept up his spine.

"I'm gonna get the girl next time," Wolfman said, sounding like a fourteen-year-old boy.

There was a tense silence. Adrenaline surged through Luke's blood.

"Good match." Wolfman nodded and disappeared into the hallway.

Relief spread across Luke's shoulders.

"Is he gone?" Lexy squeaked.

"You're safe." At least from Wolfman. Her gentle touch shot his pulse way beyond dangerous. As for other parts of his body . . .

"He's scary," she said, still way too close.

"He's gone. Now it's your turn. Get out."

She turned to him, but didn't look hurt or angry. Only confused.

"You're a strange character," she said. "You act all mean and tough, but you protected me just now."

"You're imagining things." God, how he wished she were.

"Maybe. Maybe not." She nibbled on her thumbnail and stared him down as if trying to figure him out.

"I'm taking a shower," he said, hoping to escape.

"Wait, we didn't resolve our problem."

"Which one?"

"You turning hero," she said.

"Not happening."

"You'll lose your job, your income, all the glamour and perks that go along with being a superstar."

"Perks?" He almost laughed. Instead he shifted and his knee started to give out. "Hell."

"What's wrong?" she cried, racing toward him and gripping his arm.

He grunted, she squeaked, and they both went down.

Lexy landed on her back, Luke sprawled on top of her. Not a bad move . . . if they were in the ring.

Oscar burst into the room and froze, a slow grin spreading across his face. "Foreplay?"

Luke grabbed Merlin's boot and threw it at him. Oscar shut the door just before it made contact.

Oscar poked his head in again. "Can I play?"

"Get out!"

"You never did like sharing. I'll hang a sock on the door so you're not interrupted." He cocked his head to one side and studied Lexy. "She's kinda cute. Not your type, but cute."

Luke reached for Merlin's other boot. Oscar laughed and shut the door.

Lexy stared up at him with round, startled eyes.

"You hurt?" he asked.

"I was . . . trying . . . to help," she said, winded.

Clenching his jaw against the pain, he shifted off of her and propped himself into a sitting position against the cement wall.

"Dumb idea, I guess," she said, still staring at the ceiling.

"Not so dumb. At least I didn't end up face down on the floor."

A smile tugged at her rose-colored lips. Her cheeks were flushed and her pale pink blouse stuck out from the waistband of her skirt.

He extended his hand and gently pulled her into a sitting position. He let go, but she didn't, their lips mere inches apart. He struggled to breathe, his senses heightened by the feel of her soft skin between his fingers.

"Who are you?" she whispered.

Good question. He forced a half smile and narrowed his eyes. "I'm Loverboy Luke, the baddest, sexiest pro-wrestler of them all. I can set a woman on fire with a touch of my finger."

Didn't she know it. Alexandra had a hard time breathing against the desire building in her chest. She wanted to pull her hand away, but couldn't move.

I'm Loverboy Luke, the baddest, sexiest pro wrestler of them all.

Something unsettling rang in his words. She shouldn't care, but couldn't ignore the unusual tint of his blue-green eyes.

"I don't believe you," she blurted out.

"You don't think I'm the best in the ring? Or you don't think I can light a woman on fire?" The huskiness of his voice sent shivers across her back.

Get up! Run for your life!

"Because my stats prove the first," he said "And I can easily prove the second." He leaned even closer and her breath caught in her chest. He was about to kiss her . . . or worse.

"I need . . ." she said,

"What, honey? What do you need?"

His breath warmed her skin and her lips tingled with wanting.

All kinds of images filled her mind: Loverboy peeling off her jacket, her blouse, her lace bra, touching her in the most intimate of places, stroking her skin, easing his hand lower, below the waistband of her skirt, sliding it beneath her pantyhose until he—

"Darlin'? You still with me?" he said with a knowing grin.

The same grin he shot her just before Miss Hippie USA dragged him into the locker room for a quickie.

She ripped her hand from his and scooted backwards.

"Hey, where ya' goin'?" he said.

81

"We've got work to do." She jumped to her feet and pressed her hands down her skirt.

That damn grin still played across his lips. It was almost as if she stood naked before him, and he inspected her with a slow, appreciative eye.

"Stop that," she said.

"Stop what?"

"Looking at me like that."

"I look at all beautiful women like this."

Now she knew he was playing her for a fool. Beautiful, she was not. Mildly cute, maybe, but definitely not beautiful.

"Come back here." He patted his hand on the floor next to him. "You were just about to tell me what you needed, although I think I can guess."

"I doubt it." She planted her hands on her hips.

"I'll bet you could use a night out with a sexy, handsome gentleman. I know just the guy." He winked.

"No, thank you."

"Okay, then you tell me. What do you need, Ms. Alexandra Whitford Hayes?"

"See? That's the other thing . . . how do you know my maiden name?"

He fiddled with the remaining tape on his wrist. "You told me."

"No, I didn't."

He broke eye contact and massaged his knee with both hands. His jaw twitched with pain.

"Can I get you something?" she said. She had to stay on his good side, just not too good.

"Is that an offer?" he said.

"For your knee. Ice or something."

He shifted onto the bench and a groan rumbled in his throat. "I'm fine."

And she was heavyweight champion. "I'd like to help you, if you'll let me."

"Your kind of help I don't need."

Fine, she'd extended the olive branch and he'd snapped it in half.

"Okay, where were we?" she said.

"You were telling me what you needed." He glanced up with a sparkle in those amazing eyes. "Although I'm not sure you know yourself."

She stared him down. "What I need is your cooperation."

"Now that sounds promising."

"Your professional cooperation," she clarified.

"Too bad."

He flashed a half smile and she wanted to whack him over the head with something, hard. Maybe that would break the spell and lighten the heaviness of her breasts. She hated that he affected her this way. Of all the men who could awaken this part of her, it had to be a guy named Loverboy.

But she'd never go down that road again, especially not with a macho, self-abusive ladies' man. She'd promised herself if she ever got involved, it would be with a man who would be good to Riley.

"Earth to Al." He snapped his fingers. "You sure a night of long, crazed sex wouldn't clear those cobwebs from your brain?"

"My job is to help you become popular with the fans as a hero," she redirected him.

"I already told Cosmo, I'm not turning." He unzipped his duffel bag.

"Why do you insist on being difficult?"

"Hey, lady, you're playing with my life here. I'm popular as a heel. If I turn, who's going to guarantee I'll get over with the fans? You? Hell, you know nothing about the business."

"But Cosmo does. He's assured me—"

"You don't know much about promoters either. They'll promise you free health insurance if they think it will make them money. In the end they'll sell you for scrap."

"Cosmo thinks this will improve business."

"He's wrong. I've seen too many guys lose their heat because of a crazy angle. For the past fifteen years I've been a superstar as a heel. Not a nice guy, not a sappy hero. If you do that to me, my career's over."

"If you don't follow orders, your career's over."

"Bull. I'll find another place to wrestle." He limped toward the shower.

She followed. "Like this? You can barely walk."

"I'll bounce back, I always do."

"Why?"

He flipped on the shower and glanced over his shoulder. "Because I'm in prime physical shape. No injury has kept me down for long."

"No, I mean, why do you do this to yourself?"

"Why are you doing this?" he countered.

"I need the money."

"Bingo."

"But I have a good reason to need it."

"And I don't? You know nothing about me, sugar."

Maybe not, but she sensed this wasn't just about money. It didn't matter. His motives were not her concern. All she needed was his cooperation.

"Listen." She touched his arm, thick and hard from years of weight training. She ground her teeth against the desire to touch more and squeeze harder. "I really need this to work."

He glared at her hand. "So you set me up in the ring?"

"What are you talking about?"

"Wolfman. I saw the ref look to you for direction."

"You've lost me."

He stared her down, hands planted on his hips.

"I'm not as stupid as I look. You and Cosmo set me up to lose in a hard-ass shooter match," he said.

Shooter, shooter, she scanned her brain. Right, guys who really hurt each other for a living.

"Wolfman really hurt you?"

"What the hell, lady? You think I always limp out of the ring like this?"

"I thought it was part of the job."

"Intentionally hurting each other? You really are naive. It's orchestrated violence. No one gets hurt, not on purpose. Unless someone pulls a boner and sets you up."

"Hang on, you think I—"

"You planned my fall tonight so I'd be out for a few weeks, maybe even months. That would give you and Cosmo time to destroy my career with your stupid hero plan."

Her blood pressure jumped. "You think I told that man to hurt you?"

"I saw the signals."

"But I would never—"

"Enough. I've gotta take a shower."

"We're not done."

He started to peel his shorts down over his hips.

"I'll wait out there." She raced around the corner and Luke smiled to himself. And she thought she was in charge?

As he stepped beneath the hard spray, he considered

her innocent act. As a kid she was never able to hide her feelings. He'd never forget the time Skippy Santee told the seventh grade class she reminded him of an overgrown pear after seeing her in a ballet recital. She was devastated, having "loved" good ol' Skip since the third grade.

No matter how hard she tried to convince the school she could care less about Skippy's hurtful words, everyone knew the truth. She wore her feelings on her sleeve—sweet, compassionate, tender feelings. And she couldn't lie for shit.

Could she really be an innocent in all this? It didn't matter. She still wanted to fix him, make him into something he wasn't. A familiar burn tore through his gut. He'd spent the better part of his childhood trying to be something he wasn't. He pounded a closed fist on the ceramic tile.

Bury it. Bury it deep.

That's why he couldn't work with Lexy. Her presence exposed regrets he had no use for. Loverboy Luke knew exactly what he was and he was just fine with that reality.

Lathering up, he hoped Lexy would be gone by the time he stepped out of the shower. Maybe he'd walk out buck-naked. That should scare her something good.

He couldn't avoid her forever. When Cosmo set his mind to something, there was no dissuading him.

Luke reached for the shampoo and his knee buckled again. He steadied himself just before slipping to the cold, hard tile. Yeah, right, like he could fight anywhere else. No one would have him like this.

It couldn't be over. Not yet. He had a few more things to do. Like pad Beth's bank account for the kids.

Time. You have to buy time.

He could use some time out of the ring to help heal

what was probably a minor concussion caused by Wolf-man banging his head against the ring post. He'd be damned if he'd confess his injury to his promoter. If the guy figured out just how bad off Luke was, it was all over.

It couldn't be over. Not yet.

He turned off the shower and grabbed a towel. If Cosmo and Lexy were determined to have their way, he'd pretend to go along, at least until he could heal. Then he'd move on, carve out a spot with another pro-moter. He was still a big draw. Just last year a rep from Wrestling Heroes and Kings approached him about jumping ship.

With a little down time and physical therapy, he'd be ready to step into the ring again. In the meantime, he'd keep Lexy off balance by flirting with her.

Not the most brilliant idea, Loverboy. When he'd nearly kissed her before, his emotional walls had started to crumble. He wasn't sure he could control his emotions if he got that close again.

No, he'd find another way . . . messing with her head, maybe?

He wrapped the towel around his waist, remember-ing a few of her pet peeves. Gum snapping. She'd roll her eyes up into her head when her little brother would walk up behind her and give his wad a good snap.

Loverboy always carried a packet of cinnamon gum to calm his nerves. Even after fifteen years they crept up on him, especially when preparing for a dangerous stunt. He'd chewed like crazy at last month's Pile Dri-ving Derby when Billy the Squid body-slammed him off the top ropes into a bank of TV monitors. The crowd went nuts; his legs went numb. Anything to please the fans.

He limped into the dressing area, relieved and disappointed that Lexy was nowhere in sight. Good. It would give him time to think. Gum snapping, let's see, what else? He towel dried his hair and pulled it back into a ponytail. It used to drive her nuts when people didn't believe her.

Maybe this wasn't hopeless after all. He'd drive her crazy enough to stay away from him and in the end he'd escape BAM with his heart intact.

Now he was being a sap. He didn't believe in love or happily-ever-after. That fantasy was for idiots. It never worked out.

He thought about BAM wrestlers who'd made the matrimonial mistake, Oscar being the only one not divorced by thirty-five. Luke often wondered what kept that marriage together despite Oscar's demanding schedule. Luke gave it another two years, tops.

What a shame. Luke actually liked the guy when he wasn't dousing Luke's shorts with hot sauce or setting mousetraps in his boots. The things Oscar thought were funny sometimes whipped the boys into a frenzy. But his heart was in the right place. He was just trying to make everyone laugh on grueling tours that kept them away from home and lonely as hell.

Luke opened his duffel bag and reached for his clothes. Instead of his T-shirt and sweats, he pulled out a canary yellow negligee trimmed with a bright red satin ribbon. As he stared at the blinding undergarment, snickers echoed from the other room.

"Oscar!" he called.

The blond wrestler stepped around the corner; Lexy was by his side. With his spiked white-blond hair and dimples, the guy looked like a kid sometimes. He acted like a kid most of the time.

"You pick this out by yourself? I'm impressed." Luke held up the garment and gave it a sniff. The damn thing smelled like flowers.

"It brings out the yellow in your eyes. And . . . it's edible," Oscar sputtered.

Lexy put her hand to her mouth to hide a smile.

"You in on this, too?" Luke said.

She shook her head. "No, I was just—"

"Don't bother lying to me again."

She snapped her mouth shut and he smiled to himself. Score one, Loverboy.

"Where are my clothes?" he demanded.

Oscar edged toward the door. "What clothes?"

"Sweats, T-shirt, socks."

"I left you something better." He took another step toward the door.

"Sorry, but it's not my style. I'm a lace kinda guy."

He lunged, thankful his knee didn't give out again, and applied a firm arm lock to prevent Oscar from escaping.

"Clothes," he breathed into Oscar's ear.

Oscar squirmed, but couldn't break the hold. "Ease up, man."

"I'm tired, I'm cranky and I absolutely hate yellow." He gave Oscar's arm a twist.

"Je-Sus, you've got no sense of humor."

"And you've got no sense messing with me. It's been a long day."

"Okay, okay. Your stuff's in the garbage can."

"Get it." He let go, but blocked the door.

Oscar dug through the metal bin and pulled out a plastic bag with Luke's clothes.

"Guess I won't be needing this," Luke said, tossing the undergarment at Lexy. She caught it on the fly. "Give it a try, Al. Unless it's too feminine for ya."

She glared, scrunching the silky material between her fingers.

"Lay off," Oscar said, tossing Luke's clothes at him, then putting his arm around Lexy's shoulder.

Good thing Oscar was married or Luke would have ripped it from its socket.

"She's a nice girl," Oscar said. "We had a heart to heart, didn't we, cutie?"

She grinned and Luke couldn't help shaking his head. God, she was an easy mark. If Oscar had been on the prowl, she'd be in his bed before the hour was up.

"You here for a reason other than to torture me?" he said to Oscar.

"Me? Yeah, Cosmo said I had to meet Miss Hayes. She's doing me after she's done with you."

"Doing you?" His blood pressure jumped.

"Yeah, fixing me. You know, turning me into a baby face."

"You're actually buying this crap?" He tossed his pants and socks on the bench and slipped his T-shirt over his head. "Not wise, my friend. You remember what happened to the Martini brothers and God Drilla."

"That won't happen to us. Cosmo's got new writers he hired from that soap, what was it again?" Oscar snapped his fingers twice. "*As the Bed Swirls* . . . something like that. Besides, we've got us a secret weapon." He grinned at Lexy. "This lady is gonna make sure we get over with the fans, right Al?"

"Alexandra," she corrected.

"Right." Oscar grinned.

Luke decided he'd keep calling her Al as long as it made her cheeks flush bright red.

"When do we start?" Oscar said.

"I'll get my briefcase," she said.

"No way," Luke said. "I've worked enough tonight."

"Wimp," Oscar muttered.

"Excuse me?"

"Nothing, nothing." Oscar crossed his arms over his chest and smiled.

"Since I won't be on the card for a while, let's meet at Corporate on Thursday," Luke said.

"Thursday? That's the end of the week," Lexy protested.

"I need to recuperate."

Oscar snorted.

"You looking for another broken nose?" Luke threatened.

Oscar shrugged and put his arm around Lexy. "If you want to start before Thursday, call me."

"Thanks, I might do that. Good night, gentlemen."

She slipped out from under Oscar's arm and made her way to the door. "Oh, and yellow isn't my color either." She tossed the negligee to Oscar.

She disappeared into the hall and Oscar whistled. "Man, she's something. If I weren't married—"

"You are." Luke walked to the door and shut it.

"If I didn't know better, I'd say you were turning green, Loverboy."

"Yeah, green cuz I got the crap beat out of me by a hairy lunatic." He put on his silk boxers and snapped his sweats up the side.

"That was one helluva match. Match! Crap! I'm on the card after the Tasmanian Twins do their high-wire thing." Oscar made for the door, studying the garment in his hands. "Maybe the Mrs. would like it," he muttered, hesitating as if deep in thought.

"You okay?"

"Yeah, okay. You sure you don't want to hold onto this for Al?" A mischievous twinkle lit his blue eyes.

"There's nothing going on between me and Al."

"Uh-huh." Oscar winked and left.

Now, if Luke could just keep it that way.

He had to go to the show. Just to be sure.

He paced the office overlooking the ring, frustration boiling in his chest. Damn Wolfman for not sticking to the plan. Then again, Loverboy wouldn't be stepping into the ring anytime soon, and that was a good thing.

Where the hell was Cosmo? He couldn't wait here all night. What if *she* started to suspect something?

Someone knocked at the door and he stepped back into the shadows. He gripped the silver watch at the bottom of his trouser pocket.

"Hello?" Alexandra breezed in, young and innocent looking. For a grown woman she had such childlike qualities, freckles dotting her nose, a bounce in her step a little too carefree for her age, and bangs that danced across her forehead.

He'd forgotten what it was like to be young. She glanced in his direction and he froze.

"Oh, I'm sorry. I didn't know anyone was here," she said.

He cleared his throat. "No problem."

She cocked her head to one side and frowned, as if puzzling through something. Damn, this was getting complicated.

"Have we met?" she asked, slipping her fingers around the handle of a black leather briefcase on a chair.

92

"I don't think so."

"I'm Alexandra Hayes, public relations consultant." She took a step toward him and extended her hand.

His gaze drifted to the petite fingers, nails trimmed and unpolished. She wore a garnet ring on her third finger.

Don't bring attention to yourself.

"I'm Cosmo's brother, Frank," he said, shaking her hand. Her fingers felt warm and fragile.

She'd done a fine job with Loverboy so far, challenging his persona just enough to make him question things.

"Well, nice meeting you. If you see Cosmo, tell him I'm making a lot of progress with Mr. Loverboy."

"Really?"

"Yes. He's not as tough as he looks." She shot him a smile and breezed out of the office.

"It's a good thing I am," he whispered.

Chapter Seven

Alexandra didn't know which irked her more: the fact she'd planned her week around Loverboy's schedule, or that even after everyone jumped through his hoops, he was still MIA.

Sitting at the head of the conference table at BAM headquarters, she took a deep breath and addressed the wrestlers who had showed up: Oscar the Louse, Flamboyant Floyd and his valet, Man-eating Missy.

"Let's begin," Alexandra said, passing out her preliminary report.

"What about Luke?" Oscar said.

"We've waited long enough. Please turn to page two," she said, controlling her temper. It did no good to lose it in a professional setting. "Research indicates that if BAM is to turn pro wrestling around, we'll need to use a two-pronged effort: story lines and public appearances. The new writers will create story lines geared toward children, yet suspenseful and engaging enough to entertain adults. I'll be in charge of preparing our superstars for public appearances."

As if on cue, the door burst open and Mr. Loverboy sauntered to the opposite end of the table. No apologies, no explanation. He wore skintight jeans showing off firm buns and muscular legs. Alexandra swallowed hard. On top, he was practically naked, wearing nothing but a leather vest exposing much too much skin. He took his seat, not removing his sunglasses. Must have been a late night.

"You with Beth last night?" Oscar said.

Loverboy grunted and put up his hand as if the subject was off limits.

Another woman? Geez, how many females did this man need? Alexandra would have to talk to him about his philandering, or at least his discretion. She recalled the photograph from last weekend and the woman in his arms. This Beth made three different women in less than a week. She shuddered.

"What did I miss?" Loverboy said.

To calm herself, she twirled her garnet ring, a high school graduation gift from her parents. "I was just explaining how we're going to turn BAM around."

"Inside out, you mean," he muttered.

He was determined to rile her. Well, she could be just as determined.

"In your packet there's a strategic overview explaining how the story line will develop around your new personas and how you'll make the turn to heroes. Mr. Loverboy will turn first, followed by Oscar and Floyd. All of you need to work on your public-speaking skills so you're prepared for the appearances."

"What about me?" Missy squeaked. "I'm an important part of this show. Tell her, Fuzzy."

"Fuzzy?" Alexandra looked at Floyd.

"Shush," Floyd said to Missy.

"Don't 'shush' me!" She gave his shoulder a shove and coffee spilled across the report sitting in front of him.

"Now look what you've done." Floyd dabbed at the report with a napkin. He was a handsome man, if you liked the flashy type. He wore his raven black hair slicked back off his face. The sparkle from his diamond pinky ring danced across the black conference table.

Alexandra glanced at her other two victims. Oscar sailed a paper airplane across the room, whistling through his teeth. With great fanfare it crash-landed in the pitcher of water on the refreshment cart.

"Cool!" he said.

Leaning way back in his swivel chair, Loverboy propped his sneaker-clad feet on the table and crossed them at the ankles. He'd pulled his hand-held video game from God knows where, and was focused intently on the device. *He should be focusing on me.*

They were worse than Riley's third-grade class. At least the eight-year-olds had pretended to be interested in her presentation on ecology. She cleared her throat.

"As I was saying, Missy, you'll remain Floyd's valet, but you'll have to modify your costume a bit," she said, trying to ignore the juvenile behavior.

"What's wrong with my costume?" Missy leaned forward and her breasts flattened the cream-filled donut on her plate. Floyd stuck his coffee stick in her cleavage.

"I'm confused. Are we still heels until we turn?" Floyd asked. Missy gave him the evil eye and plopped the stick back in his coffee.

"Actually, you're going to keep a low profile for a while. You'll still wrestle, but you won't taunt the crowd quite so much. It has to be a gradual turn."

"Hey, Al, can I ask a question?" Loverboy said, not taking his eyes off his video game.

"Yes, Mr. Loverboy?"

"The name's Luke."

"And mine is Alexandra. I know you're used to one syllable words, but I think with a little practice even you can get the hang of it."

Silence blanketed the room. This was it. The make-it-or-break-it moment for Alexandra.

Loverboy Luke slowly removed his feet from the table, put down the hand-held game and leaned forward. Staring at her, he slipped a piece of chewing gum into his mouth. A couple of chews later, his eyes sparkled with challenge.

"Okay, Al-Ex-An-Dra. Hey, I did it! I said her name!" He snapped his gum.

She gritted her teeth. "Let's move on. Included in your packet are lists of the charities we're going to visit, along with pointers on speaking to the media and how to handle yourself, in general."

Loverboy mumbled something inaudible.

"Is there a problem?" she said.

"Lady, I've been handling myself for over thirty years."

"And you've done such a fine job," she said, with just the right amount of sarcasm. "Your first appearance is co-hosting a charity auction for a children's hospital in Chicago next week."

"I don't do kids," Loverboy said.

Oscar snorted.

"You have something to say?" Loverboy challenged.

"Nah, not me."

"I don't understand. Mr. Lover—"

He put up his finger.

"Luke," she said. "BAM has always supported children's charities."

"Not me. I can't do those."

"Yeah, he's afraid some kid will run up crying, 'Daddy!' " Oscar said.

Alexandra's heart sank. The man probably had children scattered from here to New Zealand.

Loverboy lunged across the table and hit Oscar in the chest, tipping him over. Now she knew the real reason Cosmo had hired her instead of some high-priced firm: other agencies wouldn't put up with this lunacy.

"Since I still have your attention," she addressed Floyd and Missy, "I'd like to review the section on working with the media. There are very specific responses you'll need to memorize."

Loverboy and Oscar tumbled onto the table. Jumping from her chair, Missy squeaked and hid behind Floyd.

"What special interviews do you have planned?" Floyd asked, snatching away his plate of fresh fruit just before Oscar's elbow slammed against the table.

"During the next three months I've got some media coverage lined up with non-profit organizations. I understand you're interested in animal rights groups?"

Loverboy and Oscar rolled across the table into Floyd's chest.

"Wild animals, mostly," he said, craning his neck to see above the wrestlers. "You know, endangered species."

Floyd shoved the men back to the middle of the table.

"You're going to learn to keep your mouth shut." Loverboy shook Oscar by the shoulders, banging the wrestler's head against the table.

"And you got to stop taking everything so damn personal."

Oscar swung and hit Loverboy in the face. They rolled again and Oscar pinned Luke, a knee pressed to his back.

"Get the hell off of me," Loverboy growled.

"Not until you apologize to Ms. Hayes." Oscar looked at Alexandra and shrugged. "Sorry, ma'am. We're not usually this bad."

"They're worse!" Missy cried. "Last month, at the trading-card show in Cleveland, they trashed the three-story house of cards the fans worked on for six months!"

"Oh, shut up and comb Floyd's hair," Oscar said.

"Don't talk to her that way." Floyd dove at Oscar, all three men now in a tangle of arms, legs and cuss words.

Alexandra calmly stacked her papers, slipped them into her briefcase and walked to the door.

"Where are you going?" Oscar asked.

She glanced over her shoulder. The three of them were frozen in mid romp.

"To tell Mr. Perini none of you are hero material." She slammed the door and marched to the elevators.

Admitting to Cosmo she couldn't work with these animals was admitting failure. She had thought she was up to teaching these men how to be refined, sophisticated heroes. But she'd have a better chance of surviving a suicide jump from the top of the John Hancock Building.

If today's behavior was an indication, the only one with hero potential was Floyd, as long as no one insulted his girlfriend. Oscar acted like a twelve-year-old, and Loverboy—he was the worst of all: arrogant, insensitive, and he hated kids.

That especially bothered her. How was he supposed to be a hero and bring kids back to the shows if he couldn't stand the sight of them? Had he really left behind him a trail of children with remarkable aquamarine eyes? She sighed. Hopeless, utterly hopeless.

She should find Cosmo and argue Loverboy's role in the re-birth of BAM. The man was definitely not hero material and couldn't be trusted in public. But Cosmo was counting on her to make it happen.

Like *she* counted on another few months' retainers.

Riley. Putting up with the shenanigans of these men would help her protect her son. It was a good thing she didn't have to worry about Riley ever meeting Loverboy. If the man saw her eight-year-old coming, he'd probably run the other way.

The elevator doors beeped open.

"Hey, wait up," Loverboy called after her.

She leaped into the elevator and hit the Close Door button.

"Wait a minute!" But he couldn't get his hand between the doors fast enough.

The elevator descended to the first floor, making a few stops along the way. She stared at the industrial carpet beneath her feet, trying to figure out how to work with these men. She was at her wits' end, and she'd only been a part of their world for hours, not months.

Spoiled children. That's how they acted. Fine. She'd treat them as such. She'd scold them. Next time. Right now she needed a breather.

Upon her return Monday morning they'd all start fresh. She'd plan one makeover at a time, starting with Loverboy. Keeping them separate would prevent a repeat of this morning's altercation. Altercation? More like chaos.

The doors opened and she stepped onto the tiled lobby floor. She headed for the revolving doors, the sun beckoning to her from the Chicago sky.

"Where are you going?" Loverboy came up behind her. He must have hijacked a speeding elevator.

He touched her shoulder and heat skittered down her arm. On the other hand, maybe being alone with this man wasn't such a good idea.

"I have other clients." She kept walking.

"In Chicago?"

"My office is wherever I am. I have my laptop at the hotel. Since the three of you can't seem to focus, I have other business I can tend to."

"You're running away."

She stopped dead in her tracks and stared into his blue-green eyes. "I prefer to call it disengaging."

He backed her against a rubber plant.

"I didn't know we were *en*-gaged." His eyes narrowed, the colors blending into a clear blue.

She took a step back and the plant attacked her ear. She batted it away, then slipped around Loverboy and made for the door. She needed the fresh air, the cool breeze sure to greet her on this fall afternoon in the Windy City.

With a desperate lunge, she escaped into the revolving door. Only, Loverboy wedged himself in as well. His scent surrounded her, a spicy aftershave laced with sin.

"What are you doing?" she said.

"Stopping you from running away."

She ground her teeth. Even in her darkest days she never ran from trouble, not from David or her financial struggles. She'd learned to face problems head on. .

"I need to get outside," she said, eyeing the sun-baked sidewalk.

"Aren't you having fun?" He pinned her with his body.

"About as much fun as bungee jumping off a bridge."

"I'm flattered. You're comparing time with me to the adrenaline rush of risking your life."

They made a complete turn, Loverboy's face drifting closer, closer to Lexy's. She couldn't fight it anymore. Couldn't push him away. Her gaze drifted to his lips, the bottom one slightly fuller than the top. His mouth parted as if readying for a kiss.

She was a good mother. Good mothers didn't kiss half-naked pro wrestlers in public places, especially not self-centered, child-hating wrestlers who only wanted to prove a point. The point being he was in charge.

But when his lips touched hers, she couldn't fight his sexual charm, his sweet, soft lips. He didn't swallow her whole, like some of the men she'd dated since her divorce. His tongue didn't demand an opening or press against her teeth. This kiss was unusually sweet, yet fiery hot. Something throbbed between her legs. Strange, she'd never felt that before.

Her mind spun, or was that their revolving door routine? She couldn't be sure. She clung to his shirt, afraid to let go for fear she'd puddle to the ground. Digging her fingers into the steel-like biceps, she ordered herself to break the kiss and win back her freedom.

But she didn't feel imprisoned, controlled or manipulated. Nor did this feel anything like David's forced play of passion. She felt treasured and gentled . . . with a complete stranger.

God, she *was* losing her mind.

A loud pounding shattered their intimacy and broke the kiss. She struggled to breathe, her gaze locked on his amazing eyes, which had turned a darker shade of blue-green.

"You okay in there?" a muffled voice called.

She glanced around Loverboy and spotted a security guard on the other side of the glass.

"We'll have somebody down in a few minutes to get you out," the guard said.

She hadn't realized they'd stopped moving.

"We're stuck?" Loverboy's chest heaved in and out, struggling against the aftereffects of their kiss.

Or was it something else?

He edged into the corner of the pie-shaped compartment and slapped his palms against the glass. His eyes grew wide, his pupils flared.

"I've got to get out of here." He narrowed his eyes, took a step and rammed his shoulder into the glass. His face scrunched in pain.

"Luke?" She touched his shoulder and he stared down at her hand as if it were a three-headed tarantula.

He rammed the door again, then plastered himself against it. "I can't . . . breathe."

His trembling fingers pressed against the glass.

A crowd started to gather on the sidewalk. Not good for BAM's future hero to have a full-blown anxiety attack in public. Definitely not macho, or heroic.

She had to stop his shaking. She was a master at calming Riley, talking him through thunderstorms that snapped power lines and plunged their home into darkness.

"Luke?"

"I . . . can't . . . breathe."

104

With a firm, yet gentle grip on his chin, she turned his face to look at her. "Open your eyes."

He did, as if opening them to the blinding sun. Her chest ached at the fear she saw there.

"You're okay. But we need to sit down." She clasped his hand between her palms. "Sit down with me."

"I'm . . . I can't move."

"Keep looking into my eyes. Press your back to the glass. Bend your knees. Good. Slip down until you're sitting. That's it."

He slid down the glass and she went with him, positioning herself in the crook of his arm. His hand naturally slid around her waist. She reached for his other hand and brought it to her lips.

"Listen to my voice."

"The humming . . ."

"Once upon a time there was a little girl named April . . ."

Through the blinding haze and ringing in his ears, Luke felt the vibration of her voice. April. He remembered the name of Lexy's alter ego.

Numbness filled his body, except for his fingers, warmed by her breath. His mind flooded with the chaotic noise of panic, but her voice penetrated it.

". . . she was so inquisitive. She often ended up in a world of trouble . . ."

Trouble. He remembered. He'd followed Lexy and her girlfriends to the Spook House on Maple. He hid in the bushes and listened as her friends conned Lexy into sneaking into the garage. No one was supposed to go up there. Mummified bodies and wild snakes lived there.

"Stroke my hair, Loverboy," she said.

He wished she'd call him Luke again.

"Make it look like you're comforting me," she said.

He'd wanted to comfort her on that windy night but stayed back to take the blame for breaking into the house. The Colonel got good use out of his belt that night.

She placed his hand on her hair, his fingers gliding through the silken waves.

"Good hair-touching. Very good," she said.

"The story," he urged, knowing how it ended, but wanting to hear her tell it.

"A precocious child, April often got into trouble because she didn't have good judgment. Her mom said it was because she followed her heart, not her head. But the little girl always wondered . . ." Her voice trailed off.

"Wondered what?" He stroked her hair.

"Why she couldn't be like the other kids. She was always different. Kind of strange."

"Not strange."

She got in his face. "Hey, this is my story."

"Right." He closed his eyes and guided her back to his chest, where she fit so perfectly.

"What about April?"

"She grew up, realized her heart had steered her wrong one too many times and packed it away for safe-keeping."

"I don't like that ending." He opened his eyes.

"Okay, smart guy, how would you have it end?" She tipped her head up to study him.

"She finds a handsome prince. About six two, hazel eyes, blond hair, with a great sense of humor."

"I like that ending." She smiled.

As he looked into her eyes, the futility of their meeting again hit him full force. This relationship could never be healthy, or normal, or right. He lived a ridiculous life of spectacle and pain. She needed a man who could unlock that secret place where she'd locked her heart and show her real joy.

"And where would she find such a perfect specimen?" she said.

"I . . . don't know."

"You don't?" Confusion colored her eyes.

"It's just a story." And it could have been his. But not now.

Someone knocked on the glass. "It's not jammed anymore. You can get out," a voice called.

She got to her feet and took his hand. "We're free! Are you okay? Can you stand?"

Lexy cared? Hope shot through his body.

"Come on." She pushed the door open and led him into the warm, fall air. The audience gathering on the sidewalk applauded.

"This man saved me." She wrapped her arms around his waist and gave him a squeeze. "I was so scared."

She was protecting him by making sure the general public did *not* find out about his embarrassing fear of enclosed spaces. She might have thought she'd locked away her heart, but Luke knew better. She cared about him, about a jerk who was determined to make her days with BAM miserable.

Fans shoved things at Luke to sign, but he couldn't get his hands to stop shaking.

"Sorry, no autographs today," Lexy said. "We're late for a meeting."

She whisked him away, arm in arm. He enjoyed the feel of her holding onto him. Even though he towered over her by a good eight inches, she still kept up with his pace.

She glanced over her shoulder. "That could have really messed things up."

"Excuse me?" he slowed.

"We couldn't very well sell you as Superman if you're afraid of being stuck in a revolving door."

A blast of cold filled his chest. He jerked to a stop.

"My hotel's a block down," she said, brushing wind-blown bangs off her forehead. "I'll buy you lunch and we can go over the plan."

"Screw the plan."

"What's up with you? I saved your butt back there." She planted her hands on her hips.

"Because you want to turn me into a hero."

"That's my job."

He shook his head. "And I thought April's story was a fairy tale."

"What's that supposed to mean?"

"Forget it." He marched ahead of her, tempted to step into moving traffic. Getting flattened by a car sure as hell couldn't be any worse than dealing with this new, manipulative version of Lexy.

"Hey, we have work to do," she said, skipping up beside him.

They sure did. The sooner she felt confident he was hero material, the sooner she'd move on to the next victim. Fine by him. He'd work with her for the next few weeks; learn to speak her canned lines and to smile on cue. Hell, maybe he'd even make those ridiculous charity appearances.

But he knew two things for sure: one, he wasn't going anywhere near kids—it just hurt too much; two, he'd never be fooled into letting her touch his heart again.

Chapter Eight

"Come on, you're not even trying," Lexy protested, popping a cracker in her mouth.

Luke paced her hotel suite, cursing himself for coming up here. It reeked of Lexy, from the sweet scent floating in the air to the photograph of her son on the nightstand.

"You can't just snap your fingers and be a different person," he said, wondering how in the hell he was going to transform himself into something so opposite his nature.

"You weren't always this way," she said.

He froze. Did she remember? "What do you mean?"

"I can't picture you strutting around like a Chippendale when you were ten."

No, he just followed her around like a lost puppy.

She scribbled on her legal pad, then took a sip of iced tea. He fought the urge to touch her neck, or better yet, skim his lips down it to the hollow of her throat and . . .

Snap out of it! You're here to learn your lines so you can get away from her.

"I can't remember being any other way than the way I am now," he said.

She placed her glass on the room service tray on the table. "Well, then we have a problem, because you can't keep being who you are now."

"So you've been telling me. What's wrong with a playboy hero?"

"Cosmo is targeting kids. The last thing we want are families breaking up because the moms are running off to be Loverboy groupies."

"I can't be a geek."

"I'm asking you to be a clean cut, honorable guy."

"Yeah, right." Like *that* could ever happen.

"Let's practice."

"I'm not going to say that stupid stuff."

"It's not stupid. They're neutral responses to very pointed questions. Cosmo wants to bring wrestling into the mainstream. He can't do that if every reporter from here to the coast is attacking its authenticity. Now, when someone asks you if wrestling is real you say, 'It's a real theatrical event based on the illusion of violence.' Go on, repeat it." She slashed a check mark on her legal pad, then glanced at him.

" 'It's a real theatrical event centering around'—no, I can't say it. Violence isn't an illusion."

"But wrestling is, just like a play or movie."

He shook his head. "Stand up."

"Why?" She narrowed her eyes.

"It's time you learned firsthand what the hell you're talking about."

Her gaze darted around the room, landing on the door. Damn, she was scared of him.

"I'm not going to hurt you." He extended his hand hoping, a little too much, she'd take it.

She twirled her ring but didn't make a move to get up.

"Come on, I've jumped through your hoops. The least you can do is humor me."

She stood, pulling her navy blazer closed in front.

"This"—he turned her around and bent her arm behind her back—"is an arm lock. I'm not hurting you, am I?"

"No."

"But I could by adding a little pressure." He gently pushed her forearm upward.

"You've made your point."

"I'm not through." He turned her to face him and hoisted her across his shoulders.

"Put me down!" she squealed, kicking her feet. A shoe flew across the room and nailed the television.

"Calm down or I'll drop you on your head."

"Isn't that what you're planning to do anyway?"

"Only if you keep mouthing off."

"Please put me down."

"I'm trying to show you what I do for a living. This is my signature move, the Loverboy Lunge. I spin you around a few times . . ." He demonstrated in slow motion and she stopped kicking. Did she trust him not to drop her?

"Then I drop you flat on your back in the middle of the ring." Bending his knees, he tossed her onto the bed. He rolled over and studied her face.

"Point being?" She placed her fingers to her lips.

"Don't tell me a little spinning messed up your stomach."

She glared. "A little spinning? A few more twirls and I would have flown out the window onto Michigan Avenue."

"I'm trying to show you what wrestling is really all

about. We're not supposed to get hurt, but when you're throwing guys around like that, it's bound to happen."

"More than I need to know, thank you very much." Sitting up, she turned white.

"Easy now," he said, guiding her back to the bed with a hand to her shoulder. *Stop touching her, you fool.*

"I wish I hadn't eaten the split pea soup with lunch." She closed her eyes.

"You'll be fine. Just relax a minute."

"You're pretty proud of yourself, aren't you?"

"How was I supposed to know you had a weak stomach?"

"You could have asked."

"I'm not used to asking permission before I execute a move."

Turning her head, she opened her eyes. "Even on a woman?"

"It depends what kind of move I'm planning."

She blinked and her eyes glowed a brilliant shade of amber. He hadn't meant it as a come on, but she'd taken it that way.

"You're not going to kiss me again, are you?" she said.

Was that hope in her voice? His heart ached.

"Do you want me to kiss you again?" He couldn't help himself.

"No. Yes. I don't know."

"When will you know?"

He shouldn't be doing this. He was plunging deeper into an abyss with no rescue line in sight.

"Actually, I think I know now," she said. "I'm beginning to understand you."

"You are?" His heart slammed against his ribs.

"Sure. You control things with your sexual bravado. We're going to have to change that."

He didn't have the heart to tell her it was hopeless. Nothing could make Loverboy into the hero they all wanted.

"There isn't one damn thing you aren't planning to change about me, is there?" he said, desperate to tear himself away from her.

"I can't say for sure. I don't know everything there is to know about you."

"You know enough." He reached out and brushed a strand of chestnut hair from her cheek.

"That's inappropriate," she said.

"What?"

"Touching me."

"A second ago you wanted me to kiss you."

"I didn't say that. I said I didn't know."

"Have you made up your mind?"

"No," she whispered.

That's it. He'd scare her away before she got too close and unearthed his soul. Leaning forward, he aimed for her lips and closed his eyes. He landed face down in the pillow.

"Hey!" he protested, sitting up.

"Now, about your clothes . . ." she said, grabbing her legal pad and pen from the table.

"You're avoiding the subject."

"I'm starting a new subject. Fashion."

Fashion his ass. She was avoiding his kiss. Yet she wanted it, didn't she?

"You can't walk around like that"—she motioned toward him with her pen—"and expect people to take you seriously." She sat down at the table and pulled a few catalog pages from her folder. "This will be your new look." She stretched out her arm to hand him the pages, as if wanting to keep a very safe distance between them.

He snatched the pages and snorted at the male model dressed in a navy suit, white shirt and striped tie. "He looks like a funeral director."

"It's a classic, professional look."

He tossed page one to the floor and analyzed model Number Two, dressed in khaki pants and a beige shirt.

"Bo-ring." He crumpled and tossed it at the garbage can, still steaming about the missed kiss.

"And your earrings will have to go," she said. "They don't fit the image."

"Whose image?" He fingered the two hoop earrings and diamond stud in his left ear.

"Do you have to fight me on everything? No earrings. No half-naked vests. No skin-tight jeans that show off every bulge and then some."

"You sound like my mother."

"Good, then maybe you'll stop trying to kiss me."

"But you wanted me to kiss you."

She ignored him. "And the tattoo, can you have that removed?"

"Nope." He stood and walked over to her.

"Are you sure? I've heard there are ways to do that."

Kneeling, he took her hand. Panic filled her eyes.

"Why do you always look like that?" he said.

"Like what?"

"Like you're scared to death?"

"I'm scared of you pulling one of your flirting moves in the wrong circumstance."

"Is this one of those circumstances?"

She hesitated. "Of course it is."

"Your eyes are giving me a different message."

"You're imagining things."

"Am I?" He trailed his forefinger across her cheek and down, skimming her jaw line to her full, rose-

114

colored lips. They parted slightly and he fought for control. Damn, a woman hadn't affected him this way since . . . since he couldn't remember.

Yet this woman could ruin it all, destroy his well-crafted, safe life. The sooner he drove her away, the better. She could move down the list and convert Oscar or Floyd. But not Luke. Nothing could change what he was deep inside.

"I think you want to kiss me," he said, rubbing his thumb across her lower lip. *This will scare her something good.* "Then again, maybe you want more than kissing. Am I right, darlin'? You need more than just one . . . good . . . kiss?"

He trailed his finger lower, down her neck to where her blouse opened in front. Slipping a few buttons free, he edged his finger beneath the pale material. Her eyes widened and she licked her lips. Damn, he was getting hard. Just from a peek at her tongue. That and the fact that his hand was coming dangerously close to her breast. A breast he suspected was round and soft and would fit perfectly in his hand.

Lower, lower, his fingers undid buttons Number Three and Four and he skimmed the lace of her bra. She closed her eyes. *God, this was more erotic, more exciting than straight sex.*

But this wasn't about sex. It was about survival— Loverboy's survival.

"You like that?" he whispered, stroking her skin, teasing his finger just beneath her bra line. "You want more?" he asked, using well-rehearsed, practiced lines from years ago. Some things you never forget.

She leaned into his touch and he panicked. *Should he really do this?* His mind spun, desire obliterating good sense. He had Lexy poised on the brink of surrender.

"Luke," she whispered.

The rasp in her voice raised the hairs on the back of his neck. Not right. He shouldn't be seducing Lexy. She was innocent and naive, didn't deserve to be manipulated, used and tossed aside like yesterday's garbage.

Then again, no one deserved what he got in life. Except Loverboy Luke. He'd actually grown comfortable with his destiny of fighting for an all-too-elusive redemption.

Then Lexy walked back into his life and he ached for something else. Hell, he needed her out of his life, now.

"You want to fly with me, darlin'?" Leaning forward, he touched his lips to her ear. God, she tasted sweet. "I can make you fly higher than the sky. You want that?"

She was putty in his hands, ready to be seduced, made love to. After an afternoon of lovemaking, she'd be too embarrassed to face him.

She'd also be in his blood. Hell.

A sudden pounding made her jerk away. "The door!" She shoved at him. He fell backward and she trampled over him, nailing him in the gut in her attempt to answer the door. So much for his seduction number.

She glanced at the hotel mirror and gasped at her reflection. "My hair, my face. I look . . ." She framed her cheeks with her palm.

"You look ready for sex," he said, studying her face.

"I'm not like this. I—"

"You want me," he said.

"Don't say that."

"Why not?" Sitting up, he leaned against the bed and shot her his playboy half-smile.

"God, you're so . . . so . . ."

"Ready to get a taste of you."

"Stop talking like that. Get up. Get dressed. Fix your hair."

"I am dressed."

She shook her head. "Never mind." Running her hands through her short hair, she took a deep breath and eyed the peephole. "It's just the bellman."

She flung open the door. "Yes?"

"Delivery for Mr. Silverspoon."

Luke's heart slammed against his chest.

"Who?" she said.

"Mr. Timothy Lucas Silverspoon."

"There's no one here by that . . ." Her voice trailed off. She slowly turned and stared, mouth agape, at Luke. "Oh my God," she whispered.

"The envelope?" the bellman urged behind her.

"Right, thanks, okay." She snatched the manila envelope from his hand and closed the door.

"What? No tip?" Luke got to his feet and struggled like hell to keep a lid on his emotions.

"You're that kid from next door," she said.

He couldn't move, couldn't speak. A knot balled in his chest. He'd almost had . . . what? He'd almost had Lexy? He knew better. It wasn't Luke she wanted. Only the sex. They never wanted Luke.

And now she knew the truth. The mystique gone, she'd never find passion in his arms again.

"That's why you knew my name," she said. "Why didn't you tell me?" She rushed toward him.

He automatically took a step back. "I guess this means no more kissing."

She gave him a friendly shove with her hand. "I can't believe it, after all these years. Remember the time you parachuted an army guy out your window and it ended

117

up on Dad's grill? I'll never forget the look on his face when he brought in the burgers and held up a charred GI Joe. Or the time you sneaked into my room and glued glow-in-the-dark stars to my ceiling?"

"You were failing astronomy."

"And when you mooned Principal Myers." She burst into laughter.

He'd mooned Principal Myers because the man was rounding the corner just as Lexy was poised to pull the fire alarm. The girl was gullible with a capital G. Her friends had talked her into pulling the alarm so she could join The Cool Chicks Club. Of course, the Cool Chicks were nowhere near the action when the shit hit the fan.

"I can't believe it," she said. "Someone from Sycamore. This is great."

Great wasn't the word that came to Luke's mind. She threw her arms around his neck and gave him a hug. Not a "make-love-to-me" hug. A brotherly hug. He started to push her away, but she wouldn't give up her hold. Damn her for smelling like freshly cut roses.

"How are you?" she asked.

"I'm just peachy, thanks," he said as she squeezed the air from his lungs.

She took a step back and eyed him up and down as if seeing him for the first time. His body lit with need. Maybe she saw him as the boy next door, but he still saw her as the girl he'd loved from afar.

"You look great," she said. "To think scrawny Timmy turned into this." She gave his biceps a pinch.

"Yeah, well, a lot's happened since sixth grade."

"I'll bet. How's your mom? She made the best double-fudge marshmallow brownies. And your sister, the one that danced? Did she go professional?"

"Sheila? No. She's a mom."

"What about your other sisters? You had two older ones, right? They used to do terrible things to you."

"I've spent years in therapy trying to forget," he joked. He had to do something to cut the tension building in his chest.

"I remember the time they dyed your gym shirt pink."

"Can we skip the walk down memory lane?" he said, afraid where they'd end up.

"The oldest one, Leslie, was my favorite baby-sitter. We used to eat Cocoa Puffs and she'd tell me stories about boys in high school and—"

"Enough."

"I can't believe this. How is everyone?"

"I wouldn't know." He paced to the window overlooking the busy city street.

"What do you mean?"

"I haven't spoken to them in almost fifteen years." It wasn't a complete lie. Other than the biweekly call to Mom and occasional card to Sheila and little Katie, he hadn't kept in touch. There was no reason to pour salt in an already burning wound.

"You haven't spoken to them?" Her voice cracked.

"Nope." He struggled to ignore the condemnation in her voice.

"But they're your family. Family is everything."

"Wrestling is everything."

"What are you talking about? You loved your sisters. They took care of you, when they weren't torturing you. And your dad, he took you to work sometimes, remember? Kind of made sense since he was there practically all the time, even weekends."

Damn, he'd forgotten. He'd had to.

"Things change. People change," he said.

119

"Timmy—"

"Dammit, woman." He squared off at her. "If you call me that one more time I'm going to throw you over my shoulder again, got it? I'm not Timmy Silver-spoon."

"Sorry, it's just, I'm so excited. Sometimes I miss being a kid. Don't you?"

"I hardly remember my childhood. Let's get back to work."

"But I want to hear all about your life, your science scholarship and flying lessons. Your Uncle Ed took you out every month. You loved it up there. You told me you saw God with his poofy white hair and a round tummy, sucking on a Tootsie Pop. He sounded like a cross between the Pillsbury Dough Boy and Kojak."

His chest ached with regret. Leave it to Lexy to plunge the knife deeper into his heart. "I left home at eighteen and never went back. No college, no flying, just wrestling. End of story."

Alexandra couldn't process what he was saying. She studied him, remembering the shy boy with such big dreams.

"You wanted to be an astronaut," she said. "You were so smart. I would have failed sixth-grade science if it hadn't been for you. Mitosis and tapeworms. You sneaked notes into my lunch box. When you moved away I . . ." Her voice trailed off as dawning memory struck hard. "Oh God, Timmy, I'm sorry."

How insensitive of her. Here she was rambling about her glorious childhood when all he probably remembered was his brother's death. She walked up behind him and touched his shoulder. "I'd forgotten about—"

"Are we done here?" He pulled away from her.

"Done?"

"Work, remember? Make me a clean-cut, All-American hero?" He studied the line of skyscrapers outside.

"I guess. It's nearly five. But I'd love for you to stay. We could catch up."

"Can't." He marched toward the door.

"Tim?"

"Luke is my legal name. Use it."

"Luke?"

He turned around but didn't make eye contact. "What?"

"I am sorry for being so insensitive." Boy, she felt like a crumb.

"Forget it," he said. "What's next?"

"Next?"

"With the Hero Plan."

"Mock interviews I guess. There's a press conference next week."

"Right. I've got to go."

"Luke?"

His gaze drifted to her face, but she still didn't feel his eyes connect with hers.

"I'm sorry if I hurt your feelings. I would never hurt you," she said.

He shook his head and glanced at the floor.

She felt ashamed. "Let me make it up to you," she said. "I'll buy you dinner."

"I've got plans: a redhead, five ten, tight ass."

"Oh." She'd nearly forgotten who he really was. "I thought we could talk."

"About what? About our wonderful childhood? Our great friendship? Get off it, Lexy. I was a tagalong, the

121

geek next door with a mad crush on you. Big deal. We were kids. I'm not that kid anymore. There isn't a single part of me that resembles that kid anymore."

Something strangled her heart. "Luke, I—"

"Everything turned out fine. I never belonged in the Colonel's family. I cut my losses and took off."

"But you were his only son."

"Kevin was the only son he loved. I was an anomaly."

"Luke—"

"Enough. I have no connection to the Silverspoon family. I have no connection to anyone. That's the way I like it."

Something didn't feel right. She opened her mouth to say so, but he put up his finger to silence her.

"Let's get clear: I want to make this transformation as fast as possible. I'll do whatever it takes to get back into the ring and if that means turning myself into a pathetic, clean-cut hero, then so be it. In the meantime, I won't be talking about my sisters or your brother or anything that reminds me of my former life. Got it?"

"No, actually I don't." She crossed her arms over her chest.

"It's simple. You don't know me, Alexandra. Whoever you think you knew doesn't exist. I'm Loverboy Luke Silver and no matter how hard you try, that's all you'll ever see. Make no mistake about it, I'll bed you and abandon you just as sure as I've abandoned hundreds of other women."

She wanted to slap him, exorcise the demon out of the man standing in front of her. She wanted to find her friend. "I don't believe you."

"Whatever. Until next week." He glanced across the room. "Maybe I'll rent us the bridal suite. You bring the bubbles for the Jacuzzi. I'll bring the handcuffs."

She clenched her jaw.

"Bye, darlin'." He winked and left.

"Argh!" She threw the envelope at the door. Arrogant, self-centered, sonofabitch. Shame on him for shutting out his family. His mother had doted on him, dressed him in color-coordinated clothes and bought him supplies to make rockets that his father didn't approve of.

How could he cut himself off from such a wonderful, nurturing woman? Family was everything. They loved you, believed in you, stuck by you, and he'd abandoned his for glamour and the fast life.

"Jerk!" she yelled at the door. Her eyes caught on the envelope, the very thing that had started the argument. She grabbed her keycard, snatched the envelope from the floor and went after him. Although why on earth she should be polite and deliver his package was beyond her. He'd been rude and crude and

She turned the corner and froze at the sight of the great Loverboy Luke Silver leaning against the wall beside the bank of elevators. His back was to her, and his shoulders sagged as he rubbed the back of his neck with his left hand. She took a deep breath and watched the arrogant ladies' man turn into a broken soul before her eyes. The elevator beeped and the doors opened, but she couldn't call out. Her brain struggled to understand what she was seeing. He stepped across the threshold, lethargic and lost. She clutched the envelope to her chest.

The elevator doors closed.

"What happened to you?" she whispered.

It didn't matter. What made her think she could help a man with a troubled soul?

She turned and walked back to her room. She had

more pressing issues to deal with, like fulfilling her job requirements and supporting her son.

She'd unknowingly made bad decisions about men in the past, but this time her eyes were wide open. Tim or Luke or whatever his name was, had become a selfish, arrogant ladies' man who set her body throbbing with a need that scared the wits out of her.

Yet she couldn't ignore the kindness warming his blue-green eyes. The same kindness she remembered in the eyes of a young boy who saved her butt more times than she could remember.

"That man is nothing like Timmy," she said, wondering what had happened to the compassionate boy next door.

She scolded herself. Business was business. She was in this for the money and experience, not to help old friends or save lost souls. She couldn't help wondering if Timothy Lucas Silverspoon even had a soul left to save.

Leaning against the building across the street, he lit his pipe, keeping his gaze trained on the seventh floor of the Hartford Suites. The envelope should have arrived by now, interrupting the goings-on in Room 715.

Exposed, that's how he'd feel. When it was all over Loverboy wouldn't know which end was up. Good. He needed the kid off center and vulnerable to complete his plan.

In the meantime he'd enjoy watching the two of them dance around each other, exposing their deepest secrets and regret. It would be torture for the punk.

"Now you know how I felt, Loverboy," he whispered.

Chapter Nine

Three days later at the Sheraton in Milwaukee, Alexandra wondered how wise she'd been to bring Lulu and Riley on this business trip. She could hardly concentrate with his jumping from bed to bed, and Lulu's singing.

"I'm just a girl who can't say no," Lulu belted out.

"Please, I'm trying to concentrate," Alexandra said, scribbling notes at the desk. Although this little jaunt was a mini-vacation for Riley and Lulu, Alexandra needed to focus on work: crafting a new persona for Loverboy.

Loverboy. She had to think of him that way. It was too confusing to think Timmy was buried somewhere in that arrogant, physically magnificent creature.

"Where's—the—pool?" Riley asked, jumping from one queen-sized bed to the other.

"Riley, stop the jumping or you aren't going to the pool," she scolded.

"Ah, let the kid have some fun," Aunt Lulu said. "Here, I'll join ya'." Lulu put her bare foot on the bed and Alexandra glared.

"Maybe not," Lulu said. She snatched a purple polka-dotted swimsuit from her suitcase. "Can't wait to practice my breast stroke. Need to strengthen my arms for the lasso number in the show."

"I wanna swim!" Riley cried, his hair flying about his face as he attempted a mid-air split kick. He landed on his behind. Lulu sneaked up on him and tickled his ribs.

"Stop, Lulu, stop. I'm gonna pee my pants," he cried, giggling.

"Both of you stop. I can't think," Alexandra ordered.

"Why are you so testy?" Lulu sat on the bed and wrapped her arm around Riley's neck in a headlock. He kicked, squealed and giggled all at once.

"I am not testy."

"Are too," Lulu said, rubbing the top of Riley's head with her knuckles. "You submit, Sparky?"

"Sparky?"

"Sparky Parky. That's his wrestling name. Mine's Double L—Lunatic Lulu."

"Perfect," Alexandra said.

"Crab," Lulu muttered.

"I've got a lot on my mind."

"You won't even know we're here."

She released Riley and he climbed onto her shoulders. "Somersault pin on the bed! Come on, Lulu."

"Aunt Lulu," Alexandra corrected. "Why do I bother?" Shaking her head, she pulled out her talking points for the media. She'd only written four words.

"One . . . two . . . three . . . go!" Riley and Lulu tumbled into a ball.

"I got her! Count, Mama!"

"Riley, please."

"Go on, Alley-ooops, the kid deserves to win once in

a while," Lulu said, her chin smashed against her chest, her knees pressed against her ears.

"One, two, three, fo—."

"Ding! Ding! Ding! I won!" Riley cried.

Lulu uncoiled herself and took a deep breath. "Another minute and I would have needed oxygen."

"Serves you right."

"See? That tone. You've got something stuck in your craw. What's the deal?"

"This might be two days of swimming and room service for you, but I'm on the job. I've got to deal with a stubborn, arrogant, self-centered wrestler."

"Sounds like true love." Lulu grinned.

"Not in a million. Not with this man, not ever."

"Not ever is a long time. You couldn't stop talking about him all the way here. Admit it, you find him fascinating." She leaned forward, her eyes sparkling with mirth.

"I'm done taking on lost causes. All I want is to be a great mom who can support her child."

Riley dove into the mini-fridge. "Wow! Snickers, M & M's and peanuts. Refrigerated!"

She jumped to her feet and snatched them from his dimpled paws. "Not before lunch."

He looked at Lulu and they nodded in agreement: Mama was being a crab.

"He's got you worked up, doesn't he?" Lulu said.

"Too much sugar makes Riley crazy. You know that."

"Not Riley. Loverboy Luke."

"Can I meet him, Mom? I want to meet a real wrestler!" He curled his arms, sucked in his stomach and grunted.

"Not Loverboy." *Never Loverboy*. "I'll find someone

127

else, maybe Oscar the Louse." Oscar shared the same mentality as Riley.

But not Luke. He loathed children. She'd never expose Riley to a man like that. It was bad enough that Riley's own father found him a bother. It would crush him to be shunned by a superhero.

"I need you two to behave while I go to work," Alexandra said.

"Can I come?" Riley said.

"No, you're going to hang out with Aunt Lulu. You can do the pool, visit the zoo, all that good stuff."

"What are you going to do?" He sat on the bed beside Lulu, and bounced.

"I'll be dealing with a zoo of my own downstairs."

"Come on, the boys aren't that bad," Lulu objected.

"I meant the press. I don't think Cosmo knows what he's gotten himself into. He wants wrestling to be legitimate and better for families, yet it's all about violence. My job is to convince the public that violence is okay for kids." She snatched her briefcase from the floor. "This is insane."

"Can I watch TV?" Riley said.

"Sure." She handed him the controls, then went to the mirror to check her make-up.

Lulu came up behind her and placed a hand on her shoulder. "You'll do fine, Alley-ooops. You're a good kid, and smart too."

"If I were so smart, I wouldn't have taken this job."

"It's pretty smart to be able to pay the bills." She winked and Alexandra's heart warmed.

"You're a good egg." She placed her hand over her aunt's.

"I know, scrambled, but good just the same."

"Road Runner!" Riley cried, turning up the volume.

She glanced at the cartoon, then at Riley. Then back at the cartoon.

"That's it!" she cried, grabbing Lulu by the shoulders. "I've got it! This can work."

"Of course it can."

"It's perfect!"

"Of course it is."

"It all makes sense."

"What's she talking about?" Riley asked.

"Haven't a clue," Lulu said.

"I've got to go." She raced for the door, then ran back and kissed Riley's head of curls.

"Ma-ma," he groaned.

"You're never too old for a kiss." She gave him a hug and started for the door. "I'll be back for lunch."

"If we're not here, we'll be poolside." Lulu reached into her bag and pulled out a bright green swim cap and matching goggles.

Alexandra breezed out the door to the elevator. Fate was really in her corner today, giving her just the ammunition she needed to face the press. To think a kid's cartoon held the key.

She'd do her job, set BAM on the right track and she'd be a hero.

If only she could get Luke to warm to the idea of becoming a hero. Her brain spun with unearthed memories. He'd been a sweet kid, kinda geeky, but loyal and well-meaning. Yet he'd lost his way somehow.

Her heart went out to him. She knew it was unwise to let her guard down. History had proved just how inept her instincts were in the male department. Did she really want to trust again?

It was unfair to compare this situation to that of her marriage. Back then she was trusting and naive and . . .

She was still naive, she thought stepping into the elevator and punching the ground-floor button. She still thought she could make everything right by giving some magical part of her heart away.

She'd ignored the signs of trouble in her marriage. In the end, she'd lost her ability to trust and her belief in human nature, not to mention some self-respect.

She'd never let that happen again.

Her dealings with Timmy, or Luke or whatever he called himself, would remain purely professional. She pressed her fingers to her lips, remembering the way her body floated on air when he'd kissed her last week. A tender kiss she didn't think possible from a ladies' man.

She shuddered. She'd been fooled by David. Never again. And surely not by a womanizer like Loverboy.

Their relationship would remain strictly business, regardless of the pain she read in his eyes or the ache she heard in his voice. She had to keep it that way if she had any chance of surviving this adventure.

From the corner of the meeting room, Luke watched reporters flock around Cosmo, Lexy and the new sponsors. Sponsors they'd lured with the promise of respectability.

Lexy was all business today, dressed in a dark suit and pale blue blouse. She didn't look at him, didn't make eye contact. Just as well. Last week he'd been stunned by the look of disappointment in her eyes. The same look his mother had given him when he'd said he was leaving.

That look, those sad eyes. He thought he'd buried the pain and frustration.

The incredible shame.

He hated the feeling, the shame clenching his heart

when his father pinned him with the "glare." He'd had no choice but to leave. He didn't belong with his family. He didn't belong anywhere, until he found wrestling. In the ring he could be whoever he wanted. As a heel, he'd never felt more secure in his life. Then fate dropped Lexy into his lap.

A stranger. That's how he needed to think of her. If only she had changed more, grown out her hair or needed glasses. It wouldn't matter. He'd know Lexy with his eyes closed. Her essence still connected to an intimate part of him after all these years.

"Please take your seats," she directed the press.

"Hey," Oscar said, coming up behind Luke.

"You're late."

"What, wake up on the wrong side of the bed? Or did you miss another night's sleep?" He laughed.

Lexy glanced in their direction and Luke wondered if she'd heard Oscar's suggestive comment.

Business. This was about business.

The reporters settled into their seats and the BAM superstars sat at the long table up front. Lexy stood front and center.

"There's been a lot of criticism of wrestling these past few years," she began.

She looked incredible today, her collarless shirt accentuating a long beautiful neck.

"Mr. Perini and his sponsors are committed to changing the image of pro wrestling. They plan to take it back to the arena of family entertainment. Children will be able to attend age-appropriate shows to see their superheroes come to life, and parents will buy action figures of wrestlers their kids watched perform."

"Perform? So you're saying wrestling isn't real?" a reporter piped up.

"Let me ask you a question Mr. . . ."

"Humphrey."

"Mr. Humphrey, did you watch cartoons when you were a child?" She paced to the front row.

"Well, sure."

"And did you think they were real?"

"As real as a cartoon can be."

"And pro wrestling is as real as it can be."

"But the sexual story lines and—"

"Are going to change. BAM is committed to providing wholesome entertainment for families."

"Wholesome? It's men beating up on each other," a female reporter said.

"Do you have children?" Alexandra asked.

"Yes."

"Do they watch cartoons?"

"Yes, but—"

"Pro wrestlers are skilled athletes who provide live entertainment for children. What's more, wrestling provides heroes for young boys to admire."

"But it's all fake!" another reporter said.

Lexy flipped through her legal pad. "Three broken noses, a slipped disc, torn rotator cuff, broken wrist, two concussions and a torn knee ligament." She glanced at the reporter. "This is a list of injuries for just one of BAM's wrestlers over a seven-year period."

The room fell silent.

"I'd like to put the real-versus-fake question aside for a minute and tell you what we've got planned."

Luke watched reporters jot notes and ask questions. They weren't stupid. They knew pro wrestling was a hot ticket, although business had been slipping. At first,

Luke had blamed bookers for putting together dog matches. But as the months passed and he noticed more empty seats at house shows, he started to think wrestling had run its course in the American culture. The fans had grown cynical. And Cosmo had grown desperate.

But no one would buy Luke's heel-turned-hero routine. He couldn't be something he wasn't. The Colonel's last words to him pretty much confirmed that.

You'll never amount to any good.

He snapped his coffee stick in half and pushed the memory side.

"At this point I'd like to turn it over to Mr. Perini, owner of Brawlers and Maulers," Lexy said.

Cosmo lumbered up front. "Thanks for coming. I'd like to introduce the new heroes who will take us to great heights in sports entertainment."

He introduced Luke sans the Loverboy moniker. Luke smiled on cue, trying like hell not to wink at the ladies.

Oscar waved a mini-American flag when introduced, and Floyd stood and nodded as if accepting a bid for Congress.

"There's going to be more athleticism and less fanfare," Lexy said. "More sport and less spectacle, more of all the good things that made pro wrestling the sensation of the Eighties."

"Why the change?" the female reporter asked.

"Yeah," another asked. "Just last month you had a woman pop out of a cake wearing nothing but a three-foot candle."

Lexy cleared her throat. "We've been working with OATS, the Organization for Appropriate Television Selection. We're considering their recommendations."

"So you're making these changes out of a sense of conscience?" a reporter said.

"I'll be honest," Cosmo answered. "We've been losing good sponsors because of our programming."

"Which means big money," a reporter shot back.

"It's the American way," Lexy said. "But so is quality work. With our new direction, we've already signed three big sponsors and have plans to start production of action figures, T-shirts and other toys marketed to children."

"Can we ask the wrestlers questions?" a reporter said.

"Of course." She stepped aside.

"Loverboy, how do you feel about turning hero?"

"I guess I'll have to start behaving like a gentleman."

They laughed. Lexy glared.

Reporters fired off more questions and she coordinated answers between Cosmo and the boys. She wore an aura of confidence he'd never noticed when they were kids. He liked it, although he felt a bit threatened. He was used to being the one in control ever since he'd left home.

"This is a joke!" a young woman said from the back of the room.

The kid looked barely sixteen, wore cut-offs and a tank top that showed way too much skin, and sported a tattoo on her bare shoulder. If she were his kid he'd lock her up.

"That's all. Thank you for coming." Lexy dismissed the press and went to the girl.

What the hell was this about? he wondered.

Photographers snapped pictures and reporters asked for autographs for their kids, nephews and grandmothers. Luke signed a photo for a reporter from *Wrestler's Wisdom Magazine*.

Suddenly the girl pushed through the crowd and pointed at Luke. "He got me pregnant! My dad's going to make sure you go to jail!"

His gut twisted into a knot and his gaze shot to Lexy. He could care less about the bozo reporters, but he couldn't stand the look in Lexy's eyes.

"So much for cleaning up your act," a reporter said, cornering the girl and asking her name.

"No more questions." Lexy blocked the press from the girl. "The press conference is over."

"But this is news!" the reporter protested.

"Not today it isn't." She nodded and five burly wanna-be wrestlers cleared the reporters out of the room.

Leading the girl to the corner, Lexy placed a hand on the kid's shoulder. The kid didn't deserve to be comforted. She deserved a good spanking by her mother.

Luke stood and Cosmo waved him off. "Let her handle it. That's what she gets paid to do."

He ground his teeth. Out of control again. He couldn't control what was going on over there any more than—

"This is my mess. I'll clean it up." He headed for the women and Cosmo followed.

"I just wanted to touch him, you know, see if his muscles were as hard as they looked," the kid said. "When we got to his room he started to undress me."

"That's bull."

"Shush," Lexy interrupted, and then took the girl's hand. "I'm sure we can work this out."

"My parents don't know!" she wailed, collapsing against Lexy's shoulder.

"You're being taken in by this fairy tale?" Luke said. "Hell, you really haven't changed."

"Maybe not, but you obviously have."

Hollowness filled his chest.

"Give us space so I can calm her down," Lexy said.

"Come on, man." Oscar grabbed his arm.

Luke wrenched it away. "I don't believe this."

Storming to the front of the room, he tossed a few chairs, cursing under his breath. Usually he could care less what people thought of him. But this wasn't just people. It was Lexy.

"It had to catch up to you sooner or later," Oscar said, referring to Luke's reckless lifestyle.

"Oh, it did, brother. It surely did."

But not because of this kid. Regret had caught up to him long before this accusation of paternity and would haunt him for the rest of his life.

"Well, I'm off to find my woman," Floyd said, straightening his silk jacket. "Better get ready, Oscar. Looks like Luke's out of the picture with the little girl crying rape."

Luke whipped around and stared at Lexy. She didn't really think . . . no . . . she couldn't think Luke capable of forcing himself on a woman, much less a girl.

His heart skipped. He had to tell her . . . what? The truth? No one could ever know.

But he had to explain, or at least make the kid admit she was lying.

Lexy stood and nodded to Cosmo, who led the girl out of the conference room. Luke started after them.

Lexy stopped him. "Luke, we need to talk."

Oscar hung close by.

"Alone," she said.

Oscar patted Luke on the shoulder and left.

Luke crossed his arms over his chest and waited. His heart raced, pounding like a bass drum in his ears.

"Why didn't you warn me about this?" she said.

She paced a good ten feet away, as if she couldn't stand being too close to him.

"Or was she just one of many you couldn't remember?"

"Hang on there, sweetheart."

She spun around. "Don't you *ever* call me that."

"Don't you want to hear my side?"

"What side? You bedded a girl without her consent, reveling in her adulation, her hero-worship. God, couldn't you take a little responsibility?"

"She's not my responsibility."

"You take advantage of a young, innocent girl and she's not your responsibility?"

"And you just assume I'm guilty, that she played no part in this?"

"She's eighteen! When I was eighteen I still didn't know what third base was."

"You're kidding."

"Don't you dare be glib. You're a sexually experienced man who should have the integrity not to take advantage of a young girl." She paced a few steps away and back again.

She looked hot, her cheeks flushed, her eyes blazing fire. *She thinks you're a criminal who preys on young girls.*

Nothing he said would change her mind. He'd been there before. He wished, this time, it wasn't with Lexy.

"I didn't touch her. Not like that."

"How can you be sure? You don't even remember her, and she's pregnant with your child."

"Not possible. All right?"

"I'll have to call the girl's father and discuss some kind of settlement. If we're lucky this won't come out, but I doubt it."

"You're not listening to me."

Ambling to the table, she shoved papers into her briefcase. "Cosmo's plan is down the drain. I'll have to scratch you from the hero list. We'll have to send you off someplace for a while, maybe overseas or Mexico."

Shit, without his American fans he was nothing. Superstardom—gone. Money—gone. Ability to pay his penance—gone. His blood pressure spiked.

"I don't make as much money in Mexico."

"You should have thought about that before you screwed that kid!"

He gripped her upper arms and stared into her eyes. "I didn't get her pregnant. Why can't you believe me?"

"How *can* I believe you?"

"Look into my eyes, Lexy. You know me, better than anyone," he let slip.

"I used to know a boy named Timmy. But he was gentle and kind. He'd never take advantage of someone."

"Neither did I." He stared into her eyes, aching to see a glimmer of trust. Judgment glared back at him.

"Of course you won't own up to this," she said. "I know how you feel about children."

Her accusation was like a razor slicing open his chest. His hands sprang open and he took a step back. "What do you know, Lexy?"

"You won't do children's charities. That pretty much says it all."

"That's irrelevant. I'm not the father of that child."

Alexandra truly wanted to believe this was some kind of mistake. But she knew Loverboy Luke too well, from press clippings, well-founded rumors, and even personal experience. The man exuded sex, his body pulsated with it, drawing in unsuspecting females like moths to a flame.

"Believe what you want," he said. "Now you can take me off your damned hero list."

"So, you're admitting you had sex with her?" She couldn't bear to hear the answer.

He cocked his chin. "Sure, I was horny, she was willing."

A lead weight dropped in her stomach.

"I'll talk to Cosmo." She broke eye contact, unable to look at him. "We'll have to rethink our strategy, maybe push Oscar first."

"Whatever you say, babe."

Her gaze drifted to his hand. He cracked each knuckle, one by one, with his thumb. Her breath caught.

"You're cracking your knuckles." She looked into his eyes.

"Habit. Lots of people do it."

"Timmy Silverspoon cracked his knuckles when he lied."

"I'm not him." He clenched his jaw.

"No?" Reaching out, she touched his hand. He glared at her fingers as if they branded his skin.

"Tell me the truth," she said. "I want to hear it."

"No, you don't." He took a step forward, his eyes steely blue.

All her defense mechanisms went on alert.

"The truth is I could do you right here, right now, just like all the rest," he said, his voice low and gravelly.

She took a step back and he followed, fingering her hair. She shivered. "What are you doing?"

"What do you want me to do?"

Frustration welled up inside, clogging her lungs. One minute he was the vulnerable boy from Sycamore, the

139

next, a sexual dynamo, poised to fulfill her every fantasy.

Don't be a fool, girl. You know who he is and what he'll do to you.

"Please," she said, barely able to speak she was so flustered by his sensual assault. She'd meant "please stop." Instead, he brushed his lips over the tip of her ear. Prickles danced across her shoulders. Her breasts grew heavy with wanting.

"Please what, Al-ex-an-dra?"

He pinned her to the wall with his body. Digging her fingers into his arms, she struggled to breathe. She had to stop this. She wanted more.

No. She couldn't be drawn in by a man like this. Like what? Lady-killer and liar, or loyal protector?

"Who are you?" she said.

He tipped her chin up with his forefinger and thumb so she looked directly into his eyes. "I'm Loverboy Luke Silver. Whatever you do, sweetheart, don't forget that."

He pressed a feather-light kiss to her forehead and left the room.

Chapter Ten

Riding the elevator down to the pool, Alexandra looked forward to a mental break from work. She'd spent the better part of the morning arguing with Cosmo. He wanted to buy off the girl; Lexy wanted to challenge her.

Truth was, something didn't feel right about the girl's story, or Luke's reaction. The scene replayed itself in her head . . .

I was horny, she was willing.

Crack, crack.

No cracking when he called the girl's story a fairy tale; no cracking when he accused Alexandra of still being the same trusting soul she'd been when they were kids.

She'd changed in many ways, grown stronger in order to protect her son. But one thing hadn't changed: She believed in people. Should she believe in Luke?

A quick dip would clear her mind and maybe wash the residue of Loverboy from her body. She touched her cheeks. They'd burned at his threat to "do her" in a public place.

Admit it, girl—your whole damn body burned. She'd pictured him tossing the water pitcher and glasses to the floor and laying her on the conference table. She'd imagined him straddling her, pressing his need against her moist and wanting—

"I hope the water's cold," she muttered.

Cripes, he'd accidentally awakened some part of her she couldn't stop from careening out of control. Maybe it was time to find a nice man to share her life, a man who could blot out the enigma of Timothy Lucas Silverspoon.

The elevator doors opened and she headed for the pool. Truth was, she hadn't thought about other men since her divorce six years ago. Why, oh why, did the first man to warm her heart have to be Loverboy?

No, this had nothing to do with her heart. It was lust, plain and simple.

She pushed through the glass door to the pool.

"Mama!" Riley called, his voice bouncing off the high ceiling. He dog-paddled to the edge of the pool.

"Hey, buddy. You having fun?"

"We ordered lunch and ate by the pool. Salami sandwiches!"

"Cool." She dropped her bag beside a chair and took off her wrap.

"You coming in?"

"You bet."

"Look at Lulu."

"Aunt Lulu."

Alexandra glanced toward the shallow end of the pool. Lulu floated on her back, toes pointed, arms at her sides. A fruity-looking drink was balanced on her stomach.

"She's a good swimmer," Riley said. "She can float and everything."

"I can see that." She sat on the edge and dipped her toes the water.

"Come in, Mom," Riley said, his voice echoing off the glass walls. "Just close your eyes and jump."

"Yeah, just close your eyes and jump."

She turned at the sound of Luke's voice and something caught in her chest at the sight of him, nearly naked, walking toward her. His baggy swim trunks hung low off narrow hips, his chest was bare except for the white towel draped across his shoulders. How could he get better looking every time she saw him?

"Mom?"

She whipped her attention to Riley, who clung to the pool ledge, looking in Luke's direction. He couldn't meet Luke. She couldn't bear to see the look in her son's eyes when a superstar shunned him.

She plunged into the pool and grabbed Riley's arm. "Let's go see Lulu."

"Aunt Lulu," he corrected, glancing over his shoulder at Luke. "Isn't he one of the wrestling guys?"

"Hey, what am I? Alfalfa sprouts? Swim with your mom," she said, guiding him to the center of the pool where Lulu floated, humming a tune off-key.

Alexandra didn't miss the hardening of Luke's jaw, or the way his eyes turned cold when he spotted Riley. Whew, that was close. No matter how confused she was, she still had it together where Riley was concerned.

Luke watched them swim to the center of the pool, hesitating on his way to the hot tub. She'd grabbed her kid and swum like an Olympic competitor to make sure he didn't come in contact with her son.

Her son, the spitting image of his mother: dark hair, a round face and bright smile. Luke would have enjoyed meeting him.

He ripped his gaze from the threesome and dropped his towel onto a nearby chair. Lexy must have figured out the truth: Luke was poison to children.

Didn't matter, he thought, sliding into the steamy Jacuzzi bubbles. The water swirled around his stomach, his chest and shoulders. He closed his eyes. Big mistake. The image of Lexy, dangling her legs in the water and chatting with her son, burned the backs of his eyelids. Then something else burned, dead center in his chest.

She'd protected her son from the stupid, arrogant wrestler. The man who'd bedded a young girl against her will. The man who enjoyed being *bad* in every way possible.

He slipped deeper into the hot tub, letting the water massage his aching joints, soothe his battered muscles. It wasn't enough. It was never enough.

Nothing would soothe his broken spirit.

"Hey, man, you asleep?" The water shifted as Oscar joined him.

He hoped the guy wasn't in a chatty mood. Luke needed quiet time to purge Lexy from his thoughts.

"Hey, isn't that the PR lady?" Oscar said.

So much for solitude.

"Yep," Luke said.

"Whooo-eeee. She's a real honey in a bathing suit."

Didn't he know it. Luke couldn't help appreciating her feminine figure; she had sleek shoulders, a trim waist, and nicely rounded hips. Hips he could imagine gripping and positioning just so, to give him full access to other, more private places. Too bad they didn't make hot tubs that pumped ice water.

"Don't look now, but she's coming over here," Oscar said.

Luke opened his eyes, but she was still floating in the center of the pool with her son.

"Gotcha," Oscar said.

"Ass."

"Takes one to know one." Oscar grinned.

"You love torturing me."

"Nah, I just love you." He smacked a kiss and blew it at Luke.

"Watch it or people will talk." He closed his eyes and spread his arms across the wet cement.

"People are already talking about you," Oscar said. "What's the deal with that teenage girl, anyway?"

"Never saw her before in my life."

"Now that's a line if I ever heard one."

"I've got plenty of those," Luke said.

"You ever used one on the PR lady?"

"Sure." He smiled, his eyes still closed.

"They ever work?"

"Like a charm," he lied, wishing they had.

"Really?"

His eyes shot open at the sound of Lexy's voice. Hell, there she stood, dripping wet, the shape of her nipples obvious beneath her suit. She looked like a Playboy centerfold, only this centerfold was clinging to her son's fingers as if protecting him from the devil himself.

"Riley, I'd like you to meet Loverboy Luke and Oscar the Louse."

He wished she had introduced him as Luke.

Oscar reached over to shake the kid's hand. "How ya' doin', chief?"

"Wow," the kid said, his eyes wide, a slow grin rounding his cheeks.

145

Lexy stepped to her left, blocking Luke from the conversation. *Good mother. Protect the kid.*

Riley was having none of it. As if sensing Luke was the forbidden fruit, he stepped around his mom.

"Hi, Mr. Loverboy Luke," he said, extending his hand.

Luke's heart pounded as he stared at the boy's small fingers.

"Shake the kid's hand, you jerk," Oscar said.

Luke sucked in his breath and reached out to shake the boy's hand.

"We should leave them alone, Riley." Lexy turned her son away with two hands on his shoulders.

Luke leaned back, clenching his fist and burying it beneath the water.

"They need to relax," she said.

"Oh, bull—" Oscar caught himself. "Sorry. Come over here, kid. You ever been in a hot tub?"

"No."

"Here." Oscar grabbed the kid under the armpits.

Lexy started to reach out but Oscar already had Riley in the steaming water beside him.

"It's like sitting in a can of pop," Oscar said. "Bubbles everywhere."

"I'm boiling," the kid said.

"You'll get used to it. The trick is looking cool even when you're frying. Watch me." Oscar stretched his arms across the edge of the hot tub, leaned back and closed his eyes.

The kid imitated him, leaning back and stretching out his arms. They looked like father and son. It didn't surprise Luke, since Oscar had three kids of his own.

Too bad Luke would never . . .

Time to go. He started to get up.

"Don't leave on my account," said an older woman wearing a bright green bathing cap and polka-dotted swimsuit. With a hand on Luke's shoulder, she pushed him back into the water and sat beside him.

"So, you're the rascal causing my niece all kinds of trouble."

He glanced at Lexy, who made slashing signals with her hands. She stopped in mid-slash, pretending she'd been adjusting her bathing suit strap.

"This is Aunt Lulu," Lexy said.

"Good to meet ya." The woman shoved her hand at Luke. He had no choice but to shake it. She grinned at Lexy. "He's not so bad."

Lexy narrowed her eyes in warning.

"Stop looking all bug-eyed and hop in. The water's boilin' perfect," Lulu said.

Lexy glared and placed her hands on her hips. God, what he wouldn't give to get his arms around that woman.

"Ignore her," Lulu said to Luke.

If only he could.

"She's always so damned serious." Aunt Lulu turned to Riley. "How are ya' doing kiddo? You like hanging out with the big superstars?"

He grinned, not opening his eyes. "Yep."

"We should really get going," Lexy said.

"You just got here," Lulu protested. "Come on, get in. If anyone needs a little loosening up, it's you."

"Lulu," she warned.

"Aunt Lulu," Riley said, eyes still closed.

"I need to pick Oscar's brain about Summer Squash two years ago when the Big Cheese lambasted him with the giant mouse trap," Lulu said. "You shoulda won on a DQ." She scooted next to Oscar, leaving a smaller space between Riley and Luke.

Not to worry. The kid's eyes were still closed.

You're okay. The kid doesn't know you exist.

As if he read Luke's mind, Riley opened his eyes and stared him down. "Is the blood real or is it ketchup?"

Kids. This was another reason he couldn't stand being around them. They asked too many questions. So damned direct.

"It's—"

"Make room for Mama, Riley." Lexy practically dove into the hot tub, setting herself up as an impregnable wall between Luke and her son. This time Luke resented it.

"Did you really lock the Queen of Amoeba in the Dungeon last year because she wouldn't marry you?" Riley asked.

Shame coursed through him. The kid thought it was real, which meant he thought Luke was a . . . a what? Everyone knew he was a bastard.

"It's part of the story line, kid. It's make-believe."

"So, the blood's fake?" Riley said.

Oscar narrowed his eyes and the old lady stopped jabbering. What the hell? What did they want him to say?

"You don't really beat each other to a bloody pulp, do you?" Riley said.

"Riley," Lexy gasped.

"Of course they don't," the aunt cut in. She looked at Luke with an encouraging nod.

"Nah, it's not real blood," he said, cracking his knuckles under the water.

"What's with all the blood talk?" Oscar pinched the kid in the ribs.

Riley giggled and scooted away, pushing Lexy closer to Luke. Too close.

"Don't you want to know how I won Pandora's Power Slam contest last year?" Oscar said. "I've got special moves I use only for the big crowds. I could show you."

"Yeah!" Riley said.

"I don't think so," Lexy warned.

Luke edged away from the group. That was too close. To what? Telling the truth? Ruining the kid's fantasy that pro wrestling was safe, fun and an all-around good time?

He didn't consider himself a liar, but he sensed that was what they wanted him to do. Don't scare the kid. *Protect him.* That's what you did with someone you loved. A child you loved.

He had to get out of here. He started to get up and Lexy touched his bare shoulder. He froze.

"Thanks," she whispered.

He wanted to shoot back some cocky remark sure to keep Lexy far away from him. He started to speak, but couldn't. How many times had he ached for a thank-you after protecting her from a mishap in grade school?

He nodded, realizing her hand still touched his shoulder. Her warm fingers set his skin on fire. She had to feel it, the sparks shooting off like fireworks gone haywire in a factory explosion.

How could this be? He knew she didn't welcome the chemistry between them, and he surely didn't. Or did he?

"Hey, isn't that Beth?" Oscar said.

Luke glanced up and spotted Beth, one kid on her hip and another by her side, peering through the plate-glass window.

"I told her I'd come to the house," he muttered, standing and reaching for his towel.

"Who's Beth?" Riley asked.

He couldn't go into it, not now. Hell, not ever. He didn't want Lexy to know how bad he really was.

"I've got to go. It was nice meeting you," he said to Riley. The kid's face lit up like a fluorescent light.

"I'll see you in Houston the day after tomorrow," he said to Lexy.

"By then I'll have a plan for your situation," she said.

He hated the "naughty boy" tone she used. Good. If he hated, he couldn't love.

He wrapped the towel around his shoulders and walked away.

Alexandra sighed. The mystery woman's face brightened as he approached the window. The little girl, balancing on the woman's hip, leaned forward and slapped her palms against the glass in excitement.

Another puzzle piece. He hated kids, yet that little blonde-haired thing adored him like . . . a father. Heaviness settled around her heart. Could this be one of his many families strewn across the country? She couldn't make heads or tails of the reunion taking place on the other side of the glass. One thing was certain, this woman was no stranger to Loverboy Luke.

Why should that surprise her? It didn't. But it bothered her. Terribly.

Refocus. Making Loverboy an onstage hero is your job. Not an easy thing to do when the man has a wife and children in every state.

"Who is that lady?" Riley asked, gripping the rim of the hot tub and flutter-kicking his feet.

"A friend," Oscar said. "She used to . . ." His voice trailed off as his pale blue eyes met Alexandra's.

"Used to what?" Riley pushed.

"What are you? An investigative reporter?" He tickled Riley and the little boy's giggles echoed off the high ceiling.

Oscar might have distracted her son, but not Alexandra. She watched the scene unfold on the other side of the glass, watched Luke lean toward the woman, close his eyes and kiss her cheek. As if . . . he loved her.

She blinked, her mind a whirl of questions and her chest a knot of emotion.

"He's known Beth forever," Oscar said, tickling Riley, but looking into Alexandra's eyes.

"Forever is a long time," she whispered, knowing what forever felt like. She'd known Luke since he was six, yet the reunion on the other side of the glass made her wonder if she'd ever known him.

She hardly recognized the man who ruffled the little girl's hair, then tossed the other child, a boy, over his shoulder. The same man who supposedly couldn't stand being around children.

The truth was, she didn't know Timothy Lucas Silverspoon at all.

"They're good friends," Oscar said, as Luke and his family walked away, the young boy over his shoulder.

She glanced at Oscar and he broke eye contact. She knew there was more to the story. As the PR pro, it was her job to know it all. But as a woman, did she want to?

Chapter Eleven

Luke navigated the rental car through Houston traffic, cursing the flight's effect on his brain. Flying irritated the hell out of his concussion, yet he was thankful for this public appearance, a good excuse not to linger at Beth's.

God, how the kids had grown, even Baby Jenny. He couldn't believe Bubba had been gone four years. Not a day went by that Luke didn't remember his hearty laugh and dry sense of humor, something people weren't prepared for when they met the six-foot seven-inch beast. A burly beast, thanks to steroids and growth hormones.

He wished Beth hadn't come looking for him at the hotel. No one knew Luke took care of them like his own family. He'd smiled his brightest smile and played with the kids as long as he could stand it. Then he'd escaped, though Beth had tried, as always, to get him to stay.

Lingering amidst the love and purity of children was too hard, especially now, when he felt utterly fragile.

He swore under his breath. Fragile? He was Loverboy Luke, the biggest, baddest hard ass to step into the ring.

He mentally readied himself for today's press party. Anything to boost ticket sales for tomorrow's wrestling fund-raiser. It was the third this year to raise money for a family whose father had lost his life to the business.

Three was too many. Hell, one was too many.

He pushed aside his growing anger at the business and his life. This was what he'd wanted: to be famous, powerful and untouchable in every way.

Yet Lexy had touched him the other day, placed her fingers on his shoulder and set off a surge of emotions he didn't know existed inside his rundown body.

Thank God for the forty-eight-hour break. It had given him time to gear up for more one-on-one.

He hoped she wouldn't bring her kid. Luke wasn't sure he could stand being around the sweet, round-cheeked boy, watching that grin light up his face, fielding the boy's questions with lies, for his own good.

Just like he'd lied to his mom for the past fifteen years. "I'm doing great, Mom. I'm A-Okay, Mom," he'd lie over the phone.

"Stop," he muttered. He couldn't let the mistakes of his past eat at him. He had to refocus on his goal: jumping ship before they ruined his successful scoundrel persona.

Two weeks of public appearances as a good guy wasn't going to help. During that time he'd test the waters with other promoters to see if they had any interest. He'd explain that Cosmo was asking things of him he couldn't possibly do, like be an honorable hero. Steel's Outrageous Wrestling would understand. Their roster was made up of mostly hardcore heels, bad guys that fans loved to hate.

A sense of relief settled across his shoulders at the thought of getting away from BAM and its new direction. Getting away from Lexy and her son.

Cosmo wouldn't fire her if BAM lost one of its biggest superstars, would he? He had to stop worrying about her and think of his own problems.

Selfish bastard.

He pulled up to the hotel, swarmed by fans. The valet opened his door. "I'll get your luggage to your room, Mr. Silver. They're waiting for you in the penthouse suite."

"Thanks."

A few security guards kept the crowd under control as he made his way to the front desk. He signed a few autographs. It's what they expected.

"Hello, sir." The desk clerk slid the registration forms across the granite counter. "If you could sign here."

He glanced at the form and noticed a folded-up piece of paper. A note from Lexy, maybe?

He opened it. No such luck. It was a phone number and the name, Darla. He signed the form and pocketed the note. Then he noticed the desk clerk's name badge: Darla.

"Thanks," he said.

"My pleasure." She winked.

He had started for the elevators when he spotted a few of the guys from Steel's Outrageous Wrestling.

"Hey, Loverboy, you having fun?" said Red Rooster, a burly wrestler with a full beard.

"A laugh riot."

"This is Mooner." Red introduced a young kid, maybe twenty, who wore his hair spiked like a porcupine.

They shook hands.

"So, you're the legend, huh?" Mooner said.

"Nah, I think I'm what they call an old timer."

"Yeah, then why you got all these girls chasing after you?" He motioned to the security guards, who were keeping a dozen females from mobbing the wrestlers.

"I hear you're turning hero." Red scratched his beard and eyed Luke.

"You're hearing's not so good." Luke motioned to the security guards. "Let them through."

The girls swarmed the wrestlers, shoving notepads, visors, even panties in their faces.

Luke smiled and signed a few personal items. Suddenly, a girl pressed her body against him and a flash bulb went off, then another. Pain sliced through his skull.

"That's all," he said, backing up to the elevators.

"You don't look so good," Red said.

"Overbooked. You know the drill," he lied. He didn't want news of his concussion getting out.

He turned to face the elevator, hoping fans would get the hint and leave him alone, or at least put their damn cameras away.

He needed pain meds. He needed quiet.

The hum of the crowd grew louder, irritating the headache. He escaped into the elevator with Red and Mooner. A handful of women crowded in beside them.

"I didn't get an autograph downstairs," one girl said. "Would you mind?"

He wanted aspirin, a bed, and twelve hours of sleep.

"No problem," he said.

She unbuttoned her blouse to expose a pink lace bra. Her friends giggled. "Right here." She shoved her cleavage in his face.

Red snorted.

Luke signed her breast, blinking against the pain. The elevator stopped at every floor. He couldn't take much more of this.

Red and Mooner hopped off on four. "See you upstairs."

"Maybe." He smiled, nodding at the girls.

The elevator doors closed on Red's hearty laugh.

Luke took a deep breath. Then he felt it. Someone touching his pants. He jerked back.

"It's a condom," Miss Pink Lace said. "In case you need an extra."

"What floor?" her friend said.

"Seven," he lied. He had no intention of bringing anyone to his room.

The elevator stopped at seven and they got off. "I'm in seven twelve." He pointed down the hall. "Wait for me down there. I've got to make a personal call."

He pulled out his cell phone and walked in the opposite direction. The girls giggled and disappeared.

Shoving his phone in his pocket, he made for the stairs. He climbed them two at a time, his head pounding, and his eyes watering.

One flight. Two. Three.

He pushed through the door onto the tenth floor and leaned against the wall, sucking in air to keep from passing out. His room was twenty feet away. Might as well be twenty miles. Squinting against the gold-striped wallpaper, he leaned against the wall and took a step, then another, fumbling his way to Room 1010.

As he dug into his pocket for the key, a few dollars and scraps of paper fell to the industrial carpeting.

Leave them. His fingers curled around the key card. He popped it in the door. No dice.

"Damn." Pressing his forehead on the door, he flipped the card a few different ways until the faint green glow pierced through his mental haze. He pushed the door open and stumbled inside.

It was so damned hot. He ripped off his shirt, unsnapped his jeans, took three steps and collapsed on the bed.

Lexy was mad as hell when Luke didn't show at the press party. Better mad than worried.

She ambled through the penthouse crammed with press, wrestling superstars and promoters. She spoke with utmost confidence and charmed the pants off each and every guest. Inside she burned.

Luke knew the importance of this event, an ideal opportunity to help him cross the line from heel to hero.

To think she'd been ready to apologize for thinking him guilty of rape. Lexy had confronted the girl, who finally admitted she was pregnant with her boyfriend's baby. She'd figured no one would doubt her story, considering Loverboy's reputation.

Alexandra raised her glass at a passing reporter. She should have believed Luke, but Oscar's comment about him impregnating women worldwide hadn't done much to boost her confidence. Nor had that scene the other day with the blonde woman and her children.

"You've done a fine job," Cosmo said, walking up to her, his nose aflame with the effects of alcohol. He snagged another glass of champagne from a passing waiter.

"Thanks," she said. The penthouse door opened and she craned her neck to see if Luke had finally arrived. Instead, Floyd and Missy sauntered in, the press hovering like ants on melted ice cream.

"You lookin' for someone?" Cosmo said.

"Just our main star."

"Stop worrying. The mystery creates interest. Besides, we don't want to overexpose him."

"With what he wears, I doubt that's possible."

Cosmo's hearty laugh drew stares. "You sure are something. And thanks for clearing Luke's name. Didn't even occur to me the girl might be lying."

"Let's just hope a million other girls don't pop up in the meantime." She placed her glass on a coffee table.

"A million? Nah. A handful, maybe," he chuckled.

"Wonderful. I feel much better."

"I've gotta grease some palms with the boys at WHAK."

She watched him make his way to the other side of the room. Cosmo shook hands with a tall cowboy who had a cute, auburn-haired woman on his arm.

She strolled to the window and glanced across the city. Where the hell was Luke? Something wasn't right.

What was "right" about Loverboy Luke? She'd never know. The boy she remembered was long gone, replaced by a man who overpowered her one minute with raw sexuality, and needed her the next with a kind of vulnerability that seemed to shock even him.

"Silver is one lucky sonofagun," a male voice said.

Her ears pricked.

"How many girls you figure he's got up there?"

"They came in a pack."

"Like beer?"

"Yep."

"Lucky bastard."

Only when Lexy found herself racing down the hall toward the elevator did she realize she'd left the party. What was she doing? Her job was to charm the press.

No, right now her job was to find out what the heck Loverboy was up to. He couldn't be holed up in a room with a pack of females.

Now who was the sucker?

She took the elevator to the tenth floor. When she got her hands on him she was going to . . . to what? Shake some sense into him, that's what. He kept making the same mistakes over and over.

And she didn't? What about her overblown concern for a man who couldn't be bothered with responsibility of any kind? Sounded a little too familiar.

She stepped off the elevator and marched to Room 1010.

"Open up, Loverboy." She banged on the door. "I know you're in there."

Pressing her ear to the door, she glanced at the floor and spotted a foil packet. She picked it up. " 'Get Lucky' " was written on it in permanent marker.

She clenched both fists and pounded even harder. "Open the damn door. I'm not going away."

Bang. Bang. Bang.

"Timothy Lucas Silverspoon!"

Bang. Bang. Bang.

"Do you hear me!"

The door swung open and she stumbled inside. She gasped at the sight of the disheveled bed. Had he really been with a pack of women? Spinning around, she eyed Loverboy, half-naked, standing behind the door.

"What are you doing?" she said.

He squinted, cradling his head between his hands. "Trying to get you to shut the hell up."

"Where are they?"

"Who, they?" He ambled toward the bed, his eyes barely open.

She struggled to ignore the ripple of back muscles, the expanse of shoulders that took her breath away. She could see why a woman would want a piece of this man. Or why six women would want . . .

"Did you really bring girls up here?"

He flopped onto the bed and grabbed the pile of sheets. Untangling them, he pulled the linens haphazardly across his stomach.

"Luke!"

"God, woman, keep it down." Rolling onto his side, he covered his head with a pillow.

She marched to the other side of the bed and ripped the pillow off.

"Dammit, Lexy."

"I found this"—she waved the condom in his face—"outside your door."

He squinted, but didn't respond.

"Well?"

"Geez." He clasped his head again, closed his eyes and lay back against the pillow. "Some broad slipped it in my pocket. Nothing happened."

She believed him, dammit. She didn't want to. But he didn't look like a man ready to bed six women. He looked . . . broken.

She stood over him, waiting. For what, she didn't know. The tangled sheets didn't quite cover his broad chest, and his unsnapped jeans slipped low off his hips, revealing burgundy boxers.

"Was there something else?" he said.

"You were supposed to be upstairs an hour ago."

"I can't do this right now." He groaned and rolled onto his stomach.

Silence rang in her ears.

"I was hoping to see you upstairs so I could apologize." There, she'd said it.

He opened one eye. "What?"

She sat on the other bed. "The girl from the other day admitted she never slept with you."

"Oh." He closed his eyes and rubbed his nose against the pillow.

A few seconds passed.

"Luke?"

"Yeah," he rasped.

"I could use an apology."

"For what?" He curled the sheets between his fingers and brought them to his chin.

He looked like a little boy, shielding himself in a cocoon of linens.

"The press party is very important to us right now."

"I know. I'm sorry."

"Do you know how worried I was when you didn't show?"

He opened his bloodshot eyes and her heart skipped. Only then did she realize he could touch that part of her she'd locked up the day she found David drinking apple martinis in their bed with another woman.

Jumping to her feet, she paced to the bureau and back again. *He's a ladies' man. Don't you dare give him the power to hurt you.*

"I thought, maybe you'd been hurt." She picked his shirt up off the floor and put it on the bed. "Then I heard the wrestlers talking about you with a six-pack of girls—"

"And you assumed I'd brought them up here to get laid," he said, his voice flat.

"Yes. No. I don't know," she said.

His blue-green eyes pierced her heart like a needle.

"What do you expect? You strut around flirting with every female you meet. You're accused of getting girls pregnant and Cosmo buys them off. That girl from the other day was a liar, but what about the next one? How many children do you have littered around the country?"

He closed his eyes. "I'm not worried."

"Well, maybe you should be." She seethed, remembering David's excuses via cell phone as Riley sat on the porch swing waiting for his dad. What was it about these men who fathered children but wouldn't take an ounce of responsibility for their emotional well-being?

"Children need their fathers," she said. "How can you turn your back on them?"

"I'm not turning my back on anyone." He rolled over.

"I know what it's like to look a child in the eye and explain that his father isn't coming because his golf game is more important. Do you know how devastating it is to a child to feel like leftovers? Like an unwanted shoe?"

"Yeah, I know."

She stilled. Of course he did. Luke's father had adored his older brother, but had had little time for Luke.

"Do you realize what you've become?" she asked.

"Don't."

"You're just like the Colonel."

He bolted from the bed, backing her against the wall. His lips were so close, his eyes intense. But she wasn't afraid. Anger protected her, anger at Luke for turning out like his father and her heartless ex-husband.

163

"I'm not like him," he said. "I'd never be that kind of father."

"How can you say that? You have no idea how many girls you've gotten pregnant, do you?"

"Dammit, woman, I can't *have* children, okay? I'm sterile." He staggered back. "Hell."

She grabbed for his arm just as he went limp and collapsed on the bed.

"Luke?" She sat next to him and pressed her fingers to his neck. His pulse beat strong and steady, yet he looked so beaten, so vulnerable.

And sterile.

A heaviness settled in her chest. She couldn't imagine life without the special love of a child.

"Luke?" Young, virile men didn't pass out unless something was seriously wrong. Her hands trembling with panic, she reached across him for the phone.

"Don't," he croaked, touching her arm.

"You need a doctor," she said, stroking his hair.

"No doctor. I just need to get rid of this headache." He reached for a bottle of Ibuprofen on the bedside table. "Could you get me some water?"

"Sure." She rushed into the bathroom, catching a glimpse of her worried expression in the mirror. It was just a headache. He'd be fine. Luke would be okay.

Hurrying back into the room, she found him fiddling with the bottle cap, his fingers shaking.

"You ever have a bad headache?" he said, squinting as if looking into a blinding light.

"Yes."

"Times that by twenty. Shit." He dropped the bottle to the nightstand and fell back against the pillow.

She grabbed the bottle, lined up the arrows and popped the top. "Here."

He opened his eyes and extended his hand. She tapped two pills into his palm. He motioned for more, his eyes bloodshot and pleading.

"It says to take two every six hours," she said.

"Please, Lexy. It hurts."

It was the voice of a child who needed his mom.

She dug out a couple more and handed him the glass of water. "You need to see a doctor."

"I'll be fine." He downed the pills and gulped water like a dehydrated man in the desert. "Thanks. I need to sleep. You don't have to hang around. I'll be okay."

Something in his voice said otherwise. She stood and pulled the sheets to cover him, her fingers brushing the warm skin of his shoulders. She fought the awareness, reminding herself this was a Florence Nightingale mission.

"You . . . hate me, don't you?" he said.

She froze, her hands below his chin as she turned down the pristine white sheet. Her gaze drifted to his blue-green eyes, grayed with pain or fatigue, or both.

"Why do you say that?" she said, sitting on the bed and folding her hands in her lap.

"Because of what I am, because I can't have children."

"I don't hate you. I feel bad for you."

"Don't. God knew what he was doing. You said it yourself. I'd be just like the Colonel."

"When I said that I didn't—"

"It's okay, Lexy. I'd be a horrible father." He closed his eyes. "Besides, I've screwed up enough lives."

"I don't believe that."

Silence filled the room.

"Luke, how did you become sterile?"

"Steroids."

"Oh." She didn't know what to say.

"I was young and stupid. I got what I deserved."

More silence. Horrible, deafening silence that made her want to check his pulse again. Instead, she counted his breaths and ached to hold him, to make it all okay. There was more of Timmy Silverspoon in this man than he'd ever admit.

And Timmy would never have children. No wonder he couldn't stand to do charity functions for kids.

He rolled over and dragged a pillow across his face. He must be in incredible pain. She suspected the headache didn't come close to the emotional scars criss-crossing his heart.

She studied her childhood friend as he turned onto his back and groaned. He didn't deserve this pain, re-gardless of what he'd become.

Wanting to help, she went to the bathroom and ran a washcloth under cold water. She couldn't imagine not having a family, her mom, dad, Riley, Aunt Lulu and even her aloof brother, Christian.

Squeezing out the washcloth, she thought about Luke's family, his gentle mother, cute sisters and star brother. Bits and pieces of the accident flooded back, especially the day she found him in the tunnel with the family dog.

She turned off the water and her heart raced with the memory. She'd handed him her bandanna. He'd said he didn't need it. He wasn't crying. It was just his allergies.

But she knew what had happened. Mom and Dad had told her that the neighbor boy had been killed by a drunk driver. At twelve she hadn't known quite how to process the news. To Lexy, Kevin represented the com-munity hero who'd led Sycamore's high school football

NAME: _____

ADDRESS: _____

_____

_____

TELEPHONE: _____

E-MAIL: _____

_____ I want to pay by credit card.

__ Visa   __ MasterCard   __ Discover

Account Number: _____

Expiration date: _____

SIGNATURE: _____

Send this form, along with $2.00 shipping and handling for your FREE books, to:

Love Spell Romance Book Club
20 Academy Street
Norwalk, CT 06850-4032

Or fax (must include credit card information!) to: 610.995.9274.
You can also sign up on the Web at www.dorchesterpub.com.

Offer open to residents of the U.S. and Canada only. Canadian residents, please call 1.800.481.9191 for pricing information.

team to the state championship. He wasn't a real person to her.

Until she found Luke curled up in the tunnel, sniffing into his dog's mass of black fur. When she saw her guardian angel balling his eyes out, the air rushed from her lungs. With red, swollen eyes, he'd looked at her and said he should have died in that accident instead of his brother. Scared, she'd wanted to run away.

Somehow she'd mustered the courage to offer him her bandanna, then touched his hand. She'd never forget the look on his face as his gaze drifted to their hands, then up to her eyes. It was a scene frozen in time, buried in her memory. The look of a wounded, lost boy.

She ambled toward the bed, washcloth in hand. Sitting beside him, she gently removed the pillow from his face.

"Huh?" he breathed, struggling to open his eyes.

"Shhh. This will help."

"Lexy . . ."

"Shhh."

Placing the cloth over his forehead, she realized nothing had changed. A wounded, lost man lay on the bed, only now the wounds were deeper, maybe even irreversible.

Remember why you got involved in this crazy business: to provide for Riley.

She adjusted the washcloth over his eyes and he moaned.

"I'm sorry." She pulled away.

"No, it feels good." He wrapped his fingers around her hand.

The sirens didn't blare this time, nor did her breasts

tingle with wanting. The touch awakened something deeper inside, something sweet and safe.

He peeked out from the beneath the washcloth. "You don't have to stay."

Don't go, she heard.

"It's okay. I want to stay." The least she could do was ease his pain for one night.

"You . . . do?"

She nodded. "Just relax."

He closed his eyes and she adjusted the washcloth. He clasped her hand in a gentle grip and a few minutes later, his fingers relaxed, as if he'd fallen asleep.

She stared at his shoulders, broad and muscular, a long scar running down his chest beneath the covers. She would never understand his life choices.

Suddenly she wanted to. She wanted to know it all: why he left home and why he became a pro wrestler.

It would help her mold him into a better hero, she told herself. It had nothing to do with sympathy or compassion. Those emotions were lost on a man like Loverboy. He'd said so himself, when he'd warned her never to forget who he was.

But, did *he* know who he was?

He stood in the corner of the penthouse and sipped champagne. Loverboy didn't come. Unfortunate. The thought of being close enough to touch him shot adrenaline through his body.

He wasn't the only one who'd been waiting expectantly for Loverboy. The woman hadn't been able to keep her eyes off the door, disappointment creasing her forehead each time someone other than Loverboy stepped into the penthouse.

Could she be falling in love with him? A smile crept

across his lips. This was turning out better than he ever could have imagined.

"Another glass of champagne?" a waitress asked.

"Absolutely." Victory. He could taste it.

Chapter Twelve

Luke opened his eyes and blinked a few times to focus. Where was he again? New Jersey? Detroit? The hotel rooms all looked the same after a while.

Panic squeezed his lungs and he closed his eyes. Nothing to worry about. He'd figure it out in a minute, when his senses cleared.

"You're awake," a woman said.

Not just any woman. Lexy. Hell, he hadn't. Had he? He couldn't remember. His brain was so scrambled, he couldn't even remember a night of making love to Lexy. Why else would she be here?

Taking a deep breath, he braced himself and opened his eyes. She stood over him, wearing a Loverboy Luke T-shirt that hung to her knees. Naked knees. Shit.

"They gave these out at the press party and I didn't have anything to sleep in, so . . ." Her voice trailed off.

Embarrassment reddened her cheeks.

What have you done, Silver?

"How about some coffee?" she said with a bright smile, handing him a mug.

How about a shotgun so I can kill myself?

He sat up and took the mug, careful not to let their fingers touch. With a tentative sip, he wracked his brain for details of last night.

Glancing at the other bed, he nearly choked on the coffee. It was messed up as well, as if one bed hadn't been enough. A condom lay on the floor, still in its foil packet. Hadn't they had the sense to use protection? Lexy was too smart for that. She wouldn't let anyone get her pregnant, something she didn't know he was incapable of doing.

"How's the head?"

She sat beside him on the bed, the shirt riding up her thighs, beautiful, soft thighs.

Could this get any worse?

"Luke?" she said, concern in her voice.

"Listen, about last night . . ."

"It's okay. You had a migraine. Don't feel bad about not coming to the press event."

"I'm not talking about that."

"Oh, you mean that other thing." She studied her fingers interlaced in her lap.

He sensed it was tearing her up inside. Hell.

"I'm sorry," he said.

She cleared her throat and studied the clock radio sitting on the nightstand. "Me too."

"I didn't mean to—"

"Don't worry. I'll keep your secret."

Good God, what had he done to her?

"Lexy, I want to apologize for . . ."

For what? He couldn't remember anything. Had he

forced himself on her? Seduced her like the other women in his early years as a superstar?

"There's nothing to apologize for. I'm glad I was here for you." She reached out to touch his thigh and he jerked back. "What's the matter?" she said.

"You're not . . . mad?"

"Mad? No. Maybe a little disappointed."

This was going from bad to worse. Not only had they had crazed sex, but she'd hated it.

"I guess," she said, touching the feather comforter, "I feel sorry for you."

"It was that bad?" he whispered, struggling to remember something, anything, about last night. On the other hand, maybe it was better that he didn't.

"Was what that bad?" she said.

"Last night, us, in bed."

Her eyes grew round. "You mean you think we . . ." She trailed off.

"Didn't we?" He placed the mug on the nightstand.

"Heavens, no!" She burst out laughing.

If his ego hadn't been mutilated before, it was now.

"I don't see what's so funny," he said.

"You were in no condition to do anything but moan, and I don't mean out of pleasure. I took care of you, remember? Your headache?"

He remembered pain, but not much else.

"How is that head of yours?"

She reached over to touch his forehead and he batted her hand away. "I'm fine."

"I doubt that."

"If we didn't . . . um . . . do it, what did we do?"

She sighed, a strange look in her amber eyes. "We argued, then we talked."

"About what?"

"I'm really worried that you don't remember."

"Not as worried as I am. What did I tell you, Lexy?"

She folded her hands in her lap. "You told me about being sterile."

"Hell." He dragged the pillow over his face.

"Luke?"

"Go away," he said, shame curdling his insides.

"If you're sterile, who was that woman the other day with those kids?"

He whipped the pillow from his face and propped himself on his elbows. "She's off limits, got it? You can bat those innocent eyes of yours all you want, but I'm not going to pour my heart out to you."

"I do not bat my eyes."

"Sweetheart, you do more than just bat them. How else did you get me to spill my guts last night?"

She strode toward the room service tray on the desk. "I came up here to give you a much-deserved lecture and we got in a heated argument. Just before you passed out you told me you're sterile."

Great. Could he be any more vulnerable to this woman?

"How about a muffin?" She analyzed the plate of pastries.

"A muffin? We're talking about my inability to father a child and you want me to eat a muffin?"

"When was the last time you ate something?"

"Dinner last night."

"Liar. You've been asleep since yesterday afternoon."

He crossed his arms over his chest.

"Come on, eat something." She set the plate on the bed next to him.

"You sound like my mother," he said.

"Thanks." She held a blueberry muffin to his lips.

"I don't want it."

"How about some bacon?" She fingered a strip.

"No."

She studied the tray. "Fruit? Toast?"

"I don't want anything."

She sighed. "Okay. I'd better change." She started for the bathroom. "You really should see a doctor."

"Yeah, yeah," he said, watching her hips sway right, then left, then right. Oh, he knew what he wanted all right. He wanted Lexy to care about him and not because Cosmo paid her the big bucks.

If only he did something more respectable, something she could be proud of. He wished . . .

Wishes were for fools. He couldn't change. He'd spent his childhood trying to be someone else, trying to be his older brother.

You are who you are. Hadn't he learned that lesson by now? He was nothing more than a self-centered bastard who'd never let anyone close. Until Lexy. Damn, why had he let the truth slip about his sterility?

She came out of the bathroom, wearing a form-fitting turtleneck and slacks. Round, sleek and utterly touchable.

"Can I use your phone?" she said.

"Help yourself. I'll give you some privacy." He slid out from under the covers and went into the bathroom, hoping a splash of cold water would clear his rattled brain. He stared into the mirror, his eyes puffy and bloodshot, his skin pale. A shower was out of the question, not with Lexy in the next room.

He wanted her gone. She didn't care about him. She was just doing her job, checking on the talent. He opened the bathroom door and froze at the sound of her voice.

"I know, sweetie," she said into the phone. "I'll be home later, promise. Hug Aunt Lulu for me . . . Love you, too." She smacked a kiss into the receiver and hung up.

His heart ached. She missed her kid. Because of him.

"I know what I want," he said, flopping on the bed and analyzing the food.

"What? More eggs? Bacon? A doctor?"

The hope in her voice made it nearly impossible to do this. But it was best.

"I want you to leave." He picked at the food she'd placed at his bedside. He didn't look up. He couldn't.

"What? Why?"

"I know Cosmo promised you a bonus for checking in on me. Fine, you checked. I'm alive and breathing." He bit into a blueberry muffin. It tasted dry and tart.

"Cosmo did not pay me to spend the night," she said.

"No, that was your idea." He grinned. "Sorry I couldn't comply with your secret fantasy."

She snatched her purse from the desk. "What is with you this morning?"

"Give me a few minutes and I'll be back to my old, sexy self."

She stomped her foot. Good, it was working.

"What, I'm not recovering quick enough?" he said.

"You . . . you're such a . . ."

"Go on, say it."

"Ungrateful, self-centered . . . bastard."

The very reaction he wanted. It felt like a knife plunged into his chest.

"Our next event is Monday night in Chicago." She slung her blazer over her crooked arm. "Black tie, if you know what that means."

She stormed toward the door, whirled and stared him

176

down. "For a second there I really thought I had my friend back." She slammed the door and his heart cracked.

Those were words he hadn't expected. He'd never thought anyone could see the goodness of that nerdy kid buried inside Loverboy Luke.

Leaning against the headboard, he realized there was another plate on the desk. She'd ordered breakfast for herself but hadn't had a chance to eat.

Guilt tangled his insides. She took care of him, force-fed him carbs this morning, and tended his physical and emotional needs last night. And what did he do? Chased her away.

Someone pounded on the door. He got up a little quicker than he should have, afraid to admit how much he wanted it to be Lexy. He'd ask her back in for breakfast, maybe even explain why he'd been such a jerk. He whipped open the door and found Oscar grinning back at him.

"Hey." Oscar brushed past him into the room.

"What are you doing here?"

"Orders from the PR lady. I'm supposed to make sure you take a shower without passing out."

"Get out of here. I don't need a baby-sitter."

"That's not what I heard." Oscar settled on the bed and pinched a slice of toast between his thumb and forefinger. "Anyone gonna eat this?"

"No." Luke had lost his appetite.

"She spent the night, eh?" Oscar winked.

"Why is it you think I screw every woman I meet?"

"Isn't that your goal in life? Or has the PR lady changed all that?"

"Knock it off." He took a swig of coffee.

"Oh, man," Oscar laughed. "You've got it bad."

"I don't have anything but a headache."

"Uh-huh." Oscar crunched a piece of bacon.

"Get the hell out."

"No can do. Direct orders from your lady friend."

"She's not my friend. She's a paid employee. Her only interest is in Cosmo's money."

Oscar leaned forward. "Man, you've taken one too many drop kicks to the head."

"Meaning?"

"Al sounded really worried," Oscar said. "She doesn't get paid enough to sound like that."

"I don't want to hear this."

"Why? What are you afraid of?"

Losing his life. Losing his heart.

"I'm taking a shower. Seems that's the only way I'll get you to leave. If only I could get that woman out of my life." He snatched a pair of boxers from his bag.

"I wouldn't count on that happening any time soon."

"Why's that?"

"Cosmo's worried you won't behave at Monday's charity gig. He's sending you home with the PR lady this weekend for some intense one-on-one."

"Like hell he is. Does she know this?"

"Don't think so. She was headed to the airport. She didn't talk to Cosmo yet." Oscar forked a piece of melon.

"I won't do it," Luke said.

"You'll do it."

"I can't do it."

"Why's that?" Oscar grinned.

"I'm taking a shower."

"Yeah, make it cold." Oscar laughed.

If only that would help.

* * *

Luke tried everything short of blackmail to convince Cosmo that sending him to Lexy's was a bad idea. But the old man wasn't buying. He had it in his mind that a weekend with her would round out Luke's rough edges and brighten the shine on BAM's newest hero.

He turned onto Lexy's street, glad that her place was only a couple hours' drive from his Milwaukee condo. The thought of getting on a plane and dealing with another monster migraine gave him the shakes. The flight home from Houston had wiped him out for a full twenty-four hours.

The duplexes and single-family homes lining Newberry Court resembled something out of *Better Homes and Gardens*, with front porches, hanging planters and a few American flags swinging in the afternoon breeze.

Another image came to mind, an image of Luke and his sister, Sheila, cuddling up to Mom on the front porch with their Hi-C orange punch, telling stories. His favorite was about a boy who sprouted wings and flew to the moon. He'd been obsessed with the image, gripping it like a compass to lead him to his final destination: becoming an astronaut.

But he'd lost the compass the day he'd left home. No, he'd lost it the day Kevin died and he'd tried to become his older brother to ease Mom and Dad's pain.

Mom had always said you could be anything you wanted. She'd never told him he couldn't become his older brother.

Parking in front of Lexy's home, he took a deep breath. If Cosmo hadn't threatened to cut his pay, Luke would have ignored the order to spend the weekend with her. But he needed the money for Beth and the kids.

He eyed Lexy's duplex: a white picket fence wrapped around a small garden of yellow flowers, and lace curtains framed the windows from the inside. Then his eyes caught on a baseball bat and glove on the porch. His shoulders kinked with tension.

He hoped the kid was visiting a friend so Luke wouldn't have to look into his eyes and face the fact he never would have a child of his own. That he and Lexy could never share a child.

Where the hell had that come from? The concussion must have him spinning in fantasyland.

Walking to the front door, he glanced at the adjoining unit. Beads dangled from the front window and the flowerbeds were decorated with ceramic gnomes on ice skates. He especially liked the gnome with her skirt flipped up. Talk about wacky neighbors.

He rang the doorbell and noticed the "Welcome" wreath of dried flowers. Lexy had probably made it. He looked away, his gaze drifting down the street. People really lived like this: normal, safe and happy. A little girl pedaled past on her bike, a terrier yapping at her back tire.

The door creaked open. Riley peered at Luke. "Wow!"

He couldn't speak. The kid was cuter than he'd remembered, freckles dotting his nose, cheeks rounding in a heart-warming smile.

"Who's there, Riley?" an older woman called. "Is it that damn vacuum-cleaner salesman again? I'm getting the rolling pin! Hear me?"

The kid smiled at Luke and he couldn't help smiling back, even as his heart splintered into a million pieces.

"My Hoover will beat your contraption any day," she

said, her voice growing louder. "You'd better stop coming 'round or I'm going to whack you till you're purple."

The door swung wide and Aunt Lulu stared at him. "Sorry, I thought it was Roy. He's been trying to sell us a vacuum cleaner, but I suspect he's hot for my body."

"Aunt Lulu!" Riley scolded her, then glanced at Luke. "Did you come to show me some moves?"

"Actually, I'm here to see your mom."

"Oh." Riley glanced at his shoes.

Luke wished he'd lied.

"Come on in." Aunt Lulu whipped open the door. With a firm grip on his arm, she led him into the living room and pushed him into a thick-cushioned easy chair.

"My niece will be back soon. In the meantime, you can tell us some war stories." Sitting on the sofa, she sat Riley beside her. "That move you put on Killer Kanon at the Figure Four was as illegal as hooch in the Twenties. Ref Hooper is always looking the wrong way."

"Actually, the abdominal stretch is—"

"I saw the way you pulled on the ropes for leverage. I thought he had you after the Airplane Spin Toss over the top rope. I didn't think anyone could get up after that, except The Crawler. That guy gets up after everything. Even saw him get up after he'd been clocked with a fire hydrant. Where's he at now?"

"He retired last year."

"No kidding? Well, he was getting up there."

"He's thirty-six."

"Yes, sir, there comes a time when you have to know

181

the show's over. The show!" She jumped to her feet. "I've got rehearsal." She raced out the door.

Great. It was Luke and the kid. Alone. And the kid wasn't talking.

The ticking of a clock echoed off the walls. What should he say? He'd played with Beth's kids. It wasn't like he didn't know how to talk to a kid. But this was different. It was Lexy's son.

"Did you have a good summer?" he asked.

"Uh-huh." The kid chewed his lower lip.

Damn, he wished that crazy aunt would get back here and take the kid away.

"I beat Cal Spits in the fifty-yard dash," Riley said.

"That's great."

"He's a fourth-grader. I'm going into third."

"Awesome."

A few minutes passed. He noticed a cluster of pictures on the far wall, mostly of Riley, some with his mom.

"I play third base in Little League. Mom says if I do good in reading I can try soccer, but not football. She doesn't want me playing football." He paused and cocked his head to one side. "I wonder if she'd let me become a pro wrestler?"

"Soccer's good," he said, not wanting the kid to get any ideas.

"Does your mom come watch you wrestle?" Riley asked.

Luke cracked his knuckles. "Yeah, sometimes."

"My mom comes to all my baseball games."

"Of course she does. You're her Number-One star." He had the urge to ruffle the kid's hair.

The door burst open and Aunt Looney Tunes raced across the living room. She'd transformed herself from a mildly eccentric woman into Annie Oakley. She wore a cowboy hat, bandanna around her neck, jeans and studded denim shirt.

"We've gotta go, kiddo. Rehearsal's at five." Aunt Lulu scribbled a note on the kitchen chalkboard.

"Not another practice," Riley complained.

"Practice makes perfect. Ask Mr. Loverboy."

"But I'm not practicing, you are. And it's boring." Riley crossed his arms over his chest.

She knelt next to him. "Come on, kid. Give an old lady a break."

"This is the fourth one this week."

Luke felt bad for the kid.

"How about a ride on the Zamboni?" she bribed.

"That guy smells."

"Rotten cigars," Lulu muttered. "I'll bring quarters for the vending machine."

"All's they got is black licorice and stale pretzels."

"I think Lynea Martin will be at the rink today."

"Yuck! She tried to kiss me last week."

"I'll watch him." The words slipped from Luke's mouth. Damn concussion.

"You will?" Riley said, his eyes bright.

Aunt Lulu stood. "The kid can be a handful."

"I wrestle three-hundred-pound men. I can handle an eight-year-old boy."

"Good point. I owe you one," she said.

"I'll collect, count on it," he shot back.

"Ally-oops was supposed to be home by 4:30. Must be running late." She hesitated at the door. "You're not such a bad guy, no matter what my niece says."

"Gee, thanks," he said to the slammed door.

"Come on, I'll show you my room." Riley grabbed his hand and pulled him down the hall.

They passed what he guessed was Lexy's bedroom, decorated in pale pink and purple wallpaper. White lace pillowcases graced the canopy bed. It seemed to speak of Lexy's gentleness. He wanted to linger.

Instead Riley pulled him into his bedroom. Warmth from the kid's hand shot up his arm and wrapped around his heart. He'd always maintained a certain detachment when interacting with Beth's kids. But this guy . . . he could melt your heart with his smile.

Riley pointed toward his bookcase. "This my trophy for winning the safety poster contest in first grade . . . this is my autographed Chris Singleton baseball . . . this is a toy my dad brought back from Bermuda. It's broken . . . this is my stuffed dog, Duncan." He shoved the golden retriever at Luke, giving him no choice but to grab it. "He sleeps with me because he's afraid of thunder."

"He looks pretty tough to me," Luke said.

"Here's my Steve McNair Beanie Baby . . . here's my 'most improved' certificate from basketball camp . . . here's a jumping elephant I won at the carnival last year . . ."

As Riley handed him each item, Luke sensed the kid's need for male companionship. He needed someone to celebrate his accomplishments, someone other than his mom. Moms were expected to be there for every baseball game, skinned knee and first-time milestone. Obviously, a man's attention was special for Riley.

Arms filled with toys, trophies and other treasures, Luke glanced outside into the neatly trimmed backyard. The neighbor kids shrieked and ran inside to get out of a sudden shower.

". . . Mr. Deptula said if I practiced maybe I could sing a solo next year in the variety show." He gripped a piece of sheet music in his hand.

"You sing, too? You are one talented guy."

"Dad thinks I should stick to baseball. Dads know best." He shrugged, put the music back on his desk and continued, not missing a beat.

Luke knew better. He read the pain in the kid's eyes at the thought of not measuring up to his dad's expectations if he sang instead of swung.

"These are rocks from Lake Michigan . . . this is a picture of me and my friend Jimmy . . ." He glanced out the window. "Uh-oh." Riley snatched the stuffed dog from Luke's arms and sank to the floor. "I hate this."

Luke unloaded the treasures to the bed and sat beside him. "Hey, buddy, what's going on?"

"It's raining. That means it's gonna thunder."

"Not necessarily."

"And there might be a tornado, and the lights will go out, and I won't be able to see, and the roof will blow off, and the basement will flood and—"

Luke pulled him into his arms. "It's just one of those quick rain storms. Nothing's going to happen to you, kid. I won't let it."

Riley whimpered into Luke's shoulder. Luke remembered what it was like to be scared, to need someone to make it all better. What he wouldn't give to have someone help him get through the day, tell him he'd heal and live to see forty.

Maybe Luke didn't have someone like that in his life, but he knew how to comfort Lexy's son.

"It's okay," Luke said. "I'm here."

Riley leaned back, the stuffed dog clutched in his hand. "But you can't stop lightning."

"Hey, I'm a superstar, remember? A real, live hero. I can do anything."

Riley blinked his blue eyes and for a split second he thought the kid believed him. He laid his head against Luke's shoulder and didn't whimper this time.

The storm grew stronger and more angry, raindrops pelting the window. The boy's grip tightened around Luke's neck. A wicked crack of thunder made him jerk.

They must have sat there for fifteen minutes, Riley gripping his stuffed dog with one hand and holding onto Luke's ponytail with the other. Luke felt a slight tug with each clap of thunder. He didn't mind. He was touched that the kid found comfort in holding onto him.

Leaning against the bed, he squeezed the boy in his arms. How could this feel so right?

Patting Riley's back, he thought about the times he'd ached for his father to hold him like this. Luke closed his eyes and wondered who was more comforted by the embrace, Riley or himself.

"Riley!" Lexy called from the living room.

"Hey, buddy, it's your mom," he whispered.

"Riley!" The bedroom door swung open and she froze in the doorway. "What are you doing here?"

Her tone stung. "Waiting for you to get home."

"Where's Lulu?"

"Aunt Lulu," Riley whispered against Luke's shoulder.

"Riley, honey, come here." Her face drained of color and she extended her arms.

Did she think Luke would ruin her son in the short time they'd spent together?

Riley nuzzled Luke's neck. "It's thundering."

"I know, honey. I got caught in the storm."

"Lulu had rehearsal. She said you'd be home."

"I'm sorry, sweetheart."

"It's a good thing Loverboy Luke was here."

Lexy nodded. "A very good thing."

He studied her eyes. Did she mean it?

"Riley, are you okay?" she asked.

Well, that blew that theory.

"I'm fine." Riley squeezed Luke's neck.

Luke's chest ached at the look of shame in her eyes. She had nothing to be ashamed of. She was doing a fine job raising her little boy, mostly by herself.

"Hey, buddy?" Luke whispered. "Your mom looks like she could use a hug."

The boy looked up at Lexy. "You okay, Mom?"

She sighed. "I've had better days."

"Me too." He flew off Luke's lap into her arms.

Emptiness filled Luke's chest.

"You're okay, Mom." Riley patted her back.

"Oh, you think so?" Her voice hitched.

Riley leaned back and looked at her. "Sure, Loverboy Luke's here."

Chapter Thirteen

Lexy closed her eyes and swallowed back the shame burning her throat. Riley had needed her and she wasn't there. But Luke was.

With her son wrapped snugly in her arms, she admitted for the first time in years just how much Riley needed a man in his life, someone to offer security and protection.

It could be anyone, she consoled herself. There wasn't anything special about Luke.

Opening her eyes, she studied the man sitting on the floor, cradling a stuffed dog in his hand. Then her gaze drifted to his aquamarine eyes and compassion filled her heart. What emptiness must he feel at this very moment, knowing he'd never have a child of his own.

"Listen." He stood and tossed the dog onto Riley's comforter. "I'll come back later."

"No!" Riley cried, snapping his head around. "The streets are wet from the rain. Your tires could slip and you could crash. You have to stay. Please?"

189

"Kid, I'd like to but—"

"Pretty please?" Riley cut him off. "With sugar on top? Whipped cream? M & M's? Reeses Pieces? Hot Fudge? Mini marshmallows?"

Luke squinted. "Mini marshmallows?"

Riley nodded. "A hundred and ten."

"Okay, I guess. If it's okay with your mom."

"It's okay," Riley said, before she could answer.

"I'd like to hear it from your mom."

Luke's expression, so humble and lost, touched her heart. She wanted him to stay, for Riley's sake.

How selfish of her. It had to tear Luke up inside to be around a child, to hold a child close and feel the magic when he knew it would never be his. She couldn't imagine living with that kind of emptiness.

"Sweetie, Mr. Silver and I work together. He's not here to play with you."

Something dimmed in Luke's eyes. To think the mention of playing with a little boy caused that kind of sadness. She ached for him.

"I'll come back tomorrow morning." Luke started for the door.

Riley squirmed out of her arms and jumped in front of him. "No, wait! You have to stay for dinner, right, Mom? Remember when Lulu's cousin Squirt came from Atlanta and stayed for dinner because he came from so far away? Loverboy Luke came far, too, didn't you?"

He smiled and touched Riley's hair. Air rushed from her lungs. Such a gentle, fatherly touch.

"You've gotta stay and try my chicken," Riley said. "I make great cheesy chicken, don't I, Mom?"

"Yes, honey, but—"

"I'll go start dinner." He raced out of the room.

"Riley," she called. It was no use. He'd decided Luke was staying for dinner and conversation, and who knows what.

"Don't worry, I'll go." He shoved his hands into his jeans pockets, but didn't move.

She glanced into his eyes and read the pain there. "I'm sorry."

"You're a good mom. You're trying to protect him."

"Protect him?"

"I wouldn't want him around someone like me either."

Her heart pounded in her chest. "That's not what I meant."

"I saw the look in your eye when you caught me holding him." He moved toward the door.

"I was—"

"Horrified, I know."

"No." She touched the bare skin of his forearm, welcoming the heat burning her fingertips. "I don't know what you think you saw in my eyes but—"

"Lexy, stop. I know you're getting paid to make nice, but don't lie to me."

She squeezed his arm, leaning closer. "I've never lied to you."

"Let me go," he rasped.

"Not until I properly thank you for taking care of my son."

"I'm not a complete bastard."

"I don't think you're a bastard at all." She stood on tip-toe and kissed his cheek, leaning into him. It was all she could do not to stay there, absorbing his scent, for a very long time. A minute would do. She'd never felt this way before, as if she belonged right here, against his rock-solid chest.

"You've got a short memory," he said, a bare whisper against her skin.

"I know I called you a bastard yesterday. I've been doing a lot of thinking since then. I understand now."

With hands to her shoulders, he broke the connection. A flash of something dark filled his eyes. "You don't understand a thing."

He rushed into the hall as if he couldn't get away quick enough.

She followed. "Then explain it to me."

"Forget it. Cosmo wants you to give me a crash course in gentlemanly behavior this weekend. I'll call tomorrow morning and we'll make an appointment. That should give you time to make arrangements for your son."

They passed the kitchen, where Riley was mixing something in a metal bowl. He froze when he saw them. "Where are you going?"

"We'll be right back," she said as Luke stormed to the front door and out onto the porch.

He turned and stared her down. "See what I've done? Now you're lying to your kid because of me."

"I'm not lying."

"I'm leaving."

"No, you're not."

"Car keys, see?" He dangled them in the air and she snatched them from his hand.

"Lexy," he warned.

"He really is a good little cook," she said, backing away. He took a step toward her. She grinned and sprinted down the steps. It was like they were kids again, like neither of them had been touched by personal tragedy.

He lunged and she stumbled, falling to the damp grass. She gasped as the wind was knocked from her lungs.

"Lexy?" He gently rolled her onto her back. "Are you all right?"

Catching her breath, she thanked God for the genuine concern she heard in his voice. "Yeah . . . all right."

"You sure?"

She nodded and sat up, brushing off her clothes. "I'm all soggy. The least you can do is stay for dinner."

"I'm not hungry." He lay on the grass beside her.

She wondered what to say next. A few minutes passed.

"Please have dinner with us." She didn't know why, but she felt desperate for him to stay.

"Why are you doing this?" he asked. "I know you don't want me here."

"That's not true. I'm just worried about you. It must hurt terribly to be around children, to comfort a child like you did Riley."

"It's fine." He covered his face with his arm.

"Now who's lying?" she said. "I'm sorry you're in pain."

"I'm not in pain."

"Good. Then you won't mind staying for dinner."

He pulled his arm from his face and looked at her. "I can't."

She placed her hand on his chest. His heart beat steadily beneath her palm. "Riley has had so much disappointment and he's only eight."

"I'm a bad influence." He looked away.

With her forefinger on his jaw, she turned his face to look into his eyes. "I disagree."

"Lexy, I'm—"

"A broken soul who used to be my protector."

"Don't romanticize this."

"I owe you. You took care of my son and he's really taken to you, Luke. I haven't seen him bond with a man since his Uncle Chris stopped by last year."

"Where's his dad?"

"Long story. I'll tell you all about it after dinner." She stood and extended her hand to help him up. The gesture was a joke: There was no way she could pull this incredible creature to his feet.

"Will you stay?" she said.

I want to get to know you again, share memories and mend past hurts.

She voiced none of these reasons. She just stood there, letting her thoughts linger between them.

"Cosmo said you were determined as hell," he said.

"This isn't about work." She yanked his hand and he stood to his full six-foot-plus height.

"What is it about, Lexy? Because I'm tired of games. So damned tired."

"It's not a game. I guess I've just missed you." She wrapped her arms around his waist and squeezed.

She hoped this was the right thing to do, that her instincts about him were on target. She'd spent a sleepless night going over the past week, finally realizing he clutched this silly Loverboy image like a shield. He didn't want anyone to know the real Timothy Lucas Silverspoon.

Interlacing her fingers behind his waist, she leaned back and looked into his eyes. Only then did she realize he wasn't returning the embrace.

"What's wrong?" she said.

"I . . . I can't—"

"Oh." She snapped her arms to her sides and forced a smile. "We should go in and help Riley. We don't want him to burn the house down." A nervous giggle escaped her lips. She wanted to crawl into a hole.

It was David all over again. Not wanting to touch her or hold her. Luke must have sensed her "problem" as David had coined it, and found it repulsive. It didn't matter. She was hugging Luke as a friend.

If that were the case, why did her chest hurt?

"You *will* stay for dinner, right?" she asked.

"Yeah, I'll stay."

"Thank you." She reached out, then drew her hand back. No more touching. She didn't want to scare him off.

"I'm going to change into something more comfortable—jeans, I mean jeans." Now she sounded like an idiot. She took a step back, then another.

"Lexy—"

She did a quick turn to escape into the house but stumbled over Riley's Squeeze 2000 Double Impact squirt gun. Luke's firm grip around her waist prevented her from falling again. How embarrassing.

"I'm just falling all over myself." She started to pull away, but he held firm.

"You sure you're okay?"

"Why wouldn't I be?" She blinked a tear from her eye. Must be a high pollen count today. "You can let go now."

God, how he wanted to. But Luke needed to hold her for a few seconds more. He'd barely maintained control when she held onto him before. It would be dangerous to return the affectionate gesture, one he knew she meant only in friendship.

As he grasped her waist and inhaled her sweet scent, he knew the time for friendship was long gone. He wanted so much more from this woman. So much he could never have.

He wanted it because she *did* understand him. More than he understood himself. She cared about his feelings and his pain. When was the last time anyone truly cared about Timothy Lucas Silverspoon?

"Excuse me," a man said.

Luke jerked his hands away as if he'd been caught doing something criminal.

"David." She squared her shoulders and crossed her arms over her chest.

Overprotectiveness shot through Luke's blood. She didn't like this man. Or was she afraid of him?

"Public displays of affection? How out of character," David said.

He wore a dark suit; his muddy brown hair was slicked back off his forehead. Glasses framed the guy's square face. He probably wore them to look intelligent.

"What are you doing here?" She took a step toward him, but only one step.

"I'm dropping off Riley's basketball jersey, remember? You'd called in a frenzy saying he *had* to have it for Scoops and Hoops on Monday?"

"Oh, right." She reached for it, but David tucked it under his arm.

Control freak. Great.

"And this is?" He eyed Luke.

He felt like he should puff out his chest. He didn't move.

"David, this is Luke Silver, an old friend."

Luke wondered why she didn't tell the truth and admit she'd been hired to reform him.

He extended his hand and David clasped it, putting extra force into the shake. Dweeb. The guy probably couldn't bench press fifteen pounds.

"Nice to meet you," Luke said.

"Old friends? I don't remember you mentioning him."

"From way back," she said.

"Dad!" Riley came running from the house.

A slow ache curled through Luke's chest at the sound of the kid's voice, filled with admiration and love.

"Hello, Riley," David said.

The kid was about to launch himself into his father's arms when David held out the jersey to stop him. "Just came by to give you this."

Riley's smile faded. Couldn't the guy see what he was doing to his son? Breaking his heart. He acted like the only reason he'd come by was to drop off the jersey, not because he wanted to see Riley.

With a crestfallen expression, the boy took the jersey.

"I drove all the way from downtown to bring you this," David said in a shaming tone.

"Thanks." The boy threw his arms around his father's waist and squeezed, as if the man had just said *I love you*.

"Okay, okay. You'll be ready for Scoops and Hoops." David patted his son's shoulder in a dismissive manner and stepped back.

Clueless. The man didn't have a sensitive bone in his entire body. How could he not see that the boy needed some good, old-fashioned love from his dad?

"I'm making dinner for Loverboy and Mom. Can you stay?"

"Loverboy?" David said, quirking a brow.

"My stage name. I'm a pro wrestler."

"Really?" The ex eyed him over the rim of his glasses.

"Loverboy protected me from the storm," Riley said. "Stay for dinner, Dad, puh-leese?"

"Riley, don't whine. I'd love to, but I can't. I've got a seven o'clock meeting up in Libertyville."

"Oh." Riley pursed his lips.

"None of that attitude." He tipped his son's face up with a forefinger beneath his chin. "We're set for next Saturday, shopping with Darcy, remember?"

"Oh, okay."

Riley didn't sound thrilled.

"Go wash up for dinner. I need to talk to your mother."

"Okay."

David gave him a swat on the behind, sending him on his way without a hug or kiss. Luke bit back his temper. He'd been there, felt exactly what Riley was feeling. He'd forgotten how much it hurt.

The boy glanced over his shoulder at Luke. "You're staying, right?"

"Absolutely."

He smiled and raced into the house. Luke was a sorry replacement for the kid's father, but he'd do his best.

"We need to talk," David said to Lexy, then eyed Luke. "Alone."

Luke hesitated, waiting for Lexy's cue. He wouldn't leave her side, not unless she wanted him to.

"Could you go help Riley?" she asked. "He's got the mixing part down, but I don't let him turn on the oven."

He read defeat in her eyes and wanted to stay put.

"I'll be right in," she said, her eyes pleading for him to do as she asked.

"Nice meeting you." Luke put an extra squeeze into this handshake, taking great satisfaction in the ex's subtle wince.

He shot Lexy a supportive smile, wishing she'd let him

fight the battle he sensed was coming. Instead, he went into the house, all too aware of the silence behind him.

Once inside, he headed toward the kitchen. Riley was nowhere in sight. The bowl filled with a pale orange sauce sat on the counter.

"Hey, kid? Where are you?"

"In here."

He followed the sound of Riley's voice to the bedroom.

"Your mom thought you might need help with dinner." He paused in the doorway, watching Riley carefully hang up the jersey.

"Dad brought this all the way from the city," he said.

"Yep." Luke could barely utter the word.

"I hope he comes to see me play," he said, staring at the jersey.

"I'm sure he will," Luke said, placing his hand on the boy's shoulder. "How about dinner?"

"I'm not hungry."

"Tough. I am. If superstars don't get fed, they get downright mean." He growled, grabbed Riley by the waist and hoisted him into the air.

"Okay, okay. I give up! I'll make dinner."

"Good." He placed him on the floor. "I'd hate to have to challenge you to a hard-core match."

"I'd beat you!" Riley cried and raced down the hall.

Whew, that was intense. Luke glanced at the jersey, hanging in the corner of the closet. It was as if touching another piece of clothing would taint it. It scared him that he could relate to Riley so easily. How many times had Luke tried to gain his father's approval? His father's love?

Lexy's son deserved better.

"Loverboy Luke! Can you turn on the oven?" Riley called from the kitchen.

"Sure, kid." He ambled down the hall. "Just call me Luke, okay? No Loverboy stuff."

"Right, Mom's changing all that. What are they going to call you now?"

"Not sure." He twisted the oven knob to three hundred and fifty. "Is this right?"

"Yeah, how did you know?"

"I've been cooking for myself for over fifteen years."

"You don't have a wife?" Riley asked, pulling a package of chicken breasts from the refrigerator.

"Nope."

"Why not? You divorced like Mom?"

"Nope. Never married."

"You're smart. I'm never getting married. It's more fun that way."

Luke swallowed hard. "Why do you say that?"

Riley sliced open a plastic bag and slid a chicken breast into a shallow pan. "If you're not married you can do whatever you want: go to the movies, eat McDonalds every day, fart in public." He grinned, a twinkle in his eye.

Ah, to be a kid again.

"I'm really, really good. Wanna see?" Riley slapped his arm to his mouth, puffed his cheeks and blew. "Not bad, huh? You try."

"Uh . . . that was never one of my better skills."

"You just need to practice, come on." He grabbed Luke's arm. "You put your arm up to your mouth. It's better if you blow into the corner, right there," he urged.

With that grin the kid could talk a salesman out of his smile. Luke pursed his lips and blew. It sounded like a meow from a week-old kitten.

Riley laughed hysterically, slapping his hands together.

"What?" Luke said.

"You are really bad."

Determined, Luke sucked in a deep breath, closed his eyes and let one fly. A little better. He looked at Riley, whose eyes rounded to the size of quarters.

"What? It wasn't that bad."

A man cleared his throat behind Luke. Great. The jerk ex-husband was standing behind him. Crossing his arms over his chest, Luke leaned against the counter, but didn't offer an apology for his juvenile behavior.

"Riley, I came in to say good-bye," David said in a flat tone, brushing past Luke.

With an awkward arm around Riley's shoulder, David gave the child a less-than-enthusiastic hug.

Like Luke knew the difference? He hadn't been nurtured in years.

The ex patted his son's back to signal the end of the embrace. Riley held on. Luke glanced away.

"Be a good boy," David said, then stepped around Luke as if he were contagious. He paused beside Lexy. "This is the kind of man you're letting influence our son?"

Luke pushed himself away from the counter but Lexy stopped him with an outstretched palm. "Luke is my friend and Riley enjoys his company."

David led her into the living room with a firm hand beneath her elbow. Luke wanted to put the jerk in a submission hold that would pop the blood vessels in his eyes.

Riley curled his fingers into Luke's hand and the kitchen walls closed in. Luke struggled to breathe.

"Sorry for getting you in trouble." Riley strained to look around the corner. "I hope she's okay."

Luke knelt in front of the boy. "She's tough. I could tell you stories that would make your hair stand on end."

"Really?"

"Yeah, but let's finish dinner and surprise her."

"Well—" He peered into the living room, where angry whispers cut through the air.

"It'll make her day not to have to cook," Luke said.

"Okay." Riley went back to the counter and grabbed the scissors to cut open another package of chicken.

"Bet you didn't know about the time your mom tried to get a picture of the town spook."

"What happened?" Riley placed the last chicken breast in the pan and reached for the mixing bowl of cheesy milk.

"Here, I'll get that. Just pour it on top?"

"Yeah. What happened? Did she get the picture?"

He poured the liquid over the chicken, trying to ignore the echo of raised voices coming from the living room. "She sneaked into the garage and waited for him to pull in his black hearse. They said he kept dead bodies in the car."

"Wow. How many?"

"A dozen at least." He put the chicken in the oven. "How long?"

"Forty-five minutes. Come on, tell me what happened! Did she get a picture of the dead bodies?"

"Nah. He pulled in and she got so excited, she snapped the picture. She got a good shot of the car's grill just before the cops came."

A door slammed, but Riley didn't take his attention away from Luke. Good, he'd distracted the kid from his fighting parents.

"The cops? Really? I thought Mom was a goody-goody."

"Your mom? Are you kidding?"

"Hey!" Lexy said, standing in the doorway. "It's bad enough I have to defend you to my ex, now you're maligning me to my own son?"

The phone rang and Riley raced past him into the living room. "I'll get it!"

She leaned against the doorjamb.

"You okay?" he asked, taking a step toward her. He wanted to brush his thumb against her cheek and brighten her golden eyes.

"I'm fine." She wrapped her arms around her ribcage. "It's just hard sometimes."

"Mom! Mom!" Riley cried, racing to her with the cordless phone buried in his stomach. "It's Ian. He got a new Slim Line fold-up scooter with midnight-blue wheels. He wants to bring it over to show me, okay?"

"We have company—"

"But dinner won't be ready for forty-five minutes. Please, Mom? I've never seen a Slim Line, come on, please?"

"Well—" She glanced at Luke and he nodded his approval.

What the hell? Like she should consult him on parenting decisions?

"Okay, but—"

"Cool! Come over, come over!" Riley yelled into the phone. "I'll wait out front."

The kid took off for the door.

"I don't want any trouble when it's time to come in, mister!" she called after him.

Riley slammed the door and the house grew quiet.

"To think twenty minutes ago he was freaking out about thunder," Luke said.

"His mood swings are anything but predictable."

"You didn't answer my question before."

"Which one?"

She started toward the living room just as he reached out to touch her arm, her shoulder, something. She looked like she needed to be held.

"I asked if you were okay," he said.

"Sure, fine." She collapsed in an overstuffed rocker in the corner. Isolated and alone.

He pulled the ottoman close, sat in front of her and held her hands. "Lexy, don't lie to me."

"You were good to me when we were kids, but you don't want to hear about my problems with David."

"Sure I do."

"It doesn't matter. He's a part of my life I have to learn to deal with. I just wish . . ."

He squeezed her hands and she looked into his eyes. "What, Lexy? What do you wish?"

"That he would show more love to his son. I can't imagine what kind of damage it's doing to Riley."

"I can," he let slip.

Reaching out she traced her fingers across his cheek. "Oh, honey, I am so sorry."

Before he knew what was happening, she'd pulled him against her, and he went willingly. He dropped to his knees and pressed his cheek against her soft blouse, sliding his arms around her waist.

He closed his eyes, wishing this hadn't happened.

Another part of him thanked God that it had.

Finally, after all these years, he'd said it. He'd admitted his emptiness and wasn't greeted with shame or condemnation. Instead, Lexy offered understanding and compassion. Something that for years he didn't even dare want.

"We're quite a pair, aren't we?" she whispered, stroking his hair.

"Ye-ah," he said, the word catching on twenty years of emotional baggage.

"I'm glad we met again," she said.

"Me too."

"You think we'll stay friends?"

He wanted more than friendship. He knew he'd have nothing if she found out what he really was.

"I don't know," he said.

"What do you mean you don't know?" She pushed against his shoulders and looked into his eyes.

"I never know what's going to happen next. My life has always been like that."

"You can maintain friendships if you work hard enough."

The image of Bubba's infectious smile flashed across his thoughts. "No, you can't."

"What do you mean?" She traced her thumb across his cheek and he automatically closed his eyes.

"I mean—"

The ringing phone cut him off.

"Darned kids," she muttered.

Luke stood and pulled her to her feet. She hesitated, her breasts pressing against his chest, her eyes wide and expectant. The phone rang again.

"Probably another kid wanting to see Ian's scooter," she whispered.

"Probably," he said, unable to let go of her hand, so soft, smooth and perfect. His gaze drifted to her lips, which he guessed were also soft, smooth and perfect.

"You'd better answer the phone," he said.

She blinked, then ambled to the end table and picked up the cordless. "Hello? . . . Who? . . . You're kidding. . . . At least fifteen years." She glanced at him.

The skin pricked on the back of his neck.

"Okay, thanks. Sure, hang on."

She muffled the receiver with her palm and handed him the phone. "It's your sister."

Chapter Fourteen

"My little sister, Sheila? What's wrong? Is Katie alright?" He reached for the phone.

"No, it's Leslie."

He froze. He'd spoken to his older sister only a handful of times in the last fifteen years thanks to his father. If she was defying the old man that meant—

He snatched the phone. "Is Mom okay?"

"Well, hello to you, too."

He ground his teeth. It was just like his older sister to bust his chops.

"What's wrong?" he demanded.

"Nothing. Everything's fine. Actually," she chuckled, "you're not going to believe this, but we're having a family barbecue and Dad wants you to come."

His fingers gripped the plastic until he thought it would crack.

"I know it's wild, but I think Sheila had something to do with it. Or Mom. Hey, it's great you've reconnected with Lexy. Bring her, too."

His head spun. "I don't understand."

"It's a barbecue, burgers and hot dogs, cole slaw and watermelon."

"I know what a barbecue is."

"Good, then say you'll come."

What could he say? There was no reason to refuse other than his totally mangled pride. More than fifteen years ago he'd been disowned. And suddenly the old man wanted him back.

"I . . ." He searched for a good excuse.

"It's pot luck, so bring a dessert."

"I can't."

"Sure you can. Just pick something up at the market."

"I'm busy."

"You don't even know when it is."

"When is it?"

"Two weeks from Sunday, four o'clock. Mom and Dad's."

The house they'd moved to after the accident. The home he ran from at eighteen.

"Leslie, I—"

"I'm watching Katie. She wants to talk to you."

Hell, he'd lost touch with Sheila and his niece when the old man offered her a spot back in the family two years ago. He'd told Sheila to mend fences and not worry about him. She'd argued, but he'd managed to stay away, for her own good.

"Hello?" a soft voice said.

He gripped the phone. Katie might be nine, but she already sounded like a young lady.

"Hi, Katie."

"Uncle Tim?"

"Hey, kiddo. How are you?"

"Okay. Where have you been?"

"All over. Right now I'm near Chicago." Sitting in Lexy's overstuffed chair, he leaned forward, burying his face in his left hand.

"That's not far from here," she said.

"I know."

"I haven't seen you in a long time."

"I know, kiddo. I'm sorry about that."

"Do you still have long hair?"

"Y—Yeah." His voice caught.

"Me too. It's in a braid now."

God how he wanted to see her braid and her sparkling green eyes. "I'll bet it looks great."

"Are you coming to Aunt Leslie's party?"

"I don't know, honey."

"I'm making taffy apple salad," she said, as if trying to entice him.

"Sounds delicious."

"Grandpa says it's better than bread pudding."

Luke cleared his throat. "Then it must be great because bread pudding is Grandpa's favorite."

"I miss you," she whispered.

Tension gripped his chest like steel fingers crunching a pop can. "Me too."

"Love you, Uncle Tim."

He closed his eyes. "Love you, too."

"Here's Aunt Leslie."

He pressed the receiver to his forehead wanting to burn the sweet sound of her voice into his brain. There was no way he could bring himself to attend the barbecue.

"So?" Leslie said. "You coming?"

"Les, I—"

"You know how the Colonel is. He doesn't take 'no' for an answer. See you then, brother." The line went dead.

He tapped the receiver to his forehead. Why now?

"You okay?" Lexy said.

He glanced up. "Sure, fine, why?"

"You look pale," she said, reaching for the receiver.

He wasn't ready to let go.

She narrowed her eyes and sat on the sofa. "What's going on with your family?"

"Would love to know that myself."

"Tell me about you and your dad."

"I can't get into it." He paced to the window, his fingers still clamped around the cordless phone.

"I'm a good listener."

"Yeah, well, I'm not a good talker."

"That's not how I remember it."

Staring out the front window, he watched her son take a spin on his friend's scooter. "I don't remember much," he said. "I guess that's a good thing."

Riley gripped the handles and pumped with his right foot, speeding toward the corner.

"Luke?"

She'd crossed the room and touched his arm. It calmed him somehow. And that scared the life out of him.

"Whatever happened, it seems like your family is extending an olive branch," she said.

"Too late."

"Don't say that. Family is so important."

"I haven't seen Leslie in over fifteen years and my dad . . . I wouldn't know how to act or what to say."

"Just be yourself."

And who was that, exactly? The kid who was ostracized for not measuring up, or the playboy who abused his body for fame?

"Being myself is what got me kicked out of the family in the first place," he said.

"Tell me what happened." She ran an open palm across his shoulders. "Please?"

His muscles relaxed. He couldn't stop now even if he'd wanted to.

"High school. Senior year," he started. "I didn't know my friends had been drinking when they picked me up. A drunk driver killed Kevin. Did you know that?"

Out of the corner of his eye, he saw her nod. "Anyway, we got in an accident, hit another car. A woman and two kids were inside. They were okay, but when I got home, the Colonel went ballistic. I told him I wasn't drinking. He didn't believe me. He said he couldn't stand to look at me, that I had no right to be a part of the family. Mom tried to step in but . . ." He blinked against the burn of his dry eyes.

"What?" Lexy said.

"He said he only had one son, and he was dead."

"Tim, I'm so sorry."

"Please don't call me that."

A few seconds passed.

"Try to understand, your dad was hurting and probably scared," she said. "You could have been killed. He probably couldn't bear the thought of losing another son."

"I left that night," he said, ignoring her explanation. "Stuffed my backpack and took off." He turned and found her standing way too close. Her hand pressed against his chest where she'd been stroking his back.

211

"And here I am, a mega superstar standing in Lexy Whitford's living room."

"It's a small world."

Getting smaller by the minute. He could feel her breath tickle his lips.

"You've changed so much," she said, her gaze drifting to his mouth.

Damn, he was getting hard. Did she know she affected him like that? Nah, she still thought of him as the geek next door. Or did she?

She licked her lower lip, slowly, as if wanting to taste him there.

The front door burst open with a crash.

"Mrs. Hayes!" a kid with spiked hair cried. "Riley crashed into Mr. Wadas's station wagon . . ."

Lexy was out the door before the kid could finish.

"There's blood everywhere," he said to Luke. "You'd better call an ambulance."

"Where is he hurt?"

"His nose. It's bleeding everywhere!" The kid took off.

Luke grabbed a dishtowel from the kitchen and ran after them. He knew head wounds bled something fierce, even if the injury wasn't serious.

A half a block away he found Lexy kneeling over her whimpering son, the boy's fingers covered with blood.

"Is it just your nose, honey?" she asked, searching his body.

"Yeah."

"You didn't hit your head, did you?"

"No, just my nose. It won't stop bleeding, Mommy."

"Shhh," she soothed, rubbing his back. "You'll be fine. Let's get you to the house to get a better look."

Luke was amazed at her composure. "Here—" He offered her the towel.

"Thanks." Their eyes met and her expression made him want to stay close. She turned back to Riley. "Hold this to your nose. Can you get up?"

"Yeah."

Luke bent down. "I'll carry him."

"You don't have to," Lexy said.

"Hey, this is a piece of cake compared to the three-hundred-pound gorillas I usually throw around." He scooped up Riley into his arms and started toward the house. "Man, you sure you don't weight three hundred pounds?" he joked.

Riley chuckle-whimpered, then pressed his head to Luke's chest. He sucked in a deep breath. To feel needed like this, depended on.

"It's okay, buddy. This stuff happens to me all the time. It's never as bad as it looks."

He heard Lexy tell Riley's friend to head home.

"I'm in trouble," Riley whispered to Luke.

"I'd say that scooter's in trouble. That thing's dangerous."

"I hit Mr. Wadas's car."

"It's just a car."

"I wasn't wearing a helmet."

"That wasn't very smart, but unless you'd been wearing it on your face, I'm not sure how that would have helped."

"Mom's gonna kill me."

"Your mom?" He looked into the boy's eyes. "Nah. She's just glad you're okay."

He climbed the porch steps, breathing a sigh of relief that the kid was lucid. He walked through the living room into the kitchen and sat him on the counter.

"I'll take it from here," Lexy said, coming up behind him.

When he backed away she touched his arm and he saw the silent plea in her eyes. She needed support, his support.

"Could you get some washcloths from the hall closet?"

"Sure." He headed for the closet, the sound of her comforting murmurs drifting down the hall. He didn't belong here, he really didn't. He didn't know the first thing about tending kids. But he did know injuries. *That*, he was an expert at.

Together they cleaned up Riley, Luke rinsing cloth after cloth and handing them to her, Lexy asking Riley about the accident in a soft, consoling voice. Once the blood was washed from his round cheeks, it was obvious that the nose was not broken and the lacerations were minor.

"You're okay, kid. But maybe you should ice it to keep the swelling down," Luke said.

Lexy grabbed an ice pack from the freezer and wrapped it in a towel. "I'll get him settled in his room." With an arm around Riley's shoulder, she led him down the hall.

Smiling to himself, Luke realized how much he wanted to be here. He sat at the counter and flipped through a local paper looking for the crossword section. He felt comfortable, at home . . . like he belonged.

Penciling in the six-letter word for the capital of Saskatchewan, he heard Lexy walk into the kitchen and open the oven.

"It's coming along," she said, then opened the refrigerator and closed it. Opened it again and closed it a second time.

"What are you doing?" he asked.

She opened the freezer and closed it, three times. If he didn't know better, he'd think she'd short-circuited.

"I've got nothing to serve with the chicken. There are potatoes, but you should serve something green with every meal." She opened the refrigerator and stuck her head inside. "I can't believe I don't have anything green."

She shut the refrigerator, stood on her tiptoes and searched the cabinet above.

"It's no big deal," he said, walking into the kitchen.

She pulled down a loaf of bread. Two cereal boxes came with it, smacking her in the head, then falling to the floor, littering the tile with puffed rice cereal.

"What a mess, it's all such a mess." Kneeling, she swept at the cereal with the side of her hand.

Something was definitely not right. Knees cracking, he sat beside her and touched her cheek. Damn, why did her skin have to be so soft? "Lexy? What's wrong?"

"I have nothing green to serve my son. What kind of mother am I?"

She looked up and the expression in her eyes made him pull her into his arms.

"You're a great mother," he said, leaning against the cabinet and holding her tight.

"I shouldn't have let him ride that scooter. It's my job to keep him from getting hurt." She scrunched his shirt between her fingers.

He held her tighter. "You can't protect him from everything."

"I try so hard. All I've ever wanted is to be a good mom. I stayed married longer than I should have, thinking it would be good for Riley. I took extra work to pay for things so Riley wouldn't feel neglected. I try to fit my career around his schedule. Still, I can't help thinking I'm failing at this mom thing."

"Stop. You couldn't be any better."

"Not according to David."

"That jerk ex-husband of yours? The guy barely knows how to hold his own kid."

She leaned back and looked into his eyes. "But you do, don't you?"

Tension wrapped around his vocal chords. What could he say? Holding Riley, playing with him, felt completely natural. The kid was just plain lovable. Just like his mom.

"It's such a shame," she said, leaning against him. "You'll never have children and are so good with them, yet my ex wants kids with his new honey and hasn't a clue."

"Don't listen to that loser, especially when he's pretending to be an expert about you."

"No, that's your job," she whispered.

They sat in silence for what must have been five minutes. He wished to God he knew what she was thinking.

"You're doing great," he finally said.

"I didn't do very great tonight."

"Sure you did. You were calm and controlled."

"Yeah," she chuckle-gasped. "Look at me now."

"You look great to me."

Again, silence filled the kitchen for a good minute.

"If you hadn't been here . . ." her voice wavered.

"You would have been fine. You didn't need me."

She sighed.

He wished like hell she'd disagree.

"Just the same . . . I'm glad you were here," she said.

"Me too, Lexy. Me too."

* * *

After dinner the three of them sat at the dining room table and worked on Luke's publicity schedule for the next two weeks. No matter how hard she tried keeping things businesslike, she couldn't help pausing to smile at her friend. Who would have thought this hardened man had such a compassionate side? She should have guessed as much. After all, he was her friend, Timmy.

When Riley asked him a question, Luke's face grew animated with interest. He wasn't just Timmy from next door. He'd become much more than that geeky kid, years of life having sharpened his edges. This man was a fascinating study in how the tragedies of life can change a person. For the better.

"Show me how to do an arm lock," Riley said.

"I don't think it's a good idea, kid. You're still recovering, remember?"

"He's right." She stacked her notes and closed her folder. "Besides, it's late. You've got to get to bed."

"Can Loverboy tuck me in?"

She held her breath. Luke had been so wonderful tonight, but she didn't want to cause him more pain. Being around kids had to feel like salt in a festering wound.

"Honey, it's late. He has to get going."

"It's okay," Luke said. "I can stay."

"You sure?" she said, searching his eyes.

"Yeah." He didn't look at her. "Come on, tiger." He tickled Riley, who burst into laughter, then ran off down the hall. Luke got up to follow.

She touched his hand. "Thanks."

He smiled that boyish grin that warmed her insides and disappeared down the hall.

Clearing the coffee mugs and dessert plates from the table, she enjoyed the sounds of her son's giggles and Luke's playful growls. She couldn't remember the last time David had played with his son. This was one thing she couldn't give her son: male companionship.

She loaded the dishwasher, then caught her reflection in the chrome trim of her oven. The long, emotional day had taken its toll. She looked like hell, circles forming under her eyes, her hair flying in twelve different directions. Since when had she become so self-conscious?

With a finger comb through her hair and pinch of her cheeks, she turned to find Luke hovering in the doorway. A slow grin curled his lips. But this one didn't warm her insides like before. A completely different kind of heat started in her tummy and trailed a slow burn down low.

"He wants his mama to tuck him in," he said, leaning against the doorjamb and crossing his arms over his chest.

"I guess you have to go," she said, embarrassed that he'd caught her primping.

"I can hang around for a little while."

"You don't have to," she said a little panicked, by what she wasn't quite sure. "I mean, I understand if you have to leave. Wait, you're not driving home tonight, are you?"

"No. Staying at the Hawthorne Inn. Figured you'd want all weekend to polish me into a presentable hero."

"Oh." She swallowed hard. Could she stand to be with him for two more days? Sure she could. He was pleasant and helpful and . . .

. . . too damned sexy for his own good.

"You're not that bad, really," she said, avoiding his eyes. If he only knew how very "not bad" he was.

"Mama!" Riley called.

"Coming, honey! . . . I'd better go tuck him in."

With a sweeping motion of his hand, he granted her passage. She smiled and edged past him. Heat crept up the back of her neck, the awareness too intense, uncontrollable, and certainly not welcome. He was her friend, not a one-night stand. Besides, she knew the heat was an illusion, one that cooled and hardened to ice when a man touched her where normal women ached to be stroked.

Strolling down the hall, she wondered how she'd make it through the rest of the weekend. She had to think of him as her friend. Nothing more. Who was she kidding?

She went into Riley's room and noticed his grin of contentment. She tucked his blanket between the mattress and box spring.

"Mama?"

"Yeah, baby?"

"I like Loverboy Luke."

"Yeah?" She sat down and trailed her fingers across his hairline. "Why's that?"

He pulled his hands from beneath the comforter and counted with his fingers. "One, he's strong. Two, he knows how to fix things when you get hurt. Three, he makes me laugh, and four, he tells good stories."

"Good stories are important." She kissed his forehead and started for the door.

"Mama?"

She turned, her finger on the light switch.

"I forgot five," he said.

"What's five, baby?"

"He's nice to you."

219

She flicked off the light, glad he couldn't see the melancholy in her eyes. "Sweet dreams, honey."

"Love you."

"Love you, too." She closed the door and headed down the hall.

He's nice to you.

She heard the message loud and clear. Luke was nice to her, unlike Riley's father. Kids. They saw so many things at an early age. It scared her how much he understood, deep down.

She stepped into the living room but Luke was gone. Disappointment warred with concern. Had his time with Riley been too painful? A tapping sound made her jump. Luke smiled at her through the front window. She joined him outside.

"I poured you some wine." He leaned forward in the porch swing and handed her a glass. "Figured you could use it."

If he only knew.

"Thanks. It hasn't been an easy day, that's for sure."

The only place to sit was next to him on the swing. Not a good idea. She steadied her hip against the porch railing. "You're not having any?"

"I've got iced tea," he said, raising a glass. "Being a parent is hard work, huh?"

"More than I'd ever imagined," she said. "You're awfully good with kids."

He glanced across the front yard.

"Riley was going on and on about how much he likes you," she said. "You make him laugh."

He smiled, his gaze drifting to his feet.

"It's amazing how natural you are with him. I mean given that you don't do kids."

She waited, hoping he'd talk about the kids who'd

tracked him down at the hotel last week. He didn't offer anything. She sipped her wine.

They were growing close, very close. But she wouldn't feel totally at ease if he kept secrets from her. Why couldn't he tell her about those children and their cute mother? Was she a former lover who'd had his children before he became sterile? No, that didn't seem like him. Yet what else could it be?

"Luke?"

He glanced up, his aquamarine eyes wary.

"You've had experience with kids, haven't you?"

"I guess."

"Those kids from the hotel?"

He placed his glass on the floor and leaned back in the swing.

"Who are they?" she pressed.

"Just friends. They don't have a dad. I fill in when I can."

She sat down next to him and touched his shirtsleeve. "That's nice."

"You've got to stop doing that," he whispered.

"What?"

"Touching me."

"I'm sorry." She didn't pull away this time. Something told her he needed the contact.

"It's just," he said, "I'm not used to anyone touching me like that."

"Like what?"

"Like they care."

She saw an opening. "That woman, the mother of those kids, she touched you like she cared."

"She's grateful. I'm their substitute dad."

"They're lucky to have you."

"If they were lucky, their dad would still be around."

"Where is he?"

Luke stood. "I'd better go."

Nuts, she'd scared him off. "Here, I'll take your drink in." She reached for it and their fingers touched. The need in his eyes flared red-hot and her heart skipped.

"I'll be back tomorrow around one," he said.

Did she imagine the rasp in his voice?

"One's good." *Now's better*.

She wanted him to stay. She wanted to reminisce, tell stories. She wanted to make him laugh.

"I've gotta go." He didn't move. "Lexy?"

"Yes?"

"Thanks for everything, dinner and stuff."

"You're—"

Her words were cut off by his unexpected kiss, soft lips pressing gently against hers. It didn't surprise her. Nor did it frighten her. It was a kiss of gratitude.

At least it started that way. As he deepened the kiss, she leaned into him, wanting to grip his broad shoulders and absorb his warmth. Unfortunately, she held a glass in either hand.

He broke the kiss and stepped back. Jarred, she wavered, leaning against the railing for support.

"Sorry." He shoved his hands into his jeans pockets, as if he didn't trust them.

"It's okay."

"I just . . . the way you looked at me . . ." His voice trailed off.

"It's okay. Really." She couldn't help smiling at his sudden shyness. To think this man could act like a playboy one minute and a humble, gentle man the next.

That in itself should scare her off. It didn't.

"It felt like the right thing to do," he said. "I'd better

222

go." Avoiding her eyes, he stepped off the porch and marched toward his car.

"You're right," she whispered. "It did feel right."

She realized it had been a long time since she'd felt "right" about anything.

Chapter Fifteen

Lexy spent the morning running errands and sprucing up the place for her afternoon meeting with Luke. As she arranged a fresh bouquet of flowers, Aunt Lulu paged through a month-old *Working Woman* magazine.

Riley raced around the house, filling his backpack with a flashlight, granola bars and bug spray. Apparently he and his aunt were going on an adventure.

"Everybody's in a hurry," said Lulu, eyeing an article. "Can't even enjoy going to the grocery store. Order online; have it delivered. I like to squeeze my own melons, thank you very much."

"Working moms have a lot on their plate." Lexy rearranged the carnations, trying to balance colors.

"You're going to an awful lot of fuss for a client," Lulu said. "Or did things change while I was at rehearsal last night?"

"Speaking of which, you didn't get home until nearly eleven," Lexy countered. "I was worried."

"Oh, fiddle fudge. Something else had you pacing the floors. Your new hero, maybe?" Lulu winked.

She shoved a spray of baby's breath behind a carnation. "He's not my hero. He's an old friend." She smiled to herself.

"And I'm Queen Elizabeth."

"Luke and I can only be friends. I'm a single mom with a tenuous hold on custody of my son. He's—"

"A handsome scoundrel who I wouldn't throw out of bed for eating Jujubees."

"Lulu!"

"Calm down. I'm not after your man." She crossed one leg over the other and went back to reading.

"He's not my man," Lexy muttered.

"Uh-huh," Lulu said.

"He's not," Lexy protested.

Lulu slapped the magazine onto the coffee table and leaned forward. "You're a young, healthy woman. He's a strong, virile man. Tell me he doesn't jangle your bells."

"He doesn't," she said, fingering a carnation.

"Look me in the eye and say that."

She planted her hands on her hips and stared down her aunt. "He can jangle my bells, light my fire, even take out my garbage. So what? It's not like there can be anything serious between us."

"Ah-ha!" Lulu slapped her hands. "Finally, she comes clean. I knew it."

"Knew what?" Riley said, marching into the room, dressed in army fatigues.

"Where on earth are you two going?" Lexy said.

"On a mission. Don't expect us before ten," Lulu said. "You just take care of your business." She lifted her eyebrows, twice.

"What's wrong with your eyes, Lulu?" Riley asked.

"Aunt Lulu," Lexy corrected.

"She got a tick or something?"

"No, just a vivid imagination," Lexy said.

"Private Riley, go pack the car," Lulu ordered. "My gear is on the driveway."

"Yes, sir!" He saluted and raced for the door.

"Hey!" Lexy protested.

Riley ran back and smacked a kiss on her cheek.

"Have fun," she called as the screen door slammed behind him. "Thanks again for doing this," she said.

"Don't change the subject." Lulu stood and pointed her index finger at Lexy. "And don't be scared of feelings either. We all got 'em. Even your Loverboy."

"He's not my—"

"Alley-oops—" She placed a hand to Lexy's shoulder. "I don't usually tell you what to do, but this time I can't stop myself. Let down your hair and have fun. He's a decent man. I sense these things. And he's crazy about you."

"Where did you get that idea?"

"The crystal ball never lies."

Lulu grabbed her bright orange jacket and headed for the door.

The crystal ball? Lexy shook her head.

"And don't be shaking your head at me." Lulu spun around and Lexy plastered a false grin to her lips.

"I know what I'm talking about," her aunt said. "You've got a chance for something special here."

She closed the door and Lexy wandered to the front window where she watched them stuff her aunt's yellow Volkswagen Beetle with backpacks, a cooler, a blanket and an American Flag that stuck out the sunroof.

"Something special. Right." She looked at the flowers, their natural beauty always brightened her mood.

She wasn't in a bad mood, was she? Not bad, exactly, just pensive. Lulu was right on when she said something had made Lexy pace the floors last night.

At first Lexy had thought business pressures were keeping her awake. Yet around two this morning she'd realized her restlessness had nothing to do with work and everything to do with a hunky wrestler named Loverboy. She struggled to define their relationship: Was he friend or potential lover?

"Definitely friend," she said, walking to the dining room table and opening the BAM folder. She'd expected it would take time to change a scoundrel into a hero, but there was so much goodness in Luke, so much compassion. Not only was he a natural with kids, but when he let down his guard, he was quite endearing . . .

. . . And generous, caring and attentive. Qualities she'd once hoped for in her husband. Luke listened to her and comforted her. He never made her feel small or stupid. He'd even called her a great mother.

Smiling to herself, she realized that he reflected good things back to her, things she'd needed so desperately to see. He was a loyal and true friend.

Stop lying to yourself. He's much more than that.

"I've got to be crazy." She focused on the file.

Nothing more than friendship could come of her relationship with Luke. It wasn't as if they could be a family, what with Luke traveling three hundred plus days out of the year.

"You're getting way ahead of yourself," she said.

It's the lack of sleep. She wasn't thinking straight. Why else would she consider a man like Luke as anything but a friend? She needed a family man, a stable, trustworthy man with a solid character to fill the role of mate for her, and father for her son.

"Well, he is pretty trustworthy. And definitely solid." She closed her eyes, remembering the feel of his rock-hard biceps beneath her fingertips.

Such a hard man; such a tender soul. She shook her head. No way, no how. Lulu was right, Lexy and Luke did have something special. It just couldn't be sexually special.

Yet she felt so comfortable with him. When he'd kissed her last night . . .

Truth was, she couldn't remember the last time someone had jangled her bells. Maybe she should consider exploring the physical nature of their relationship.

"I'm a responsible mother," she reminded herself.

Responsible mothers didn't have sex with untamed pro wrestlers. Yet she ached for the closeness. Against her will and better judgment, she wanted to get closer to Luke. But how close was too close?

Luke had been on time but lost his nerve and couldn't get out of the damn car.

What was he thinking, kissing her like that? Sure, he'd done it before to intimidate her, but last night he'd left himself wide open and let her in. Dumb, stupid, idiot. She didn't belong in. Nobody did.

Staring at her living room window, he considered making up some excuse to get out of an afternoon of sheer torture. His head still ached. He could say he had a migraine and couldn't think straight. Hell, he'd stopped thinking straight the day she walked back into his life.

"Focus," he ordered himself. Not an easy thing to do with a concussion.

Goal: string her along. Objective: jumping promotions and retaining his heel status, because one thing was certain—changing from heel to hero meant the end of his career, the end of his life. After all, who was he if not Loverboy Luke?

Getting up his nerve, he opened the car door and headed toward the house. Business was business. That kiss last night had to be a "thank you" for accepting him, faults and all, and making him feel part of a family. If only it hadn't gotten away from him. It wouldn't happen again.

He knocked on her front door. Time to go in and get more lessons on becoming a hero, more reminders about just how much of a failure he was. She opened the door and his heart lurched in his throat.

"Hi," she said.

"Hi."

Damn, but she looked amazing, dressed in slacks and a sleeveless white top that showed off her sleek, bare arms. Her hair was pulled away from her face, silver hearts dangled from her ears. What a beautiful neck, full lips, amber eyes . . .

"You coming in?" she said, pushing open the screen door.

"Yeah, sorry. I'm a little spaced out today. Where's the kid?"

"My aunt took him for the day."

She smiled and he wanted to run from the porch. He was a goner if she kept doing that.

"I figured we could go over your clothes first, then work on speech and facial expressions," she said.

"I can hardly wait."

"Don't sound so enthusiastic," she teased, leading him to the dining area.

Colorful flowers had been arranged on the table. His mom always kept flowers on the table.

"Put yourself in my shoes," he said. "How would you

feel if someone wanted to completely change your personality?"

"I don't want to change you," she said, her gaze catching his.

Did she mean it?

"You're doing this to keep your job, remember?" She motioned for him to sit at the table. "Wait here and I'll get the outfits I bought you."

"Aw, you shouldn't have."

"I didn't. Cosmo did. Oh, before I forget, here's that envelope from the other day." She handed him a manila envelope, the very thing that had jogged her memory and reminded her of Tim, an honorable boy who no longer existed.

"I'll be right back." She winked and started for the back of the house.

Luke ripped open the envelope while admiring Lexy's round bottom as she disappeared down the hall. God, that woman had a touchable behind.

He glanced at the contests of the envelope and froze. It was a twenty-year-old newspaper article about Luke winning the State Science Olympiad. Where in the hell had this come from? Mom must have been cleaning out the closets and figured he wanted it. He didn't.

"Hope you're ready for this," Lexy said, coming down the hall.

This was going to be a joke. Lexy playing dress up with her favorite live doll: Loverboy Luke. His head started to throb. It was going to be a long day. He dug into his jeans for the bottle of Ibuprofen.

"Your head's still bothering you?" she asked.

"A little. Sinuses, I think."

"Promise me you'll see a doctor before the end of the week." She squared off at him.

Hell, he couldn't deny her as a kid. What made him think he could now? "I'll work it in next week."

"Good. Now, this sharp black outfit is for Monday's fund-raiser."

"I'll look like I'm going to a funeral."

"Black is classic. I figured it was either this or a tux and I didn't peg you as a tux kind of guy."

"How do you know this stuff will fit?"

"Cosmo gave me your sizes and I scouted the big-and-tall-man stores. Anyway, for the signing next Wednesday you'll wear this." She pulled a conservative gray suit from the pile. "And this is my favorite—I got you a skin-tight purple ensemble for the bike-a-thon."

"I don't do bike-a-thons." The thought of the physical strain made his head pound in anticipation.

She sat down. "It's for the Make-A-Wish Foundation. A lot of the guys will be there."

"No." He wouldn't last three minutes on a bike.

"You don't do kids, you don't do bike-a-thons. Anything else I should know about before I disappoint more fans when their hero's a no-show?"

"I'm doing the pediatric fund-raiser Monday night. That should make you happy."

"Delirious. Why are you so picky about what you do?"

"Can't talk about it."

"You *won't* talk about it, you mean. You're stubborn."

"You make that sound like a bad thing."

"Just make sure you're stubborn about the right things. Here—" she handed him the black outfit. "Try it on."

"What, here? Now?"

"Sure, why not? I need to know if it fits."

"Le-xy."

"I'll cancel the bike-a-thon," she offered.

"Deal."

"You can change in my room."

Great. The last place he wanted to be was around Lexy's things, teased by her essence.

"I'll use the bathroom," he said.

"It's too small. You're a big guy. Go to my bedroom and undress."

"Is that an order?" He crooked a brow.

"You know what I mean." She blushed bright red. "Hurry. We've got other lessons to cover, like shaving."

"Huh?"

"This—" She reached over and rubbed her fingers against his two day's growth.

He nearly leaned into her touch, but caught himself. "It's part of my image," he protested.

"Your old image. Now you're a clean-cut hero, which means a clean-shaven one. Besides"— she leaned back and opened a folder—"who'd want to kiss you with that on your face?"

Hell. Had he hurt her last night? Scraped her cheeks raw with his whiskers? He studied her face but saw no sign of redness.

"After that, I'll teach you how to smile," she said.

"I know how to smile."

"A polite smile, not your usual, 'Come to me, baby' smile," she mimicked in a deep voice.

He dropped to one knee. "Come to me, baby," he joked.

"Knock it off, we've got work to do."

"You're no fun."

"Fun later. Work now."

That sounded promising. Okay, he'd play her game. "I'll be right back," he promised in a suggestive tone.

She shooed him with her hand. He ambled down the hall and chose Riley's room to change. He had half a mind to lock the door. What was his problem? It wasn't like she was going to bust in and jump his bones. He changed and strolled into the living room like a model on a runway.

"And now, the one, the only, Luke Silver, reformed heel and overall good guy." He turned in front of her, showing off his backside. He took a few steps and faced her, planting his hands on his hips. "You happy now? I look like an idiot."

She stood and narrowed her eyes, her gaze drifting from his shoulders down to his legs and up again. It was getting hot in here.

"Wow," she said, walking around him.

She touched his shoulder, ran her hand down his sleeve. "Well, it certainly is long enough."

Oh, baby, was it ever. He gritted his teeth. He wasn't going to make it, he surely wasn't.

She ran her finger between the shirt collar and the skin of his neck. "Too tight?" she asked.

Not there. His pants on the other hand . . .

"It's fine," he said.

"You actually look normal." She smiled.

"Very funny. May I be excused?"

"Go. You're as bad as Riley," she muttered.

Great, he thought, escaping down the hall. She compared him to an eight-year-old while he got hard from her simple touch. He shucked the clothes and got back into his jeans and T-shirt. He prayed she wouldn't touch him again.

He went back to the living room.

"Here's the second outfit." She held up the conservative gray suit.

"I'll take a chance it fits."

"But—"

"Dammit, woman, I'm not a Ken doll." *And I've only got so much self-control.*

"Take it home. Let's work on this other stuff."

They got comfortable in the living room, Lexy sitting in the wingback chair, Luke sprawled across her sofa. The next three hours were spent going over his new persona, how he'd present himself in public, what he'd say and how he'd say it. It wasn't that hard to change his image, the way he talked, walked, even smiled. Every time she nodded her approval, warmth filled his chest.

Sap. *She doesn't care whether you're a flirt or the all-American boy. She's just doing her job, making you better and more suitable for the general public.*

Fixing Loverboy Luke. That familiar burn started low in his gut.

"Well—" She flipped her notebook closed. "We've covered a lot today. This was easier than I thought."

"For you, maybe."

"Is it really that hard to act like a good guy?"

No, and that's what scared him. It wasn't real. He was anything but good.

"Luke?"

"Am I excused, Teach?"

"Yeah, I guess."

He got up and stretched his arms over his head.

"Do you have plans tonight?" she asked.

"Thought I'd head home, unless we have more to do tomorrow."

"No, I think you're okay."

His chest ached. He wished she was referring to his

235

soul, not his PR skills. "Good, then I'll see you Monday night at the fund-raiser."

He headed for the door, relieved to get the hell out in one piece. He gripped the brass door handle, tasting freedom.

"Luke?"

He turned casually. "Yep?"

"Would you be interested in dinner?"

Get away, now, before you're lost for good.

"What did you have in mind?" he said.

"I know the perfect place." She fingered the manila folder. "But I'll understand if you've got to get home."

He glanced at the door. Freedom. Safety.

"Never mind," she whispered.

He heard rejection in her voice.

"I'd love to," he said.

Her eyes brightened. "Really?"

"Sure, why not?"

You're a dead man.

Chapter Sixteen

"Great. I'll get some things together."

Luke watched her practically skip into the kitchen. Was she that excited about spending more time with him? No, this was just her way of saying "thank you" for not being a complete jerk during hero practice. He was helping her do her job, that's all.

In minutes she came out of the kitchen carrying a wicker basket. She must have had this planned all day. He was glad he'd agreed to join her.

"Ready?" she said.

"I'm impressed."

"Don't be. I bought some things at a local gourmet market."

"And here I thought you cooked for me." He lifted the lid and she slapped his fingers.

"You'll have to wait until we get there."

"Where are we going?"

"Oh, just this place I found." She smiled and handed him a wool blanket.

"What are you up to?"

"You'll see." She locked the front door and they headed for her car.

To the neighbors it must look like the pair was heading out on a romantic interlude, a picnic basket on her arm, a blanket in his.

Don't think it. Don't even fantasize about it.

Between her reinvention of Loverboy Luke and their newly formed friendship, Luke's walls were slowly crumbling. Walls he needed to protect himself.

The drive was unusually quiet. He leaned back against the seat, his headache settling to a dull hum. He didn't want to get into the ring anytime soon, yet he knew Killian Steel would jump at the chance to snatch him from BAM and showcase him ASAP. Probably in a hard-core match with leaf blowers and snakes, fought inside a Dumpster, or worse.

He groaned internally, wishing for other options. There were none. Steel's Outrageous Wrestling was his last hope. He wished he didn't have to hurt Lexy in the process. But then this was about work for her, too, not personal lives or feelings. Feelings? Where the hell did that come from?

The car slowed and he opened his eyes. His breath caught. She had parked on the fringes of a local airport.

"What are we doing here?" he said.

"It's one of my favorite spots." She peered through the front window at a twin-engine plane taking off. "It's so peaceful."

For her maybe. Luke struggled to keep his emotions in check. His dream. Flying. A dream crushed by his ludicrous career. A knot tightened in his chest.

"Besides," she said, grabbing the basket from the backseat. "I remember how much you liked to fly."

She got out of the car and he sat there, dumb-founded, afraid to move. He'd dreamt of flying ever since his Uncle Ed had taken him out when he was a kid. Luke had even considered joining the military to get his start. But he'd had other obligations, like providing for his little sister and her newborn daughter.

And now it was too late. A man with as many concussions as he had could never become a pilot. Pro wrestling had stripped that dream from him as well.

Lexy flung open his door. "You coming?"

He looked at her, her eyes sparkling as if she'd done a good deed. She had, in a way. He just wished it didn't hurt so much. She couldn't know the regret that taunted him.

"Luke?"

"You got a spot picked out?" he said, putting on his actor's face and getting out of the car. She'd done something nice for him and he'd be damned if he'd screw it up.

"Riley and I came out for the air show last spring and we found a great place for a picnic, over there." She pointed toward a cluster of trees, then handed him the blanket. He walked beside her, trying to figure out how he'd make it through the next few hours.

Pretend, act, keep up the shield. You've done it for the past fifteen years. You can do it for a few hours.

They reached her special spot, a patch of grass beneath a sturdy oak tree. He handed her the blanket. "I can't believe you remembered," he let slip.

"I guess I owe you an apology for that."

"How do you mean?" He took one end of the blanket and they stretched it to the ground.

"I feel bad about not remembering you the first time I saw you, in the locker room. You just"— she glanced at him—"look so different."

"Not the nerd anymore," he said.

"No, really, really not."

He didn't miss the slight catch in her voice or the flush of her cheeks.

Don't do it, Silver. Don't even think about it.

"Lexy," was all he could say. How he wanted to touch her, to taste her again.

A low-flying plane shocked him back to earth. She ducked and laughed. They watched the plane land in the distance.

"Listen, I really appreciate the dinner and all," he said.

She sat down cross-legged and looked at him. "But?"

"But what?"

"I hear a 'but' in your sentence."

She was right, there was a 'but.' Only he hadn't a clue what came next. Something like, "don't touch me," "let's be friends" or "be careful or I'm going to rip off your clothes and drive myself deep inside of you."

He positioned himself at the opposite corner of the blanket, close enough to reach the food, but far enough away so he wouldn't be tempted to grab something else.

"Don't mind me," he said. "I'm just a little punchy."

"You need food." She popped open the top of a container, dug into it with a small knife and spread something on a piece of fancy bread. "Try this."

"What is—"

She shoved it into his mouth. Some kind of garlic spread. Not bad.

"Lexy—"

"Eat, you'll feel better."

Wrapping his hand around her wrist, he took another bite of bread. His fingers burned clear to his chest, the usual reaction whenever he touched her.

He studied her eyes. It was obvious she wanted to

make him happy. If she only knew how happy he was at this moment. Happy and lost.

"Wait until you see what I've got planned for after dinner," she said.

His mind started concocting its own version of dessert with sensual kisses, naked bodies and maybe even—

Hell. He'd never make it past the appetizer. How was he going to keep his hands off of her?

"So, how are you feeling about this family barbecue thing?" she asked.

That shocked him out of his sexual fantasy.

"I'm not feeling anything." He dug into a container marked mini-ribs.

"You're going, right?"

"Nope."

"Why not?"

"Complicated."

"Coward," she muttered.

"What was that?"

"You heard me."

"Those are fightin' words, Whitford."

"Hayes."

"Whatever." He couldn't stand to be reminded she'd been married to that jerk ex-husband of hers, that he'd kissed her and touched her in the most intimate places.

"You can't make things go away by ignoring them," she said, nibbling on a piece of cheese.

"That's where you're wrong. I can do anything. I'm a superhero."

She shrugged. "As long as you're happy."

"Whatever that is," he said, biting into a rib.

"Hey." She touched his cheek.

She was too close. He couldn't breathe.

"You deserve to be happy," she said. "You're a good guy."

He laughed and leaned away from her, needing to break the skin-to-skin contact. "It's an act, Lexy, remember? You're making me into a hero, but I'll always be a heel at heart." He reached for another rib.

"I don't believe that." She touched his arm and he bit into the rib, his teeth gnashing on the bone.

"Luke?" she said, a question in her eyes.

"Come on, eat." He shoved a rib at her. Damn, he wanted her to stop touching him, stop talking to him.

"What happened after you left home? I need to know."

"No, you don't."

"I really do. Please?"

"Don't do this, Lexy." He grabbed another rib.

"I'm sorry." She glanced at the crackers in her hand. "It's none of my business."

God, but he wanted it to be her business. He wanted her to know everything about him, to care about him. *She does, you fool.*

"The Colonel moved us so we could forget," he started. "You don't forget someone like Kevin. Thirteen isn't the best age to move into a new school. Making friends was hard enough when I was in Sycamore, me being a geek and all."

"You weren't a geek. You were smart."

"Whatever. I didn't fit in. I withdrew even further. Pretty pathetic, huh?"

"No, not at all."

They ate in silence for a few minutes. A plane landed and he watched.

"You know," she started, "you haven't changed all that much. Well, I mean physically you have." She smiled.

He usually basked in a woman's admiration of his

body. But he wanted Lexy to look past the muscles and see into his heart.

"But inside," she continued, "you're still the same nice kid I knew growing up."

Pride swelled in his chest. He caught himself. He didn't deserve to feel proud of the things he'd done. Not by a long shot.

"Nice guys finish last," he joked, tossing the rib onto a plate and wiping his fingers with a paper napkin. "They don't win wrestling matches and they never get the girl."

"Oh, I don't know about that."

Her gaze drifted to his. What he saw there blew him away. She licked her lips and his heart slammed against his chest. He couldn't do this, no way, no how. This wasn't some groupie who wanted a quick tumble.

She smiled and the wind played with a few stray bangs, brushing them across her eyes, then back off her face.

He couldn't move.

She leaned forward and kissed him, the taste—pure heaven. He'd lose it all this way: his career, protective facade, their friendship.

With a hand on her shoulder, he broke the kiss. "Lexy," he breathed against her skin, skin that tasted of sunshine and honey.

"Hmmm?" Her eyes were still closed, and her tongue darted across her lower lip, as if tasting him there.

"What are we doing?" he said, his voice hoarse.

"Kissing."

She leaned into him and they both went down, Lexy on top of him. She pressed her breasts against him, her lips to his lips. He'd dreamt about touching and kissing her, but he'd never imagined she'd be so hot and demanding. Her tongue tickled his lips, begging for an opening. A moan vibrated against his chest as his protective walls caved in, crumbling to dust.

He opened up to her, wrapping his arms around her backside, slipping his hands down low to cup her behind. It was a dream, right? He prayed he'd never wake up.

He wanted her. Completely. Wanted to roll her onto her back and strip off her shirt. He could have her right here, with planes flying overhead and God frowning down on him. But unlike past conquests, he wouldn't seduce Lexy. This had to be her idea.

And it was. Oh, man, was it ever. She swung her leg across him and straddled his hips, his body reacting in the most direct way. Did she feel his strength, the need that burned inside his jeans?

"I've never felt this way," she whispered.

Neither had he. He wanted to tell her so, but couldn't speak, couldn't even form the words in his mind.

She kissed him hard and a stream of light flashed across the backs of his eyelids. Drifting, floating, flying.

"Excuse me, folks," a deep male voice said.

Luke's eyes shot open and Lexy shrieked, burying her face in his shoulder. It took a minute to focus, but once he did, Luke found himself staring up at a security guard.

"This is private property," the guard said, aiming his flashlight at Lexy.

"Sorry," Luke said.

The security guard flashed the light at him.

"Hey, not in the eyes, okay?" He blocked the beam with his hand. A migraine was something he didn't need.

"Holy Hammerlock, it's Loverboy Luke! I hate to do

this to you, Loverboy, but you and your lady friend really can't be out here."

"No problem. We'll clear out."

She buried her face deeper into his chest.

"Shoot-fire, they won't believe this at the Legion. Don't suppose I could get an autograph before you go?"

"Sure." Like he had a choice?

The cop pulled a gas station receipt from his jacket pocket.

"To think you brought one of your females to my airport. Is she one of the BAM women? Nedra the Nymph, maybe?" He leaned forward, trying to get a better look.

One of his many females. He felt like a heel.

"We'll be out of here in five minutes." He scrawled his signature on the scrap of paper and handed it back.

The guard's eyes glowed as he studied the paper. "Boy, I wish I had my camera."

And boy was Luke glad he didn't.

The cop grinned but didn't make a move to leave.

"I think my date's a little embarrassed," Luke said.

"Oh, right. Well, I'll leave you two alone. You behave now." He nodded and headed for his truck.

Luke couldn't believe he hadn't heard the truck drive up. Then again, he'd been a little busy.

"Is he gone?" Lexy mumbled into his chest.

"It's safe," Luke said, his lips touching her hair.

She started shaking and he held her tighter. "Lexy?"

She tossed her head back and burst into laughter. What the hell?

"It's been forever since I've been caught doing something naughty," she said.

Was that how she thought of their kiss? Naughty?

Hell, he thought it mind-altering, life changing . . . perfect.

"Glad I could be of service." He eased her off of him and started shoving food containers into the basket. He needed distance. "Stick with me and you're guaranteed to experience more naughty."

"Promise?" She grinned and helped him pack the food.

He wasn't grinning. His heart ached, his mind spun and his body craved relief. *That* wasn't coming any time soon.

"Let's get out of here before he comes back with a camera." He stood and grabbed the picnic basket.

"Since when are you camera shy?" she said.

Since you exposed my heart.

"Let's go." He started for the car, wanting to get away from her, wanting to catch his breath.

She ran up beside him. "What's wrong?"

"I'm tired."

"Wait." She grabbed his arm and he froze.

He didn't want to look into her eyes, but couldn't help himself.

"I'm sorry," she said.

"For what?"

"For kissing you."

There, she'd said it. Lexy squinted, fully expecting lightning to strike her down. There wasn't a single fiber of her body that was sorry about what had just happened.

Luke nodded and headed for the car. Sheesh, she'd expected a little more like "it's okay" or "accidents happen" or "let's do it again."

She knew she wanted to do it again and again. And

not because it was naughty. Kissing Luke, holding him, felt exciting, exhilarating and so right.

He had a good lead on her, giving her time to think. Jangles didn't come close to describing the sounds flooding her brain when they'd kissed. It made her realize she was quite normal in the sex department, after all, but David had been the wrong man.

They loaded the blanket and picnic basket into the car and headed back to Newberry Court. Luke didn't speak a word all the way home. Wasn't that a kick, Luke playing the conservative one and Lexy playing thrill-seeker. The thrills weren't over. Not if she had control over things.

She'd be damned if she'd let an opportunity like this pass. A chance to let loose and discover her sexuality. But why Luke?

Because she trusted him. She knew he'd never hurt her, which was more than she could say about David.

They were halfway home when she started to freak out. What if he didn't find her attractive and didn't want her? Silly girl. His body had been perfectly clear about its intentions only minutes ago.

She glanced at the clock. Six thirty. They had hours before Lulu brought Riley home. Lexy suspected she'd only need one. One glorious hour of seduction and consummation.

Cripes. She didn't know the first thing about seducing a man. What should she do first? Perform a strip tease? Suck on a Popsicle?

Glancing at Luke, she wondered what he'd do if she threw herself into his arms. No, too pushy. She'd ask him in for coffee and dessert, then serve herself up in her black lace nightie, the one Lulu had given her when she'd turned thirty. They pulled into the driveway and she shoved the car into park.

"I've gotta go," Luke said.

He flung open the door before she could ask him in, before she could try out her seduction skills.

She got out of the car and grabbed the basket. "I could make us some coffee," she offered.

"Another time." He plopped the blanket on top of the basket as if there was no way he was following her inside.

"Do you need me tomorrow?" he said.

I need you right now.

"No, we're done but I thought if—"

"Great," he cut her off. "I've got things to do back home. I'll see you Monday night."

He walked to his car.

"But your clothes. They're inside."

"Bring them to the hotel."

He slammed the door and drove off, not looking back, not waving. Nothing. She ambled toward the front door, glancing over her shoulder.

Was she wrong? Was he just humoring her by kissing her at the airport? No, something had happened between them, and she was determined to get more of it. The question was, how hard would she have to fight to get it?

Chapter Seventeen

There must have been three hundred people crowding Chicago's Embassy Ballroom. During every miserable second of the dinner-dance and autograph session, Luke knew exactly where Lexy stood, sat and breathed.

At least he'd been able to keep his distance. Leaning against the bar, he admired her gorgeous figure from across the room. She was dressed in a form-fitting black number slit down the back to her waist. He lost count how many times he wanted to rush over and wrap his suit jacket around her shoulders to cover up her bare skin.

She glanced in his direction and his body tightened. Damn, he'd be glad when this night was over.

"Luke?"

He turned at the sound of Beth's voice. "Hey, how's it going?" He kissed her cheek. "I'm sorry I didn't get a chance to talk to you earlier.'

"You were busy being a superstar hero."

"Don't remind me." He glanced at Lexy, who stepped

onto the dance floor with some dignitary. He'd probably hand her a donation when they were done. No matter. Luke wanted the guy dead.

"What's the attraction?" Beth said.

"Nothing, sorry." He smiled at her.

"Can we talk for a minute?"

"Sure." With a hand to her elbow, he led Bubba's wife to a table in the corner.

"How are the kids?" he said.

"They're fine." She sat down and fingered the strap of her small black purse. "Had a little trouble with Newt. He won't stop fighting at school."

"You want me to talk to him?"

"Nah. It's handled."

"You can call me anytime and I'll be there ASAP."

"I know." She glanced into his eyes. "That's one of the reasons I'm here." She reached into her purse. "I needed to give you this."

She handed him a check for fifty thousand dollars.

"Je-sus, what's this? You win the lottery?"

"It's the money you've been sending me since Bubba died. I'm giving it back."

Air rushed from his lungs like he'd been punched by a four-hundred-pound grappler. "I don't understand."

"Listen, you needed to give it to me and I needed to take it. I'll admit it was nice to have just in case. But between the life insurance and my business taking off, we're managing quite well."

He stared at the check. "But it's for you, to take care of you and the kids."

"I'm grateful, really, but I can't keep it."

"It's the least I can do," he said.

"Stop talking like that. It's not your fault that he died.

Bubba made his own choices. He got caught up in the glamour and lost touch with reality."

"I could have prevented it."

"How, by hiding his supply of steroids? He would have found more. He wasn't listening to anyone in the end. Not even me."

"I thought I was helping you."

She took his hand and squeezed. "You did. You gave me the security I needed to take a chance and start my business. But it's time to stand on my own and it's time you let go."

"You . . . you don't want me coming by anymore?"

She leaned forward. "You're always welcome in my home, but I don't want you to feel obligated. You aren't responsible for my family."

The soft-spoken words drifted across the table, but didn't process in his brain. He'd always feel responsible for Bubba's death. And Kevin's.

"You're free, Luke." She slipped the check into his hand. "It's time to move on and stop trying to make up for sins that aren't yours."

The paper scraped his palm like sandpaper. This was his role in life—to atone for his mistakes, to make up for being bad.

She stood and placed a kiss on his cheek. "You're a good man."

He closed his eyes for the briefest second, trying to make sense of her words, maybe even believe them. When he opened his eyes, she was smiling down at him.

"Take care of yourself." She touched his cheek, then turned and wandered toward a group of wrestler's wives.

Fingering the check, he thought of the extra matches

he'd fought to support Beth, going months with only an occasional day off. A day off to sleep, soak in a hot tub, recover as much as he could.

A sense of loss overwhelmed him. And confusion. Although she said he could always visit, it would never be the same. They didn't need him like they used to. He couldn't ease the guilt by sending money to Bubba's family anymore. He should have seen it coming and stopped Bubba from killing himself. They said it was a heart attack. A drug-induced heart attack.

It's time to move on, Beth said. But to where?

He glanced at the crowd and spotted Lexy coming his way. He couldn't do this. Any of it. He couldn't smile and shake hands, sign autographs and act the perfect gentleman. He didn't feel like a gentleman right now. He stood as she approached.

It was nearly eleven. He'd done his part. Time to get the hell out of here.

"Hey, you okay?" she said with a smile. "You look a little pained."

"It's the suit."

"Poor baby," she teased. "Listen, Kathy Lechner, president of International Imports wants to meet you. I think she's ready to make a big donation."

"No more. Not tonight. I've gotta go."

"Hey, it's not over," she said.

"It is for me." He walked away.

"Luke, wait," she called after him.

He was having none of it. Lexy watched him storm out of the ballroom. She had realized seeing him would be uncomfortable after the kiss this weekend, but she hadn't thought he'd completely avoid her. They hadn't spoken more than ten words to each other all night.

Personal issues aside, he'd been doing quite well up to

now. He'd actually looked like he wanted to be here, acting the gracious hero. He even made people laugh.

Then it was like someone had flipped a switch. Or was it because Lexy had cornered him one-on-one? All night they'd been surrounded by people. But now, when alone together, Luke shut down, shut her out, and ran like hell.

Her gaze drifted to the blonde woman who'd been sitting with him. They'd shared an intimate discussion, the woman whispering into his ear, then slipping something into his hand. Her room key, perhaps?

No, definitely not. It was the mother from the hotel last week, the one without a husband. Luke had explained his role of fill-in father for her children.

What kind of business was this that caused fathers to abandon their children? It didn't matter. Lexy would be done with all of it in a few months.

She automatically smiled as the president of Blackwell International, Inc., approached. Speaking to the man, she said the right things and laughed when he told a joke. In truth her mind was someplace else, thinking about the end of her assignment and the end of her time with Luke.

A sick feeling rolled through her stomach. Had he left because of another headache? She suspected it had nagged him Saturday night. What if he went upstairs to down a bottle of Ibuprofen? Or something stronger?

Suddenly she wanted to get to him more than she wanted to shake another hand. She headed for the door, startled when a light hand touched her arm.

"Hi, I'm a friend of Luke's, Beth Powers." The woman extended her hand.

"Alexandra Hayes." She recognized the mother who'd been sitting with Luke earlier. An innocent kind of beauty sparkled in her eyes.

"You're going up to check on him, aren't you?"

Lexy nodded.

"Be good to him. He's had it rough."

"No, you don't understand. We're just business associates," Lexy said.

"No, you're not." The corner of Beth's mouth curled.

Lexy cleared her throat and glanced at the floor.

"He watched you all night," Beth said. "It made me feel like maybe there's hope."

"I don't know about that," Lexy half-joked.

Beth searched Lexy's eyes. "But you have to know. You have to believe in him. It will make all the difference. It will help him believe in himself."

"You sound like you know him pretty well."

"He was a very good friend of my husband's."

"Was?"

"Bubba died."

"I'm sorry." Lexy shuddered. "I didn't know."

"It's okay." She hesitated, as if trying to decide how much to say. "My husband had a heart attack. He was thirty-five."

"Oh." So young. So very young.

"Luke's been visiting ever since, playing with the kids, bringing them gifts," Beth said. "It's hard for him to be around kids."

"I know."

"Did you know he supported his sister and her baby?"

"No, I didn't."

"There's a lot no one knows about Luke."

Yeah, like what a truly good man he is. They made eye contact and a knowing passed between them.

"He's been sending me money ever since Bubba died," Beth said. "He's generous like that. But my life's on track these days. I gave the money back tonight and he seemed upset. I thought you should know."

"Thanks."

"Take care of him, okay?"

The plea touched her heart. With one last smile, Beth squeezed Lexy's hand and walked away.

Taking a deep breath, Lexy counted to ten, trying to get hold of her thoughts, her emotions and her fear. Not only fear for Luke's emotional state, but fear of something else, something she couldn't quite put her finger on.

Like a woman on a mission, she headed for the elevator, digesting Beth's tale. Luke had come to the rescue, offered his time, money and compassion to help Beth adjust to being a single parent. The man was generous beyond measure, thoughtful and caring.

Yet he didn't see it that way. He still thought of himself as . . . what? She wasn't sure. In her eyes he was a good and honorable man, and she cared so much about him. She hesitated as she approached the elevator.

She cared about him. A lot.

It didn't feel wrong or risky. Not by a long shot.

As she stepped into the elevator and punched the seventh floor, Beth's words haunted her. *He seemed upset, maybe a little lost.*

Looking back, he'd seemed lost ever since Lexy had challenged him to act the hero. It was as if two separate personalities thrashed about, wanting control of the same man. Only, which one was real?

She knew who Luke was. No matter how hard he tried to hide behind bravado, he was that sweet kid from next door. The kid who took the fall for her, and held her son during a thunderstorm.

Luke was good people, honest and generous. None of that had changed. Somewhere, deep down, he knew it as well, and it scared the hell out of him.

He didn't have to be scared. She'd tell him so and give him a safe place to explore his feelings without conditions or judgment.

The elevator doors opened and she started for his room. He'd done so much for her. Now it was her turn.

She knocked on his door. "It's Lexy. Open up!"

"Go away."

She knocked again, waited. Then pounded with her fist.

The door swung open. "What do you want?"

He loomed in the doorway, his formal shirt unbuttoned to reveal his solid torso dusted with soft chest hair. She swallowed hard.

"Well?" he said.

"We need to talk."

"I'm busy."

A round-faced blonde peeked around him and waved. "Hi," she giggled.

"Come on, I was having fun!" another female called from inside the room.

That's two. Lexy ground her teeth and pushed past Luke and bimbo Number One.

"Why don't you introduce me to your friends," she said, trying to act casual, feeling anything but. The twenty-ish brunette on the bed wore tight jeans and a leather halter exposing way too much breast. Where did he find these girls, in a biker bar?

"Get out of here, Lexy," he said, his foot still propping the door open.

"Yeah, get out of here, Lexy," the blonde mimicked.

He visibly cringed.

"It looks like I'm missing all the fun," Lexy said.

"You're not invited. Four's a crowd." The blonde sidestepped Luke and marched up to Lexy.

The door slammed. Luke took the blonde by the arm and nodded in Lexy's direction. "Forget she's here."

"Oooo, kinky," the brunette cooed. "Where were we?"

The blonde stuck up her nose at Lexy and shoved Luke to the bed. "It was my turn."

Her turn? Good God, what had Lexy walked into? She crossed her arms over her chest and leaned against the dresser, trying to look unaffected, maybe even bored.

"Let's play strip the pro wrestler," the blonde said.

Luke pushed himself up on his elbows in apparent protest. Maybe there was hope. "I know, Loverboy," the blonde said. "As long as I don't touch you."

Lexy's breath caught. Undress him, play to his ego, but don't touch him. Anything but that.

"This could be very erotic." The blonde grinned over her shoulder at her friend.

"Me next, me next." The brunette clapped her hands like a kid about to get a present on Christmas Day.

As the blonde straddled him, Lexy fought to keep her temper in check. He didn't want this, she knew he didn't. He'd brought these women up here to reinforce in his own mind his heel persona.

The blonde fiddled with his zipper and Lexy stepped into his line of vision. "I met Beth tonight. Nice lady."

He turned away.

"She must be your biggest fan," Lexy said.

"No, I'm the biggest," the blonde said, shaking her scantily clad breasts in Luke's face.

He closed his eyes and clenched his jaw.

"She had such wonderful things to say about you, how you spent time with the kids, gave her money—"

"That's enough." He sat up and set the blonde aside, rising from the bed. "What do you want from me, Lexy?" He towered over her. "I've pretended to be a hero. Now it's my turn to have some fun."

"Right!" The brunette jumped to her feet and threw her arms around his neck.

Sliding his hands around her backside, he cupped her bottom and rocked his hips forward. "Take a good look, Lexy. This is what I'll always be, no matter how much you try to make me into a hero."

With the young woman in his arms, he rotated his hips in a suggestive motion.

Lexy stared into his eyes. "I must have been thinking of someone else who protected me when I was a kid and saved my little brother when he tried to parachute out of Deadman's Oak."

The motion slowed and he narrowed his eyes. She was getting to him.

"Silly me," she continued. "It couldn't have been you who comforted my frightened son during the storm and helped tend his bloody nose."

He snapped his attention to the woman in his arms as if willing himself to ignore Lexy.

"It must have been someone else who stepped in as a father figure for Bubba's kids; someone else who took care of your sister and her baby."

"Enough!"

Breathing through clenched teeth, he reminded her of a fire-spitting dragon. She wasn't scared of a little fire. Not from this man.

The girls' eyes grew wide as they watched and waited.

"Damn it, everyone out," he ordered.

"Even me?" the blonde said with a pout.

"Everyone." Fire sparked in his eyes.

The women grabbed their belongings and ambled toward the door. He motioned for Lexy to join them.

"We're not done," she said.

"The hell we're not." He grasped her elbow and urged her out as well. "The party's over." He slammed the door.

Lexy stared into the peephole.

"Gee, thanks," the brunette said.

Lexy shrugged. "He's a lot of talk and no action. But Floyd and Marco, now there are two party animals. I just saw them downstairs signing autographs."

The blonde's eyes lit up. "Marco's yummy!"

"Let's go," the brunette said.

"Aren't you coming?" the blonde called to Lexy.

"In a minute. I left something inside the room."

The girls giggled and disappeared into the elevator. Lexy tapped at the hotel room door. "Luke?"

No answer.

"I'm not leaving."

Tap. Tap. Tap.

"Luke, come on. Open the door."

Nothing.

With her back pressed against the door, she slid to the floor, legs stretched out on the industrial carpet.

"You know what I can't figure out?" she shouted over her shoulder. "How we ended up like this." She opened her purse and searched for something to gnaw on. "It all seemed so simple in elementary school."

She unwrapped a sour ball, a gift from Riley in case she got a nervous throat.

"But life's not simple, is it? I mean, who would have thought I'd grow up to marry a complete jerk and you'd grow up and get a job beating on guys for a living?"

The door was flung open and she fell flat on her back.

He looked like a giant from this vantage point. Straining over her, he peered down the hall toward the elevators.

"It's safe. They're gone," she said.

His expression softened with relief. "Please go."

"No." She got to her feet, not an easy accomplishment considering her floor-length dress and heels. Standing her full five foot four, she stared up into his eyes. "Let me help you this time."

"I don't need help."

"Luke, pretending really doesn't make it go away."

He threw up his hands in exasperation and stepped into the room. "Whatever that means."

She followed him and shut the door. Yes! She was in.

"It means that you don't fool me or Beth. You're a nice guy. Stop pretending you're a jerk."

He raked his hand through long waves of blond hair. "What's with you? You just found me with two women I was planning to . . . to . . ."

"What?"

"Does it matter? I kissed you twice last weekend and tonight you find me with two groupies in my hotel room. Get a clue. See me for what I am."

"Only if you'll see yourself for the hero you are."

"Oh, for Pete's sake." He sat on the edge of the bed.

She knelt in front of him and took his hand in hers. He stared over her shoulder at the muted television.

"Look at me," she said.

With a clenched jaw he dragged his gaze to meet her eyes.

"It's okay to be a good guy." She brought his hand to her lips, not breaking eye contact.

"I'm not good," he said in a voice lower than she'd ever heard before.

"Says who?"

He shot to his feet, ripping his hand from her grasp. "Everybody who knows me. The Colonel, the women I've bedded, Bubba." He paced to the window.

"What does Bubba have to do with this?"

He turned. "I'm responsible for his death."

"Bull. He died of a heart attack."

"Caused by abusing growth hormones. I introduced him to the stuff. I wised up and quit, but not Bubba. He was hooked and it killed him."

"If you hadn't gotten him the drugs, someone else would have. He was a big boy, Luke. He knew what he was doing."

"The Colonel knew how bad I was. Why do you think he kicked me out of the house?"

"My guess is he was hurting."

"Thanks to me."

"No, thanks to fate. Fate took away his oldest son. Your dad couldn't stand the thought of losing another."

"You don't know what you're talking about. You weren't there."

"I'm a parent. I know how I'd feel."

"Damn it, Lexy, what about the women I slept with in my early twenties? Do you think they considered me good?"

"That depends on how well you performed in bed."

"This isn't funny."

"Look, you've done some stupid things in your life. Who hasn't? But what about the other stuff? You took care of me as a kid and I'm guessing you tried to fill some big shoes when Kevin died. You helped your sister and you've been taking care of Bubba's family. That's

261

good stuff, Luke. You're a quality man. Why can't you accept that?"

The bewildered look in his eyes took her breath away. "Because . . . I won't know who I am anymore."

Chapter Eighteen

Damn. His biggest fear, and he'd just confessed it to Lexy. She'd surely leave now, race out of here and find a normal, well-balanced man who knew who the hell he was and what he wanted to do with his life. Luke collapsed on the bed, all fight drained from his body.

She sat next to him and stroked his back. He wished she wouldn't touch him, make him believe in an emotional healing he knew didn't exist.

"I'm so sorry," she whispered.

He glanced into her eyes and couldn't stand what he saw there. "Oh, no, don't you feel sorry for me. I don't want your pity. You, of all people."

"It's not pity. But I do feel sorry," she said, running her fingers lightly across his hairline.

God, how he loved the feeling. He closed his eyes.

"I'm sorry you lost your big brother when you were only twelve," she whispered. "I'm sorry you got into a car with an irresponsible friend. I'm sorry you were chased away from your family."

She touched his cheek, feathery-light fingertips grazing his jaw. "I'm sorry you've seen such ugliness and so little beauty and you've had to deal with it all alone."

"You get used to it."

"You shouldn't have to." She leaned forward. "I'm here."

He wasn't prepared for the gentle kiss, tempting him to take her in his arms. She wanted him. He could taste it on her lips. She trailed her fingertips across his chest and his skin burned, aching for more.

A moan vibrated from deep in his throat, a sound so unlike anything he'd uttered before. He gripped her shoulders and laid her against the feather comforter, pinning her beneath him. She tasted of honey and spice.

And desire. Arching her back, she squeezed her arms around his neck, as if anchoring herself to his body. The faint tremble of her lips humbled him, telling him just how much she wanted this.

With each kiss he explored a new spot on her neck, her cheek and her lips. He couldn't get enough of this woman and it wasn't because she was convenient or uncomplicated. He wanted her because she was Lexy.

The thought paralyzed him. Sure, he'd had plenty of women in his years as a superstar, but he'd never wanted one like this.

He'd never loved one like this.

His chest tightened. There was no way of getting around it. He'd fallen in love with Lexy. Again.

"Luke?"

He glanced into her questioning eyes. Only then did he realize he'd pulled away.

"What is it?" she said, stroking his lower lip with the pad of her thumb.

"We shouldn't be doing this." He rolled onto his back.

Propping herself on one elbow, she leaned over him. "What's wrong? Is it . . . me?"

Sitting up, he took her by the shoulders. "God, no, you're beautiful. More than beautiful."

She sighed. "Good. I've been told I have a problem with . . ." She looked into his eyes and his heart ached. "Men, you know, sex."

"Whoever told you that is an idiot."

"Then why did you stop?"

"I . . ." he started. What could he say? That he was afraid he'd screw this up too?

"I don't know if this makes a difference . . ." She touched his cheek. "But I've fallen in love with you."

It made all the difference in the world—it made it impossible for him to do this.

"Please, talk to me," she said. "Is it that you're experienced and I've only been with one man?"

This was getting worse by the minute. "That's not it."

"What then?"

"I don't know how to do this," he blurted out.

"Have sex?"

"Make love. I've had sex. But this is *different*." He studied his hands, trembling in his lap. He was falling deeper and deeper.

Lexy eyed Luke and realized he was humbling himself to her. Her heart ached. She loved this man. She wanted to touch him and kiss him—everywhere. How much simpler could it be?

"Trust me," she said. Casting her own fear aside, she urged him back to the bed. She ran her hands across his chest, then kissed him there, over his heart. His moan vibrated against her skin and she smiled to herself. This was so right, so easy. So natural.

With a passion she hadn't thought she possessed, Lexy nuzzled kisses across his chest while inching her hand lower, brushing the outside of his pants. She stroked and squeezed, ever so gently. The bulge grew beneath her fingers.

He wanted her.

She couldn't remember being wanted like this, especially not by a man she loved. She didn't have to think about what to do or how to do it. With gentle determination, she unzipped his pants and slid them down, off his body, then feathered kisses up his thighs.

"Lexy." Her name was a plea, a cry for completeness.

She climbed on top of him, and his need pressed against the soft spot between her legs.

"Unzip my dress," she demanded, moving forward then back. Wetness pooled between her legs.

His fingers slid the metal across the teeth and a rush of cool air blanketed her back. In a slow, sexy motion, she slipped the dress over her head, letting it fall to the floor. She noticed his eyes were closed.

"Open your eyes," she said.

He did and swallowed hard.

"It's me," she said. "And it's okay."

As if he wasn't sure, he broke eye contact and glanced at her breasts.

"You like what you see?" she asked.

He throbbed with appreciation.

"Then touch me," she demanded.

His cool fingers brushed the tips of her nipples. She gasped for breath and leaned forward. He laved her right breast and she nearly came apart. Amazing sensations shot across her nerve endings.

"You need to be naked," she breathed, her mind a blur. She slipped his boxers off his hips and ran her palm across his hardened need.

"God, Lexy," he rasped.

He returned the favor by easing his fingers between her panties and skin, trailing the silk gently down off her behind. He ran his hand up her inner thigh until it touched her feminine mound. A gasp escaped her throat.

He froze. "Did I hurt you?"

"No," she breathed. "Touch me."

She rocked forward into his hand and his fingers made a kind of magic that shot stars across the backs of her eyelids. More, she wanted more.

"I want to feel you," she said. "Inside me . . ."

His manhood responded, teasing her opening, driving her insane.

"Wait." He reached over and grabbed a condom from his duffel bag. She slipped it on him and repositioned herself to feel him against her.

"Now," she demanded, rocking her hips forward and opening fully.

He entered with slow, deliberate precision. A little more . . . more. Her body ached for completeness. She braced her hands against his shoulders and sat up to look at this incredible man. His eyes were shut, his face turned as if ashamed by their lovemaking. She wouldn't let him feel guilty about this, as he had with other women. This was beautiful, amazing and right.

"Look at me," she said, struggling for breath.

He blinked slowly and opened his eyes.

"Make *love* to *me*." She thrust again. His jaw clenched as if trying to retain control.

"Love . . ." she croaked.

She rocked forward again. A ball of emotion rose in

her throat, strangling her vocal cords. She squeezed his pecs and thrust forward, driving him deeper into her.

This was right. This was love.

"God, Lexy!" he cried as he brought them both to completion with one last thrust.

She collapsed against him, the aftershock vibrating against her chest and across her body.

Burying her face in his neck, she felt a tear trickle down her cheek. Such wonder. Such magic. Shared with an incredibly complicated, yet good man.

This was the way it was supposed to be. The way it should have been with her ex. But it had never been like this. Not even close.

Because Luke was the man she loved.

She snuggled against him and he held her close, one hand cupping her behind, the other flung across her back. She wanted to stay right here, skin to skin, heart to heart, never breaking physical contact.

His breathing slowed and his heartbeat pounded a steady rhythm against her. He needed her. He needed someone to take care of him, protect him and love him.

She'd do all those things, and more. She wouldn't let anything hurt him ever again.

Warmth. Incredible warmth.

Luke wasn't cold anymore, wasn't alone. A warm, wonderful woman had sprawled across him, possessing him in every way possible.

Lexy.

Slowly opening his eyes, he still couldn't believe she lay next to him. Hell, he couldn't believe any of what had happened last night. Did he dream it?

No. It really happened. Every stroke, every joining.

How many times had they made love? Three? Four? The woman was incredible.

It wasn't until four this morning that he'd been able to coax her under the covers. That wasn't easy with Lexy clinging to him, her arms locked behind his neck as if he was her salvation.

In reality, she was his.

Stroking her hair, he relived their night together, the touches and whispers. The incredible surrender. What came afterward had been even more powerful: being held all night by someone who loved him.

She loved him. Fear pricked the back of his neck. Love was a tricky, if not terrifying, proposition. It had let him down way too many times.

Glancing at the beauty snuggled against his chest, he hoped she didn't freak when she woke up. Would she regret their lovemaking? He didn't know if he could stand that.

She stirred against him and he stroked her back to urge her back to sleep. A few more minutes, just a few more minutes. He didn't want the magic to end.

In his mind, he analyzed the possibilities for a future together. As a hero he could take fewer risks and be given lighter matches. He'd have to scale back a bit to be more available for Lexy and her son.

Lexy and her son. He took a deep breath. Was it possible? Could they really be a family?

It hit him like a metal garbage can to the head: not if he wrestled. It wasn't healthy for a family to be without a father. Oscar was proof of that. Luke suspected the wrestler's family was falling apart, but he didn't want to talk about it. Who would? Failing as a father had to be the worst failure of all.

The Colonel's image popped into his mind. Failing as a father. That must have been how he'd felt when the police brought Luke home. One son killed by a drunk driver, the other picked up on a joyride with his drunk buddies.

Fate took away his oldest son. Your dad couldn't stand the thought of losing another.

Was that true? Was fear behind his father's bitter words on that cold winter night? Words that were not easily taken back, especially after each year passed.

"What are you thinking about?" Lexy said, her voice hoarse with sleep.

"Life."

"Don't think. Sleep." She nuzzled against his chest.

"Lexy?"

"Mmmmm?"

"What happens now?" He stroked her back.

"Now . . ." She leaned close and smiled, "I kiss you!" She planted kisses on his cheek, his neck, and his chest.

"Come on." He patted her behind. "I'm serious."

"So am I," she mumbled against his skin, her hand trailing lower and lower.

"Stop," he half-laughed. He grabbed her hand and placed it on his chest over his heart. "We've got to talk."

She moaned in frustration, giving his chest one last nip. She propped herself up on her elbow. "Fine, what do you want to talk about?"

"What happened last night."

She blushed and bit her lower lip.

"You're not sorry, are you?" he asked.

"You're kidding, right?"

He shook his head.

"Oh, sweetheart—" She touched his cheek. "Last

night was incredible. I love you so much. Don't ever forget that."

He brushed a copper brown strand of hair off her cheek. She loved him. Everything was going to be okay.

"It's still . . . hard to believe."

"Believe it, Mr. Loverboy."

He shot her a death glare.

"Sorry." She smiled. "Listen, we were meant to be together. I guess I knew it somewhere deep down all the time. You were always there for me, loving me as a little girl, and now as a woman. Nothing can change that."

"I have nothing to offer you. Hell, I don't even know who I am anymore."

"You're a smart and generous man. And you're mine."

She kissed him, long and sweet, and her words penetrated his fear. They belonged in each other's arms.

She broke the kiss and pressed her cheek to his chest. "The rest will work itself out. I promise."

"I'll hold you to that."

"Mmmm."

"Hey, don't fall asleep on me. I don't know about you, but I've got to get home."

"What time is it?"

He glanced at the clock. "Almost eleven."

"No way! I've got a one thirty plane." She jumped out of bed, racing around the room, picking up her clothes. He propped himself against the headboard and enjoyed the show, her hips wiggling and breasts jiggling.

"What are you smiling at?" she said, stepping into her panties.

"Nothing," he chuckled.

"Then get over here and help me into this dress."

271

He tossed the sheets aside and swung his feet to the floor. He'd moved too fast. He gripped his throbbing head. It would be okay in a minute. He took a deep breath. The bed shifted and her warm hand touched his shoulder.

"Remember your promise."

"I know, I know. I'll see a doctor." He forced a smile and stood. "I'm okay. How about that dress?"

She stood and turned her back to him. His legs wobbled and he struggled against the pain. Everywhere. His body just hurt all over. Like usual.

He focused on her zipper, cursing his shaky fingers. "Pretty tricky stuff," he said, finally getting it zipped.

She turned around and cocked her head to one side. "You sure you're okay?"

"Fine. Go catch your plane. I'll call you tonight."

"Okay," she said, but she didn't move. Instead, she stood on tiptoe and kissed him.

Suspended in time. That's how he felt whenever she kissed him. She grabbed her purse and headed for the door. His legs gave way and he sat on the bed. She turned just before she reached the door.

"I'm okay," he said. "You just wore me out."

She raised an eyebrow, her gaze traveling his body from his eyes down to his private parts.

"You're giving me a hard-on," he said.

She smiled, blew him a kiss and flew out the door.

Luke fell back onto the bed. God was being awfully good to him these days.

He fantasized about many more days wrapped in Lexy's arms. Okay, so it was a complicated relationship. But they'd make it work.

They had to.

Chapter Nineteen

The next morning Lexy got up early, made her family breakfast and was on the road by eight for a meeting at BAM. She didn't have to explain her good mood to Lulu and Riley. They'd figured it out: She was in love.

Riding the elevator to the sixth floor, she wondered if she'd see Luke today. She hoped so. She wanted to see him every day of her life.

"You're in trouble," she whispered to herself.

The elevator doors opened. Cosmo was waiting.

"We gotta talk about Luke." Worry creased his brow.

"What's wrong?" Her heart plummeted to her feet. Had he collapsed in the shower? She knew his headaches were worse than he let on. Damn, she wanted him out of this business. She wanted him safe.

"What is it?" she said as Cosmo led her down the hall.

"My biggest backer is pulling out unless the guys start touring this week."

She panicked. "This was supposed to be a slow conversion."

Cosmo led her into the conference room. Cosmo's brother sat at the head of the table.

"Mr. Perini," she said.

"Huh?" Cosmo said.

"As I was saying," the brother started. "The new heroes need to start touring day after tomorrow. Especially Loverboy Luke."

"I've got a schedule right here." Cosmo pulled a sheet of paper from his jacket. "Even got a few double headers."

"Two matches in one day?" Her legs weakened and she grabbed hold of a chair. Luke would never make it.

"We could do some hard-core matches," Cosmo continued. "Nothing like a hero going up against an opponent who prefers hacksaws to body slams."

The room closed in. She struggled to breathe. The thought of Luke in a ring with a hacksaw-wielding maniac set her nerves reeling. She couldn't let this happen. She couldn't lose him to this crazy business.

"We'll start Luke in a cage match day after tomorrow, followed by a ladder match or two," Cosmo said.

If you love him, protect him.

"He can't," she said.

Both men looked at her.

"Why do you say that?" the brother asked.

She sat across from him and leaned forward. "The fans aren't stupid. We've got a lifetime of womanizing to counteract."

"But he's learning to be more discreet," Cosmo said. "He's not shoving it in people's faces. He's doing it in private."

No kidding. A flush started at the base of her neck.

"He's not ready," she said, remembering his childlike voice begging for more pain pills.

"That's disappointing," Cosmo's brother said.

Cosmo stood. "The fans care about what we tell them to care about. He's in and that's that. We'll start him in a cage match, with Wolfman, Brutus and Gargoyle."

Luke wouldn't last five minutes in a cage. She stood, desperate. She had to stop this. And she knew how.

"He'll never be a believable hero!"

Cosmo swallowed hard. His brother narrowed his eyes. Had she spoken too forcefully to her clients?

Cosmo motioned to someone behind her. "Luke, come in."

The wind was knocked from her lungs. She closed her eyes.

No God, please, say he didn't hear me.

"What the hell are you doing here?" Luke said.

She turned, but he wasn't looking at her. His eyes burned a path straight to Cosmo's brother.

In four steps he was across the room, brushing by Lexy as if she were invisible. Cosmo's brother stood.

"You two know each other?" Cosmo asked.

"Why wouldn't they? He's your brother," Lexy said.

"I don't know where you got that idea," Cosmo said. "This man's been BAM's silent backer for months."

Silence permeated the room. Every exposed muscle in Luke's body was stretched taught, his hands clenched by his sides.

"What's going on?" She touched his arm and he jerked away.

"Don't play me for a fool, Lexy," he said. "He's been behind this all along, hasn't he?"

"He, who?"

"God, you're so believable," he said.

Nobody moved. Nobody breathed.

"So, you're the one who dreamed up this hero thing," Luke said to the mystery man.

"I've invested in this company. I'd like to see it show a profit."

"Why *this* company?" Luke said.

The mystery man didn't utter a word.

"To destroy me," Luke said.

"You *would* see it that way."

"Wait, nothing's been destroyed," she cut in, reaching for Luke's arm, but not quite touching him.

"Naive little girl." Luke's voice sliced open her heart.

"Excuse me?" she said.

"Like I wouldn't have found out you were working for him?"

"I work for Cosmo."

"You really must think I'm gullible. Sorry, kid, but our tumble last night didn't blow my mind completely. I see what's in front of me. I know the score."

"Then tell me."

He broke eye contact with the mystery man and stared her down, the anger in his eyes burning straight to her heart. "You guys want me out, so you dreamed up this heel-turned-hero thing to confuse the fans and sabotage my popularity. Fine. I can take a hint. I'm out. I get Cosmo's reasoning, he suspected my injuries were worse than I let on and I'd end up costing him in the end. And this sonofabitch"— he motioned toward the mystery man—"I even understand *his* motivation. But you? What was your payoff in all this? To prove you could have a man like me? Call the shots for a change? Or was it all about money?"

This wasn't happening. Her chest ached, the pain burning her eyes. "Luke, you don't think—"

"I think you'd better find another job, because this

one's over. Unless you want to hang around and ruin Floyd or Oscar's lives. I'd better warn you, Oscar is happily married, so don't expect a repeat of our little adventure last night."

The air rushed from her lungs. "How dare you!"

"Me?" His full belly laugh shot goose bumps across her shoulders. "You are too good. You come in here, ruin my career and unearth my secrets, all for a buck."

"This isn't about money and you know it."

"No? Then what is it about?" He aimed his question at the mystery man.

"I did what I thought was right," the man said.

"Don't we all." Luke walked toward the door.

"Luke," she said.

"Tim," the mystery man called.

Her breath caught.

Luke glanced at Cosmo. "Killian Steel will make me an offer. I'm out of here."

Luke stared deep into Lexy's eyes. "Congratulations, kid. You really had me believing in myself for a second there."

She started towards him.

"Don't." He put out his hand. "Just stay away from me."

Her heart split into pieces.

He ripped his gaze from hers and glared over her shoulder at the mystery man. "Congratulations, Colonel. You got your revenge."

Chapter Twenty

Luke threw five more punches at the bag, the contact resonating in his head.

"I've got you on the card against Vile Kyle on Friday," Killian Steel said, checking his clipboard. "Kyle's into barbed wire these days. Think you can handle it?"

"I'll handle it." Luke threw a few punches.

"Man of many words, aren't you?"

He paused, and placed his gloved hands on the bag. "Did you hire me to fight or talk?"

Something flared in Steel's dark eyes. "Cincinnati, Friday."

Luke resumed his annihilation of the bag. The damn thing would be whacked to pieces by the time he got through with it. Bring up the anger, surround your soul, deaden your heart.

Punch. Punch.

Forget about her. She was a mistake, a bad judgment call.

But he still loved her.

Punch. Punch. Punch. He ground his teeth and threw so many punches he thought he'd pass out. He'd welcome unconsciousness over the dull ache in his chest.

Damn, he didn't see it coming. He didn't see any of it. The Colonel . . . Cosmo . . . Lexy.

Her betrayal stung the worst.

"I suppose you see my face on that thing."

Luke froze at the sound of the Colonel's voice. The old man loomed in the doorway.

"Take your best shot," he said. "I deserve it."

A surge of emotions tied Luke's gut into a knot.

"Can we talk?" the Colonel asked.

"Nothing to say." He could barely speak past the anger clogging his throat.

"I have a lot to say."

"What if I don't want to hear it?"

"Let me do this one last thing. Then I'll leave you alone."

Grabbing a towel, Luke ambled to a nearby bench.

The Colonel followed. "I blew it."

Luke sat down, gripping the towel between his hands. He studied the Colonel's eyes, still blue as the sky.

"My worst mistake was loving too much," he said.

"Right. Kevin." He really didn't want to hear this.

"Not Kevin. You."

Luke clenched the towel.

"This started as a way to bring you back into the family, for your mom. I was kidding myself. *I* wanted you back. I was just too damned proud to say so."

He shoved his hands in his gray trouser pockets and glanced at the floor. "I couldn't walk back into your life after all these years and demand you quit wrestling.

God, how I wanted to. I know about your injuries. The thought of your being a cripple at forty . . ." his voice trailed off.

The room started to spin. The Colonel cared? His father . . . loved him?

"I picked up the phone a thousand times, but never got past the dialing part," his father said. "You hated me. I couldn't blame you. I was horrible that night."

"You disowned me."

"Words, Tim. Words uttered by a terrified father who'd lost one son and was about to lose another."

"I wasn't drinking."

"I was losing you just the same. I kept pushing you away, figuring if I didn't love you too much, I wouldn't die inside if anything happened to you. It's how I dealt with things."

"You were the one who set me up in the ring."

"No, that wasn't the plan. Wolfman had his own agenda. I'm sorry about that. God, I'm so sorry," he said.

Luke hardened his heart. "You sabotaged my career."

"I didn't want to see you hurting. I thought as a hero you wouldn't take so many risks."

"You can't just go around messing with people's lives like that, Dad. It's not right."

His father's eyes misted over. "You called me *Dad*."

"I can't do this." He started for the door.

"Wait," his father pleaded. "Be mad. That's good, be mad at me. But don't take it out on the rest of the family. Come visit sometime, the barbecue, maybe. I don't have to be there."

"I'll think about it."

"And Tim, I don't suppose I could do anything to stop you from getting into the ring?"

Luke took another two steps away from the old man. "Son?"

The sound of this one word spoken from his father's lips snapped something in Luke's chest.

"Alexandra knew nothing about my involvement. I was hoping she'd bring you around somehow. You always admired her."

"That was a lifetime ago," Luke said. "Good-bye, Colonel."

He stormed out of the room, enraged that after all these years the old man thought he could walk back into his life, screw around with it, apologize and everything would be okay.

Everything was definitely not okay.

Luke headed for his car. But he didn't want to go home, wherever that was. He hardly knew anymore.

Sure he did. Lexy's place was home.

"Damn!" He tossed his bag into the passenger seat and slid behind the wheel.

The woman might have been duped into ruining his wrestling persona, but she'd known exactly what she was saying when she'd claimed Luke would never be a "believable hero."

Of course not. After spending days and nights with him, she'd seen all his non-heroic traits.

Yet when they'd held each other she'd said just the opposite.

"Forget it."

Pulling out of the lot, he knew he couldn't go to the condo. Lexy had called a dozen times over the past twenty-four hours. He couldn't stand listening to her messages, messages that started with a plea and ended with a demand. "We're going to talk, even if I have to drive up there and bang down your door."

Another reason not to go home. He couldn't talk to her. Not now, not next week. Maybe not ever.

The thought squeezed his heart. Never talk to her, see her eyes light up, hold her in his arms. Never play with her son, take them out for a dinner and spend the evening in front of the television eating popcorn, laughing.

Lexy and her son. The family he'd never have.

Nothing would stop her. Not the weather, not her better judgment, not even her fear of confrontation. Lexy waited in the Cincinnati locker room, preparing to catch Luke before he stepped into the ring for his first Steel's Outrageous Wrestling match. Good thing she'd found an OW wrestler to help her with the plan. Red seemed to be a good man, if more than a little scary to look at.

She and Luke would talk face-to-face, before he put himself at risk again. With a little luck, maybe she'd get through his thick skull and convince him he didn't have to do this anymore. It was okay to be Timothy Silverspoon. A hero to so many people.

The door was flung open and she held her breath. It was only Red, her accomplice.

· "He just pulled into the lot," Red said. "You might want to hide around the corner until he comes in. I'll hold the door shut so you can talk."

"Thanks," she said, rubbing her hands together.

"Don't forget our deal."

"I haven't." Red wanted an interview with Cosmo, a small request, considering what he was about to do for her.

"Go on, get behind there."

She stepped around the corner by the sinks and clasped her fingers together.

Don't you give up. That boy needs you something bad.
Lulu's words energized her.

Truthful words resonating deep in her heart.

"He needs me," she whispered, clasping her fingers tighter. And he'd been there for her so many times.

She heard the door open.

"Hey, Loverboy," Red said.

Luke's grunt echoed off the cement walls.

The door crashed shut and Lexy took her cue. She stepped into the room.

"Hi, Luke."

He spun around. "What are you doing here?"

"I told you. We have to talk."

Flinging his bag over his shoulder, he headed for the door. He gave it a push, but it wouldn't budge.

"You're not leaving until we talk," she said.

Luke shouldered the door. It didn't budge.

"Coward," Lexy said.

His bag dropped with a thud and he turned in what seemed like slow motion. He charged her, slamming his hands to the wall beside her head. But he didn't touch her.

"And what makes me a coward?"

"Your fear."

"Of what?"

"Of yourself."

"Oh, that's perfect." He took a step back and planted his hands on his hips. "Spoken by the expert on the great heel Loverboy Luke."

"Nope. I'm the expert on Timothy Lucas Silverspoon, the hero."

"Then you're an expert of nothing. You said so yourself. I'm no hero."

284

"Don't you know why I said that?"

He stared her down.

"Because I love you," she said.

"I'm not listening to this."

Shielding her heart, she drove on. "And you love me."

"I'm leaving now."

"I said you'd never make a believable hero because I couldn't let them send you into the ring. You never would have survived. Luke, I know you're in physical pain most of the time, but you're so damned scared of trying something else you'd risk your life to stay safe in wrestling."

"You call this line of work safe?"

"Isn't it? You hide behind the persona of a heartless ladies' man who lures women into your bed."

"I lured you, didn't I?"

"Nope."

He stepped closer and fingered her hair. The touch sent shivers down her spine and her eyelids grew heavy.

"What do you call this?" he said.

"Love."

"No." He stepped back. "Loverboy Luke doesn't know true love. He knows desire and lust and—" he pressed his body against hers. "Need."

He gripped her shoulders, threatening to force a kiss. Something flickered in his eyes and he froze.

She wrapped her arms around his neck and kissed him hard, moaning her pleasure at tasting him again. Her hips rocked forward, her nipples hardened.

He broke the kiss, breathing heavy against her. "Don't. This can't happen."

He let go and she nearly pooled to the floor. "We can't stop this from happening. It was meant to be. It's love."

"Then I want no part of it." He stepped away from her. "My own father ruins my career in the name of love and you're right there with him. You're nuts if you think I'm buying that love crap."

"I know you called your mother every other Sunday for the past fifteen years," Lexy said. "Did she know about your injuries, your steroid abuse, your friends who died?"

"Hell, no."

"Did you tell your sister how many matches you fought to support her and her baby?"

"It was none of her business."

"What about Beth? Did she know you fought three hundred and forty days one year to support her family? That you fought with a blown knee and a concussion?"

"Of course not."

"Why didn't you tell them the truth?"

He stared at her, his jaw clenched.

"Because you were protecting them," she said. "Because you care about them. Well, guess what, big guy, that's why I told Cosmo that you'd never make a good hero. I wasn't about to let you walk back into the ring with a possible concussion, bruised vertebrae and who-knows-what else. I love you. I was trying to protect you, just like you protected the people you loved."

"I've got to get ready for my match."

She searched his eyes. "Don't you get it? I couldn't watch you get back into the ring and kill yourself out of some misplaced sense of guilt."

"Enough!"

She grabbed his hands. "It's okay to be who you are. It's okay to be a *good guy*."

The door burst open. Red and a tall, thirty-ish man came in. "You ready, Silver?" the tall man said.

"Yep." Luke tore off his jacket.

"Don't do this," she whispered, her fingers digging into the flesh of his arm.

"What's the angle?" Luke said to Killian Steel, not taking his eyes off Lexy.

"You're the Silver Stallion, Stud du Jour. You'll walk out with four females, tie each one to a ring post. Winner takes the women."

"Luke, you know who you are," Lexy said. "Don't betray yourself."

The tears in her eyes tore at his heart.

Standing on tiptoe, she kissed his cheek, then walked quickly out the door.

"I'd like to tie her to a ring post," Steel said.

"She's too good for you," Red said.

"If she's too good for me, she's sure as hell too good for him." He motioned toward Luke.

Something cracked inside Luke's chest. Killian Steel couldn't be more wrong. Luke knew this deep in his soul. He also realized he was pushing love away with both hands.

All the anger and confusion flooded from his body. It was over. And it was okay. He tossed his pants back into his bag.

"What are you doing?" Steel said. "You're on in twenty."

"I'm not wrestling tonight."

Or any other night.

"What the hell are you talking about?"

"It's not being taped. You can change the card." They did it all the time. He zipped up his duffel and walked past the guy, hoping to catch Lexy.

"Hang on, Silver. I've got big plans for you."

"So do I, man. So do I."

287

As he raced down the hall, his mind blurred with panic. Where had she gone? He had to find her, thank her . . . love her.

It had been so long since he'd been free like this, and not just from wrestling. The guilt anchor had dragged him down for so long.

Lexy had changed all that.

He tried not to think about their uncertain future. He focused on the possibility of having a family to love, his family with Lexy and her son.

He grabbed a security guard. "I'm looking for a short brunette."

"I saw one run through there a minute ago."

"Thanks." She was running?

He pushed the door open and the fresh night air chilled his bones. He spotted Lexy getting into a cab.

"Lexy!" he cried, racing up to her. "I couldn't do it."

She turned around, her face wet with tears.

He took her in his arms. "Sweetheart, please don't cry."

"It kills me to see you hurting," she said.

"Shhh, it's okay. I'm not going into the ring anymore." A new flood of emotions pounded his chest. "Come on, honey, don't cry. It makes me crazy."

She leaned back and hiccupped. "Crazy enough to come home with me?"

"Home. Yeah, that sounds nice."

"I love you, Timothy Loverboy Luke Silverspoon."

"Just Tim to you."

He held her close and thanked God for another chance.

.

Epilogue

"When's Lulu coming out, Mama?"

"Aunt Lulu," Luke said, nudging Riley.

Lexy smiled. It felt like a dream, the three of them sitting together in the dark rink waiting for the final number of the skating show.

"Here, kid," Luke said, pulling something from his jacket. "I meant to give this to you before."

Her breath caught at the sight of the red bandanna.

"Wow, I'm like a real cowboy!" Riley said.

"I've had it for a long time." He smiled at Lexy.

"Cool!" Riley struggled to tie it.

"Here, honey, I'll help." She tied it behind his head, never taking her eyes off Luke. He'd kept her bandanna. Somewhere, deep down, he must have always known they would reconnect. And boy, did they.

He looked amazing tonight, dressed in conservative slacks, turtleneck and a jacket.

"What are you looking at?" he said with a wink.

She smiled, a flush tickling her cheeks.

"Behave," he warned.

"There she is!" Riley cried, hitting Luke in the thigh. "This is when she gets to shoot her gun."

"And they say wrestling is violent," Luke muttered.

Lulu sailed out from behind the barroom set. A dozen skaters dressed as saloon girls followed close behind, skirts flaring, legs swinging.

"There's no business like show business, like no business I know . . ." the chorus rang over the public address system.

Dressed in a denim skirt, jewel-studded cowboy shirt, and skates dolled up as cowboy boots, Lulu stroked from one end of the rink to the other, where she performed a spin.

The group of showgirls glided into a single line and began their kick routine. Wild Bill jumped out from behind the cardboard mountain waving his gun.

"There's no people like show people, they smile when they are low . . ."

Bill's gun went flying, tripping showgirl Number One and setting off a chain reaction of falling fluff. Lulu glanced at the audience and shrugged, then took Wild Bill by the arm and led him into a pairs number. With hands crossed in front they butterfly jumped down the rink. The audience cheered with delight, then Lulu let go of Wild Bill and he crashed blade-first into the saloon set. It flattened to the ice. The girls lined up, Lulu front and center, waving her gun.

". . . Let's go . . . on . . . with . . . the . . . show!!"

BANG! BANG! BANG!

The crowd roared and jumped to their feet. Riley grinned, clapping his hands and straining to see between the spectators standing in front of him.

"Here." Luke hoisted him onto his shoulders.

Lulu bowed four times, then led the cast off the ice for the reception.

"That was awesome!" Riley cried.

"And no one got hurt," Lexy said.

They glanced at the rink where a showgirl was extricating Wild Bill from the barroom set.

"Can we come back tomorrow, Mom?" Riley asked as they filed down the steps towards the lobby.

"I'm not sure, kiddo. Your father might want to spend some time with you on Saturday."

"Nah, he's busy making baby plans with Darcy. They don't need me around."

Luke squeezed her hand and smiled. Things couldn't be working out any better, from her ex's obsession with his wife's pregnancy, to Luke pursuing a teaching career. He wanted to be a high school wrestling coach. He'd be great.

Sure, he'd agreed to stay on Cosmo's payroll for a while to train some new guys in the art of outrageous, yet safe wrestling moves. But slowly Luke would pull away from pro wrestling. He'd be safe.

"Look, there she is!" Riley cried.

A swarm of fans surrounded Lulu, waving programs in her face for autographs. Lexy studied Luke's face, a mixture of resignation and peace. And maybe a little envy.

"You miss it, don't you?" she said.

He lowered Riley to the ground. "A little. But it's nice to be a normal guy for a change."

"Hot dog! There's my boy!" Lulu cried, parting the crowd and giving Riley a hug. "How'd I do, kiddo?"

"Great! You're gonna be famous."

Everyone laughed.

"Where's that crazy Lulu!" a man cried.

Wild Bill pushed through the crowd, his hat askew, his shirt torn at the shoulder. "I told you not to throw me into that dang bar. What's your problem, woman?"

A hush fell over the crowd. Luke took a step forward.

"Wait," Lexy said with a hand on his arm.

"I can't help it if you're too cheap to get your blades sharpened," Lulu said. "You keep losing your edge."

Wild Bill, an older gentleman with a lean build and pointed nose, stared her down. "Lulu Amaryllis Dumacker, would you like to go to dinner a week from Sunday?"

"Only if you leave your guns at home." She slapped him on the back and he lurched forward. "I'd better check with my niece. Alley-ooops, you need me a week from Sunday?"

"No, I'll be home."

"Actually she won't," Luke said. "She and Riley will be with me, at a barbecue."

Lexy wrapped her arms around his waist. "I'm so proud of you. And I love you so much."

"Hey, watch it with the public display of affection. I'm a shy kind of guy."

Leaning back, she looked him in the eye. "Now there's a line if I've ever heard one."

"Stop it, you two. You're showing me up," Lulu said.

"Is that your niece?" Wild Bill asked.

"Yep, that's Alley-ooops and her friend—"

"Tim," he said looking into Lexy's eyes. "I'm Tim Silverspoon."

"You certainly are," Lexy said and kissed him.

MR. COMPLETE

SHERIDON SMYTHE

Lydia Carmichael is looking for proof that the drop-dead gorgeous date provided by Mr. Complete Escort Services is a gigolo. All she has to do is lure that bad boy into her bed and she could put the slimeballs out of business.

But Lydia soon learns she isn't cut out for this kind of under-the-covers work. Luke is not only Hot with a capital *H*, he is also a considerate, caring man. As she discovers there is a lot more beneath the surface than his sexy underwear, she finds herself wanting to leave her tidy white-cotton life behind. If her secret wishes could come true, their bought-and-paid-for beginning would lead to a happily-ever-after end that has nothing to do with money and everything to do with love.

- -